Lara Temple was three years old when she begged her mother to take the dictation of her first adventure story. Since then she has led a double life—by day she is a high-tech investment professional, who has lived and worked on three continents, but when darkness falls she loses herself in history and romance…at least on the page. Luckily her husband and her two beautiful and very energetic children help her weave it all together.

Also by Lara Temple

The Wrong Way to Catch a Rake
'Snowbound with the Earl'
in *Regency Christmas Parties*
The Earl She Should Never Desire

The Return of the Rogues miniseries

The Return of the Disappearing Duke
A Match for the Rebellious Earl

The Sinful Sinclairs miniseries

The Earl's Irresistible Challenge
The Rake's Enticing Proposal
The Lord's Inconvenient Vow

The Lochmore Legacy collection

Unlaced by the Highland Duke

Discover more at millsandboon.co.uk.

THE SCANDALOUS LADY MINA

Lara Temple

MILLS & BOON

All rights reserved including the right of reproduction in whole or in part in any form. This edition is published by arrangement with Harlequin Enterprises ULC.

This is a work of fiction. Names, characters, places, locations and incidents are purely fictional and bear no relationship to any real life individuals, living or dead, or to any actual places, business establishments, locations, events or incidents. Any resemblance is entirely coincidental.

Without limiting the exclusive rights of any author, contributor or the publisher of this publication, any unauthorised use of this publication to train generative artificial intelligence (AI) technologies is expressly prohibited. HarperCollins also exercise their rights under Article 4(3) of the Digital Single Market Directive 2019/790 and expressly reserve this publication from the text and data mining exception.

® and TM are trademarks owned and used by the trademark owner and/or its licensee. Trademarks marked with ® are registered with the United Kingdom Patent Office and/or the Office for Harmonisation in the Internal Market and in other countries.

First published in Great Britain 2026
by Mills & Boon, an imprint of HarperCollins*Publishers* Ltd,
1 London Bridge Street, London, SE1 9GF

www.harpercollins.co.uk

HarperCollins*Publishers*, Macken House, 39/40 Mayor Street Upper, Dublin 1, D01 C9W8, Ireland

The Scandalous Lady Mina © 2026 Ilana Treston

ISBN: 978-0-263-41878-1

04/26

Printed and Bound in the UK using 100% Renewable Electricity at CPI Group (UK) Ltd, Croydon, CR0 4YY

This one is for my very own
second-chance romance partner—my brilliant Andy.

Chapter One

1880, The SS Aquitania, *not far off the coast of New York*

'You did what?'

The fine china cup with the SS *Aquitania*'s emblem embossed in gold slipped from Max Cavendish's hand, bounced off the carpet, and rolled back towards his shoe like a well-behaved puppy come to heel.

Across the table, his Uncle Septimus Cavendish lowered the edge of his newspaper and smiled, pressing his gold-rimmed reading glasses back up his hawkish nose.

'I said—I hired Mina Davenport to act as Eliza Serena's companion on the way back to England. Polish her a little, help her through all the hullabaloo.'

'Mina Davenport. As in Lady Wilhelmina Davenport,' Max clarified, hoping he'd misheard.

'I don't know of any other. Peter's Mina.'

Peter's Mina.

'You're mad.'

'Nonsense. Makes perfect sense. My *La Serena* could be the greatest success on stage since Madame Vestris and Adelina Patti. It's not only her vocal skills, a dozen singers have that, it's the emotion. Makes you believe in heartbreak.' The pages rustled as Septimus folded the newspaper and leaned forward, his face alight. 'I'm planning to put on that poor fellow Bizet's *Carmen*. London is yearning for something different, something on a grand scale. And Eliza has the voice for that—she can make you believe a twenty-year-old slip is a hardened streetwalker.'

He heaved a sigh and went across the state room to the upright piano in the corner, running his fingers over the keys in a bright arpeggio. 'Problem is, off the boards she's still wet behind the ears. The damned wolves in London will strip her bones and use them for toothpicks. Carmen is a woman on a grand scale. Can't have Eliza blushing and stuttering every time a countess deigns to address her. She needs poise. Aplomb. Needs to look down her nose at people when they cross a line. Mina could do all that in her sleep.'

Max ignored nine parts out of ten of his uncle's speech. Partly out of long practice and partly because only one aspect of it struck him as utterly, outrageously wrong.

'That is the worst idea you have yet concocted, and you have had quite a few, Sep.'

Septimus frowned and closed the piano lid.

'Not that many. I would say no more than four out of ten, and as you well know those are fair odds. Not every business deal you've brokered has been a success.'

'No, but believe me, I never knowingly walked into a lion's den with raw chops hanging around my neck.'

'Not a very pleasing image,' Septimus considered judiciously.

'Slightly more pleasing than the image of Peter coming face-to-face with the woman who broke his heart ten years ago. We're talking about your nephew whose wife died barely a year ago, Sep. Bringing Mina Davenport back to London, and now of all times...' He broke off, jerkily rising to his feet. 'This is a hell of a way to treat your favourite nephew.'

Septimus smiled a little as he poured himself the remains of the coffee.

'I don't choose favourites, Max, my boy. I love you all.'

'You have a damned strange way of showing it, then.'

'Peter is a grown man, with two lovely children. He can fend for himself. Besides, I hired Mina to act as a companion to Eliza in London, and Peter is with the children at Fairweather. There is no reason for them to even meet.'

'Do you mean to say it is done? She is actually aboard the *Aquitania* now?'

'Why, of course. She has a berth in Eliza's state

rooms. There would hardly be a point to hire her and not bring her with my new investment to…er, pump some bravado into her.'

'Well, Mina Davenport certainly has that in spades,' Max retorted as he continued pacing the confines of his private parlour. He loved ships, but sometimes they felt too much like a cage, dredging up unwanted memories. He slowed his pacing, his breathing, and concentrated on the pattern of the carpet, following lines, isolating shapes. It had taken years of practice, but it usually worked quite well. Not so well today. He went to retrieve his cup from the floor and pressed the steward's bell. He needed more coffee.

'Well, I do hope so,' Septimus responded cheerfully, ignoring his nephew's roaming. 'She is rather altered. Ten years is a long time, Max.'

'This is a mistake.'

'Perhaps. As you said—I've made a few. I don't think this is one, but one lives and learns. One lives and learns.'

He clucked his tongue and picked up his newspaper once more, a satisfied smile curving his mouth. Septimus definitely lived far more than he learned.

Max resumed his seat. If there was one thing *he* had learned, it was that crying over spilled milk was not only a waste of time, but tended to turn that milk sour even faster. The best course of action was to walk away and milk another cow.

But walking away was hardly an option on the SS

Aquitania, despite its fame as the longest ocean liner currently plying the Atlantic. He picked up the other newspaper, but the words were as elusive as the shapes on the carpet.

'How the devil did you even come across her, anyway? I thought she and Lady Bascombe were in Brazil.'

'I haven't heard all the details yet. I was rather rushed preparing everything for the voyage. But naturally I had to make one last visit to the museum, which was very fortuitous because there she was, with three children.'

'She has...three children?'

'Not hers. She was their governess. Horrid little beasts, but she had them well in hand. Stopped them from bringing down the Temple of Dendra in a pile of rubble about their ears. Told the chubbiest one that if he carved his name into the stone, the guardian mummy would cast a curse on him. That caught their attention and naturally they wanted details, so there they were, cross-legged on the floor as she concocted some rather gruesome tale about giant crocodiles and moldering mummies rising to life on winged camels and whatnot, so naturally I stopped to listen. Some marvelous ideas there for a stage setting. Good visuals.'

Max held on to his patience, barely. Septimus was known for his digressions and trying to shove him back on track only prolonged them.

'But my point...' Septimus continued, smoothly inserting himself back onto the main rails, 'was that I recognised her, and while the three horrors were stuffing their rotund selves with some sugary concoction in the tea shop, I went to speak to her. It seems her mother ran off to Mexico with some fellow after they arrived in San Francisco and Mina had to make her own way. She was a teacher and a nurse and goodness knows what else and was in New York acting as governess to one of those overdressed women who delight in being patrons of the arts but couldn't tell Verdi from Mozart.'

He paused to allow Max to support his outrage about such heresies, but when Max maintained his smoldering silence, Septimus continued.

'Well, I told her about Eliza and my worries that she will find it hard to assume the persona I have decided would best serve her in England. When she asked me what persona, I told her—quite off the cuff, mind you—that I wanted her to be just like you—meaning just like Mina—at least the Mina she was back at Fairweather. Decisive, charming…alight. Serena must light up not only the stage, but every room she enters. She has that in her, but she lacks confidence. We must drum that into her.'

Only Septimus, who had confidence in frightening abundance, would treat it like something to be stoked and damped at will, like feeding coal into a boiler. Max didn't debate the likelihood of drumming confidence into anyone. He was too busy battling fury.

'So to further your business pursuits you are willing to risk Peter's heart again?'

Septimus sighed. 'I repeat. Peter is a grown man. I have more faith in his fortitude than you appear to, Max.'

'Almeria will have your head on a platter when she hears of this. She despises Mina even more than I do.'

Septimus clicked his tongue. 'My sister-in-law is far too proper to resort to such bloodthirsty methods. As for despising her... I don't think that is the correct word.'

'She said from the start that Mina was wrong for Peter.'

'She wanted her to be wrong for him, as you well know. Mina upset Almeria's plans for Peter to marry Emily, and she was worried Mina might not be content as a country matron.'

'Worries which proved well-founded.'

'So they were,' Septimus replied easily. 'And we must be grateful that for whatever reason Mina broke the betrothal before it was too late.'

'"*For whatever reason*"?... Call a spade a spade, Sep. The girl eloped with her lover. Though I daresay you forgive her that as well since she did it in a sufficiently melodramatic manner.'

'It is not for me to forgive her, Max. She did me no ill.'

'She did Peter a great ill. If she'd left Peter to marry the man her father had chosen for her, then Society would have smirked a little at his expense and moved on. But to elope with some unknown she must have been communicating with behind Peter's back... She not only broke his heart, she humiliated him.'

'Ah. Which is the greater sin?'

'I'm not playing your games, Sep. I'll take your point that Peter is no longer a boy, but losing Emily so suddenly last year has left him alone and vulnerable. Throwing Mina Davenport into that mix...'

'You exaggerate, my boy. Besides, I am hardly planning to take her down to Fairweather. She shall remain in London with Eliza and guide her through the treacherous shoals of London Society while I help her through the far less treacherous shoals of a London theatre.'

'This won't end well, Sep.'

'You think not? I rather think Eliza Serena will be the success of the season. Mark my words.'

'I'm not worried about your damned opera singer! I am—'

A soft knock on the door interrupted Max.

'Ah, fresh coffee, I hope,' said Septimus with pleasure.

Max shoved to his feet and stalked out onto the private veranda that adjoined the state rooms. He was wasting his time. Septimus was a brilliant impresario, but he could be as blind as a bat about everything else.

It would be up to him to minimise the damage his uncle's latest whim might cause. That meant keeping

Lady Wilhelmina Davenport as far away from the Cavendish family as possible.

He was damned if he was going through all that again.

Chapter Two

'I'm dying! I want to go *home!*'

The groan was heartbreaking. And the retching that followed was stomach twisting.

Mina stood in the cabin door as Mrs Oakes, Eliza Serena's capable nurse companion, tutted around her charge. Two of the ship's maids hovered in readiness to provide new basins and towels, while they basked in the glory of serving New York's beloved new operatic star *La Serena*, even diminished as she was by sea sickness.

There was little for Mina to do at the moment, but she felt obliged to be in readiness for her new mistress. Actually, not obliged. It had been a while since she'd felt that sensation, but there it was—her readiness was not merely a matter of duty, but tinged with concern. Eliza Serena had that effect on people. If she hadn't looked and sounded so awful right then, Mina might have felt a twinge of envy. Eliza Serena was not only fabulously talented; she was also…nice.

Which made Mina worry all the more about Septimus Cavendish's plans to introduce the girl to London Society.

'How is she doing?'

Mina turned at the theatrical whisper behind her. She hadn't heard Septimus slip into the suite and she shooed him into the parlour. Eliza would definitely not appreciate having her agony witnessed by her impresario.

He went tamely, tucking his thumbs into the pockets of his extravagant waistcoat. This one was covered in lyres and musical notes in shades of pink, silver and indigo. He noticed her inspection and grinned at her, patting the embroidered fabric lovingly. She smiled back without thinking, just as she had when she'd seen him approach her at the museum tea shop. It had been the first time she'd smiled, truly smiled, in a long while, and it had frightened her.

'She is rather miserable, I'm afraid,' she said briskly, forcing herself back to the moment.

'That's a pity. Poor lass,' he said, his voice low and sympathetic and Mina felt her eyes prick. Sometimes, in his less theatrical moments, he reminded her of Peter.

'If she can rest she'll probably feel better in a couple of days.'

'Probably. Can't she hold down some laudanum?'

'No, but even if she could, she doesn't wish to. She told me her mother died an opium addict.'

His brows rose, rumpling the wrinkles on his forehead.

'She told you that?'

She shrugged. 'She knows I'm here to help her. She's not loose-lipped if that is what concerns you.'

'Oh, I know she's not. That's why I was surprised...' His brow knitted as the moaning from the cabin penetrated the parlour door. 'Well, she'll just have to brave it out, then. It does get better. You're not ill yourself?'

She shook her head, but his gaze moved over her, noting her pallor.

'You're doing no good here. Leave her to Mrs Oakes and take a turn in the fresh air. Best thing for being a little green about the gills. There's a brisk wind and no rain yet. Off you go.' He pulled a coat from the hooks by the door and before she could point out it was Eliza's, he had coaxed her into the corridor, draped the coat over her arm and aimed her towards the stairs. 'Off you go,' he said again, and closed the door.

Mina stood for a moment, unsure whether to laugh or be annoyed at being shoved around like a piece of furniture. She stroked the fine cashmere of the coat. It was a lovely shade of dark wine and Mina slipped it on and gave a sigh of pleasure. It had been a long, long while since she'd worn anything so fine.

Her plain straw hat was still in her room, but she didn't want to reenter the state room, so she tucked the flying tendrils of her unruly tawny hair behind her ears and went out into the immensity of the sea and sky.

There were fewer people than she'd expected on

the deck. Probably because Septimus Cavendish had grossly overstated the state of the weather.

The Atlantic Ocean itself looked a little seasick.

She walked to the farthest end of the promenade deck and leaned over the railing to watch the churned wake.

'It's a single screw.'

Mina turned in surprise at the gruff voice beside her. A girl, probably no older than ten, had come to lean on the railing and was frowning at the ship's wake.

'I beg your pardon?' Mina asked, a little annoyed to have her quiet moment so swiftly interrupted.

'The propeller. Single screw. This is the longest liner on the Atlantic line. Length to beam of eleven to one. Did you know that?'

'I didn't. Is that a good thing?'

'It is neither good nor bad. It is special.'

'What else is special about it?' Mina asked, more curious about the child than the ship.

'Two-cylinder compound steam engine. That's not special, but she can reach fifteen knots and hold it. That's special. That is why she has a blue riband. Did you know that?'

'I didn't. I'm afraid I don't even know what that is.'

The girl turned to face her. Her gaze was very direct and unblinking, but rather than meet Mina's eyes it seemed to settle on a spot on her forehead, just a little to the left. Mina resisted the urge to reach up and see if there was some smut on her brow.

'Most people don't,' the girl answered, still addressing Mina's hairline. 'Fastest voyage time. Seven days, eighteen hours, two minutes. That was to Queenstown in Ireland.'

'That is very accurate.'

'It is important to be accurate in order to win a blue riband. That is more than fifteen knots on average.'

'Are we travelling that fast now?'

'No.'

'I see. Perhaps that is best. It is already quite choppy.'

'Less than usual at this season, but there is a storm expected on our route. I heard the stewards speaking. At the current speed and if the weather patterns are true to the season I calculate a voyage time of eight days and twenty hours…' The girl appeared to struggle to hold back, but then the words rushed out nonetheless, 'and fourteen minutes.'

'What is your name?' Mina inquired, forestalling a possible inundation of more sailing statistics.

'I am Anne Seymour Garfunkel.'

'Anne Seymour. I like that.'

'Garfunkel.'

'Garfunkel. I am Mina… Davenport.'

The girl frowned, her brown eyes flickering to Mina's for the first time, but only for a moment.

'Did you forget your name?'

'No. Sometimes I wish I could, but it is the only one I have.'

Humor, or at least inept humor, was clearly lost on the girl.

'I like your name,' the girl declared. 'It has lots of blue and purple and green in it.'

Mina's mouth opened a little in surprise. She took a step towards Anne Seymour Garfunkel.

'What...what is the purple?'

'The *M* and the *V*, though the *M* is rather more burgundy than purple. Like your coat. Is that why you have that coat? The *D* has a little purple, but it is mostly blue. Mina is a happy name. Purple and pink and white and pale blue. Pretty. Who are you and why are you listening to our conversation?'

The question stymied Mina, until she realised it was addressed not to her, but to someone behind her. And someone much taller by the angle of Anne's Seymour stare.

'I'm Max,' said the intruder. 'And I am listening because I am curious.'

'About what?' Anne Seymour asked, clearly more interested in facts than manners.

'About ships. And about letters having colours.'

'Letters and numbers,' the girl clarified. 'Max is a good name.'

'It is?'

'Purple and two blues. Light blue like a robin's egg and grey-blue like the sky over a lake before the sun is high. Not grey like your eyes. Blue-grey like Mina

Davenport's eyes.' She repeated Mina's name as if she was connecting it all together as she spoke.

Mina hadn't moved, but Max Cavendish came round her and went to lean on the railing on the other side of the girl. There was no expression on his face other than mild interest. No surprise, no dismay, no anger. Nothing of what was grabbing Mina by the throat.

'Yes, I agree, that is a very different kind of grey,' he said at last.

'It is a prettier grey than yours,' Anne Seymour elucidated and he smiled at her.

'Undoubtedly.'

'Yours is dark. It will be dark soon.' Her voice switched, returning to some personal reality and not a pleasant one.

'Not for another couple of hours,' Max replied, his voice calm and calming.

'I am not fond of the dark. I am not allowed to read after dark.'

'That is a pity. What do you do after dark, then?' Max asked.

The girl frowned.

'I must sit with Nanny and have my tea and then say my prayers and get into bed and sleep. It is very…hard. May I join you again tomorrow, Mina Davenport?'

The direct address shook Mina out of her stupor, but it was the resignation in the girl's words, expecting rejection, that brought her fully to the surface.

'When I am not working and am allowed on deck, certainly you may.'

'You work? What is your work?'

'I am companion to a young woman.'

'Is she as young as I? Or younger?'

'No, not so young.'

'Good,' the girl said and Mina smiled without thinking. The girl's gaze locked on her face and she smiled back. It was a strange, tentative, almost sad expression, as if aware in advance it would not do. Impulsively, Mina held out her hand, and Anne Seymour placed hers, giving it a single firm shake before leaving the deck.

Mina hugged the *M*-coloured coat around her and forced herself to meet Max Cavendish's gaze.

Ten years is a long time, but somehow it wasn't. Time pinched and shrank and suddenly she was back in the library at Bascombe Hall, facing a younger version of this man as he furiously denounced her for what she had done to Peter.

Like Septimus when he'd appeared before her at the tea shop, Max Cavendish looked utterly familiar at first glance. But as quickly as the memory came, reality pressed it aside.

He'd changed.

He was probably even more handsome now than he had been at twenty-five. Maturity suited some men more than others, and the deepened lines that bracketed his sharply defined mouth added gravitas to his already serious face. He seemed far taller than her memory, though that made little sense. But she had seen him at his lowest point back then, just as he was now seeing her at hers.

His eyes, however, were the same. As Anne had pointed out, they were a dark grey with shards of silver, and could, when he wished, convey a numbing coldness.

Mina felt that frigid blast and wished she'd remembered that impulsiveness was a luxury she could no longer afford. If she'd known Max Cavendish was travelling with his uncle she would never have accepted the position. The last time she'd seen him had been on the very worst day of her life. It had taken years for that memory to fade sufficiently until she no longer felt ill when it resurfaced. The thought of a week in this man's company was...

She couldn't find a word for it, but it made her feel some of the symptoms of seasickness.

Still, she'd learned the best way to face life's curses was head-on.

'Good afternoon, Mr Cavendish.'

'Good afternoon, Lady Wilhelmina.'

She felt the frost of tension climbing up her cheeks. Just get it over with.

'I am travelling under the name of Mina Davenport. I would prefer you not use my title, Mr Cavendish.'

'Unless it serves your purpose. As I would guess it did to secure your position as governess in New York?'

'As it did. But right now it serves my purpose to be Mina Davenport.'

'Does it? I rather thought it serves my uncle's purpose for you to be precisely what you are, Lady Wilhelmina.'

He knew she'd always hated that name. Sometimes Peter called her that to tease her, but then Peter's teasing had been warm and full of love. This man's barbs had a completely different purpose. She shoved her hands deeper into her pockets. They were cold despite the warm wool—a cold that was coming from inside her as her past bloomed back into existence, fuelled by the contempt and dislike he'd veiled until Anne Garfunkel left.

Not that she was surprised he hated her. He had every reason to do so. Far more surprising was that Septimus hadn't regarded her with the same disdain. When he'd approached her at the museum tea room she'd expected polite gloating at the very least. The fact that he'd treated her with warmth was the prime reason she'd agreed to his outlandish proposal. It had been so…disarming.

So enticing.

Basking in the balm of Septimus's sympathy, the urge to go home, even though she had no home, had been overpowering.

Impulsive, foolish, but undeniable.

But Septimus Cavendish was the exception, not the rule. And Septimus had not seen her at her worst as Max had. *This* was the reality. The cold contempt in Max Cavendish's eyes was what she must expect from most people she would meet back in England. She could hardly complain. After all, she'd earned it honestly.

Ten years was a long time, but some things did not change.

Max had wondered if he would recognise Mina Davenport after a decade. After all, she'd been barely nineteen. But she looked very much the same. Older certainly. Quite a bit thinner. Her face, too, was leaner, her cheekbones more marked, and there were fine lines beside her eyes.

But mostly the difference was in her expression.

Or lack thereof.

Peter had often joked that he did not need to engage in exercise—physical or mental—he had Mina. Unlike her refined older half-sisters, known in London as the Bascombe Beauties, Lady Mina Davenport had suffered from an inability to sit still and her face had been a constantly shifting stage for her thoughts. In that sense the woman facing him, still and watchful, was a pale copy of Lady Mina, darling of Society and notorious flirt. At least that was what she'd been until to everyone's surprise she'd accepted the proposal of a younger son with nothing but the Cavendish name and a sweet disposition to recommend him.

'Do you think it wise to return to England, Mina?' he asked, dragging his thoughts back to the present.

Her eyes widened at his direct approach, but there was nothing else there. Young Mina would have fired up immediately, knocked down his shot across her bow and retaliated with a fusillade of her own.

'I think I hardly need share my thoughts with you, Mr Cavendish.'

'Well, allow me to share more of mine with you, then. My uncle is an excellent impresario, but he can sometimes have a rather naive view of Society. He actually believes you can smooth his new project's path in Society.'

'Your uncle hired me to help her acquire the tools to do so, not for me to do it for her. I made my limitations quite clear to him.'

'Your limitations?'

'I am certain you have your own list of my shortcomings, Mr Cavendish. I need not supply you with mine.'

'I most certainly do have my own list, but the only item that concerns me is what you did to Peter.'

An ache in his hand made him realise he was gripping the railing so hard a screw was embedding itself into his palm. Her calm was only feeding his anger, as if they were back in the village square outside Fairweather, where she'd publicly jilted poor Peter and shredded the boy's heart with brutal efficacy. Except Max had still been too shocked at that point to be angry. The anger had come later that day in the library at Bascombe Hall when he'd discovered just how viciously mistaken they'd all been about her.

She turned to watch the frothing scar of the ship's wake, the tilt of her aristocratic profile making it clear he was dismissed. He remembered that too—when something displeased her she could transform into a human suit of armour—infuriatingly impenetrable. Peter had always floundered when this happened, fluttering about her like an anxious moth tossing itself at a windowpane. Ten years on Max could see it for what it was—not a strength, but a weakness, a last resort.

'Cold shoulders don't work on me, Minnie. Keep in mind that in returning to England you're returning to the battlefield where you lost the war. Your father is dead and your half-sisters turned their backs on you and your mother when you ran away. You're no longer the darling of Society, but a pariah. Septimus is doing you a favour by employing you, but he's a volatile man and might as easily discard you if he thinks you'll endanger his precious project. And if you find yourself without a position in London, you'll have a far harder time finding gullible matrons to hire you because of your title. You made a sore mistake leaving New York.'

Her face remained utterly blank, but she could do nothing about her eyes. The blue-grey the little girl had so admired had darkened to dusk with fury and hatred.

'Is there a point to this lecture, Mr Cavendish?'

'There is. Stay away from Peter. If you are cherishing any ideas about approaching him and trying to rekindle what you burned to ashes ten years ago now he is widowed, then banish them. You make any overture to him, anything at all, and I will repay you the favour of destroying you as you did him.'

'Aren't you being a tad dramatic, Mr Cavendish?' she scoffed.

'Try me and find out.'

'I don't think I care to. Try you, that is.' Her voice dripped with distaste and against his will he felt a quiver of laughter at her twisting of his words. He'd forgotten that about her—snappish as a turtle and slippery as an eel.

'We agree on that at least, Minnie.'

'Are you planning on maintaining this discourse for the remainder of our voyage, Mr Cavendish?'

'I don't repeat myself, Minnie. For the remaining eight days, nineteen hours and however many minutes I plan on ignoring you.'

'Marvelous. Finally, we agree on something. Maxie.'

Max cursed her roundly in silence as she stalked off, but his disgust soon turned on himself. He'd always kept his temper well leashed and had no respect for people who lost theirs. He had no time for fury and certainly not for a wasteful emotion like hatred. But right now, watching that tawny hair tangling in the wind as if laughing at him, he felt the choking effect of both.

Chapter Three

After the previous day's disastrous encounter with Max Cavendish, Mina was not in the least looking forward to her conversation with Septimus Cavendish. The note summoning her to his state rooms, which the ship's steward had delivered that morning, looked innocuous enough, but she had no doubt Max had spoken with him and had probably convinced his erratic uncle to dismiss her without delay.

Well, he might dismiss her, but if he thought he could evade paying her wages he was in for a battle she had no intention of losing.

She raised her chin and drew to a halt as she reached a split in the corridors and realised she had no idea where she was or where Septimus's cabin was. She was about to return to ask Mrs Oakes when a steward appeared.

'Excuse me, can you direct me to Mr Septimus Cavendish's state room?'

The steward hesitated, casting an expert eye over

her plain dark blue dress, which lay straight to the ground without a single flounce or furbelow.

'The Cavendish state room is private, miss.'

Mina's cheeks heated a little at the man's dismissive tones.

'I appreciate that, but he is my employer and sent word I join him. I'm afraid I am not yet familiar with the layout of this ship.'

And never will be, most likely, she thought ruefully.

'Of course. In that case, you may follow me, miss.'

At the end of a corridor the steward knocked on a door. For a moment there was no sound and Mina could feel the steward's suspicion mount. But then the door opened and Septimus beamed at them.

'About time. Come along then.' He pulled Mina inside and fished in his vest pocket for a coin for the steward. 'We've work to do.'

Mina followed him down a wood-paneled corridor. She ought to have felt relief that he was clearly not about to dismiss her, but her thoughts were overtaken by surprise as he led her into a lounge that would not have been out of place at the Fifth Avenue Hotel.

She stood still for a moment, gaping. Rugs in earthy colours covered the wooden floors and grounded the endless expanse of sea and sky visible through large windows that opened onto a private veranda. Bookshelves and delicate watercolours covered the internal wall and an upright piano stood in the corner, it's top covered with stacks of dog-eared sheet music.

A different hand from the rest of this ship had decorated the room, someone with an eye to comfort and light and no patience for frills and heavy furnishings.

She loved it.

If she'd been wealthy she might have chosen to live in just such a place. Always sailing between worlds because she belonged in none. Stopping occasionally in some new city, tasting it and moving on. She'd lived like that for many years now, but always worried, always wondering if she would have enough.

This room was like her life, but with wealth and a dream woven into it.

'Do you like it?'

Septimus still stood in the doorway, his hands on his hips like a little boy asking her what she thought of the sandcastle he'd built. Today his waistcoat sported pyramids with what might have been either camels or malformed rabbits standing on their peaks. *Aida*, perhaps?

'The parlour or the waistcoat?' she asked and he grinned, patting the exuberant fabric.

'I never ask people what they think of my waistcoats, though all too often they tell me nonetheless. I meant this room. Do you like it?'

'Very much. I didn't know such rooms existed on ships.'

'Oh, this is special. Let's go sit on the veranda while the weather is still perfect.'

She did as she was told, settling into the deckchair

he indicated. From here the sea was even more dominant, as if she was hovering above it. The veranda was narrower than the promenade decks, just wide enough for a tall person to stretch out on a deckchair, but it was encased on both sides by metal walls. She felt like she'd stepped onto a completely separate ship with no one on board but herself. Even the chair was of a far finer quality than the ones on the open deck. It was cushioned and she felt as if she could easily curl up here, a book in her lap, and...

She sighed.

'Beautiful day, isn't it?' Septimus grinned at her and lit a cheroot, flicking the match over the rail and shoving one hand into his waistcoat pocket. 'Soak up all the sun you can, love. London weather is rarely this benign.'

The reminder dimmed her pleasure and she straightened.

'Shall we begin, Mr Cavendish?'

It was his turn to sigh. 'I do wish you'd stop treating me like that Vandertoot woman.'

'Vandermoot,' she corrected reflexively.

'Not much better. Point is, I might be your employer, but I need you as much as you need me. How's my investment feeling this morning?'

'Much better. She had some tea and toast and held it down. I think she will likely improve from here. Especially if this weather holds.'

'Good. Good. I want her to make an appearance tonight if she is up to it.'

'You wish for her to sing?'

'No, not yet. Certainly not so soon in the voyage. Everyone knows she's on board and they're hoping she might sing, but you know as well as I that spoiled children tire of the object of their desire if they are given it too soon. I want to tantalise them first. For the moment all I wish is to see how she does on the social stage before we reach London. Captain's table, a few amicable drinks among friends, nothing too demanding. Her previous manager kept her out of the social scene because he knew it was beyond his connections and intelligence to manage. But I happen to think she has the right material to learn. Think she can do it?'

'Most definitely. She has a good heart and sweet disposition and she's been through enough in her life to understand the need for hard work. But you know this already.'

'I do. Just wondering if you saw it as well. Wouldn't have taken her on otherwise. I've reached a point in life where I won't take on just anyone, and certainly not one of those people who believe they're superior to everyone else, even if that kind of confidence often convinces people they are. But confidence is exactly what Eliza lacks. I need you to teach her.'

She swallowed, feeling like an utter fraud. 'Confidence isn't something one can teach.'

'That's what Max said. But keep in mind that every

great opera singer is also an actress. Teach her to act with confidence, even if she doesn't feel it, and in time it will seep into her, fill in the cracks, so to speak. All she has to do is watch you. You've always had an abundance of confidence.'

She stared at him. 'Mr Cavendish, up until this moment I thought you a very clever man.'

He laughed out loud, tossing the stub of cheroot over the rail, and Mina had the worrying image of it landing on someone's hat.

'And so I am, Mina. Now stop funning and let's get down to business. I've already prepared a schedule of activities and training for the duration of the voyage. All I'm waiting for is for her to feel better to set it in motion. Mrs Oakes will do the voice training…'

'Mrs Oakes? I thought she was her nurse.'

'Well, she is, but she was also once a music hall singer. So, Eliza shall have sessions every morning with her, and spend the afternoons with you. What you and I need to decide on is precisely what ground we wish to cover. Deportment, how to talk to a duke, practice conversation, that kind of nonsense. And all the while I want her watching you and soaking you up like a sponge.'

Mina laughed at the absurdity of it all. Still, at least all the nonsense that had been drummed into her in the nineteen years of being raised to be auctioned off to the highest-paying bidder would come in useful for someone.

'Very well. I shall do my best.'

'I know you will. Always did. Where are my lists… Ah, damnation, I left them yesterday with Mrs Oakes. Wait here. I'll be back in a hop and a skip. Help yourself to…whatever.'

Mina had half begun to rise, but he was already gone so she sank back with a laugh. She'd forgotten just how energetic Septimus Cavendish was. She'd met him often during the summer she'd been engaged to Peter and found him amusing, but he'd seemed so much older than her then, and his mercurial moods made him hard to gauge. It was strange to think that he had only been thirty-five at the time.

Max Cavendish would be thirty-five now.

Things looked very different from the perspective of time.

She snuggled deeper into the deckchair and raised her face to the sun and sea breeze. She did not mind if he took his time. She was quite content to…

'Good morning.'

No.

No, no, *no*.

She straightened even as Max Cavendish settled into the deckchair beside her.

'I am waiting for your uncle,' she said stiffly. 'He went to fetch his lists.'

'Was that where he was rushing off to? I was beginning to wonder if the ship was sinking. Good morning,

Lady Wilhelmina,' he said again, with emphasis, as if she was a child to be schooled in manners.

To hell with that.

'Does your uncle know you stroll in and out of his rooms at will, Mr Cavendish?'

'My uncle has been strolling in and out of rooms all his life. He can hardly object when one does the same to him.'

She could feel him watching her, but she refused to turn. She owed this man absolutely nothing. Not even courtesy. From now on her good manners had to either be earned or paid for.

'Well, I can. I am here to work, Mr Cavendish. Not to act as a dart board for your ill temper.'

'And here I thought I was in a particularly good mood this morning.'

'And here I thought I was also in a good mood until…' She raised her fob watch. 'Two minutes ago.'

He laughed and the deckchair creaked as he shifted it to an angle that brought him into her line of vision.

'Are you going to keep this up the entire voyage, Minnie?'

'You took the first shot, Mr Cavendish. You don't get to dictate the terms of a war you began.'

'I see. We are at war then?'

She turned to him, registering with a slight burst of shock that he was not fully dressed. Or at least not wearing anything other than trousers and a linen shirt that was not yet fastened at the throat or cuffs, its sleeves rolled up to reveal his forearms, tanned against the sharply white linen.

A horrid thought occurred to her. The doors leading off from the inner corridor she had passed through...

She was in enemy territory.

The urge to run was followed immediately by a stronger urge to stay and fight.

'Yes, Mr Cavendish. I think you could say that. If you wish to negotiate a treaty of armed neutrality, I am willing to discuss terms.'

He leaned back in his chair, locking his hands behind his head. His shirt rose, just flirting with the waist of his expensive trousers.

'Are you? What would such a treaty entail?'

'Happily ignoring each other. That was *your* suggestion after all.'

'So it was. And I fully intended to act on it, but it is rather hard to ignore an attractive woman one finds sunning herself in one's own deckchair first thing in the morning.'

She ignored the faint flattery. She knew this version of Max as well. He never bothered being charming unless he was trying to obscure something or fob someone off.

'I was not aware that you shared these rooms with your uncle. Had I known...'

'You would have run like the devil was at your heels?'

'I never turn my back on the devil, Mr Cavendish.'

'Interesting philosophy. What would you have done then?'

'I would have told your uncle to meet me in the ship's lounge.'

'How disappointingly prosaic. I was hoping for something more creative. You could, for example, invite me to admire the view and push me overboard.'

She smiled. 'What a coincidence. I imagined that same enticing image earlier, though in my fantasy there were sharks involved. But that would require I sully my hands by touching you.'

His mouth quirked.

'I see you've found your claws, tigress. I was beginning to wonder if a decade of disgrace had leached the Bascombe arrogance from your veins. Apparently not.'

'My refusal to turn the other cheek at your snide barbs doesn't mean I'm arrogant, Mr Cavendish. It means my patience and my manners have their limits.'

'Your manners?' He laughed. 'You always had the manners of a hellion, but so long as you were amusing and had your father's name behind you, people forgave you everything. Well, not precisely everything.' He paused, his gaze flitting over her face and he leaned forward, just brushing the crest of her cheek with his fingers. 'It amazes me how quickly you can blush, Minnie. That hasn't changed, at least. But it's never shame that causes it, is it? Just rage or embarrassment. I presume that's the colour of rage this time. Or do you have something new to be embarrassed about, Lady Wilhelmina?'

'Perhaps I'm merely embarrassed for you, Mr Cavendish. Your manners are showing clear signs of having been indulged far too long by sycophants interested in your wealth.'

'Perhaps. I admit I was a trifle harsh when we met on deck. I was…taken by surprise.'

It wasn't much of an apology. She didn't know whether to accept his rather leafless olive branch or resent him even further. Fair play demanded she make some equivalent gesture, but it stuck somewhere below the red-hot thudding of her heart.

'At least you had the grace not to show your true face in front of Miss Garfunkel.' She winced at her own words. She was sinking to pettiness and she hated that above all. She drew a deep breath and made her own effort at an oblique apology. 'You were quite kind to her.'

'Perhaps that was part of some dastardly strategy of mine.'

'No. You aren't quite that conniving. Unless business is involved.'

'I always play fair in business,' he objected and she gave an unladylike snort.

'I spent two months acting as your secretary that summer. *Fair* was a term you employed when it suited you. I doubt you've changed for the better in this respect when you clearly haven't in any other.'

He smiled out at the horizon. 'At least I never cheated anyone.'

She was about to say that neither had she, but thought better of it. Instead she said: 'Well, bravo. And since we are speaking of fairness—I never did receive recompense for all the hours I spent managing your correspondence while you were still too weak to do so. Perhaps I should even receive double pay for having to read aloud all those endless reams of technical papers people insisted on sending you even though they knew you were ill. Fine friends you had.'

'Make an account of it and I'll reimburse you. Just be sure to deduct something for all the interruptions and questions about those technical papers I had to field while you were helping me.'

'Very well. But I shall also be sure to add ten years of interest for lack of payment, shall we say at…ten per cent?'

His smile softened suddenly. 'Clever. But I'm not offering to more than double your pay because you were tardy on collection. There are many areas in which you might not wish to emulate your father, chief among them his underhanded financial dealings.'

'I wish you would stop mentioning him. Lord Bascombe is dead.'

'If you are trying to make me feel guilty, I'm afraid you're off the mark, Minnie. From what I heard of him, the world is a better place now he's gone. It would have been far better for you if he hadn't infected you with his avarice and ambition. You should have married Peter while you could.'

She swallowed and turned away from his clever grey eyes. She hated that he'd been there to witness the worst moments of her life. She could still hardly comprehend the enormity of what had struck her that day. At nineteen she'd been on top of the world and then, in a matter of hours, at the bottom.

The urge to tell him the truth rose in her like the waves rolling towards the ship. She could almost see herself rise, chin up, her words striking him like arrows: I saved your precious cousin and your sanctimonious aunt from the scandal of finding out Lord Bascombe's daughter wasn't his daughter at all, but mostly likely the bastard of one of the footmen her mother entertained. Imagine how that would have looked on your vaunted family tree!

That would show him.

Mina would have smiled at the childish addendum if she hadn't felt so miserable and angry. She didn't want to remember those bitter days when Lord Bascombe had summoned her and told her the truth. There had even been some relief that she finally understood the disgust and dislike she'd so often seen in his eyes.

But both shock and relief had been overtaken by his next command. Not only was she to break her engagement with Peter, but she was to marry Sir Godfrey Renfrew within the week. A man more than twice her age and as wealthy as Croesus. As Lord Bascombe put it—he was finally going to get some return on not kicking her and her mother out on the street when she was born.

That memory—his face, his words—were as crystalline today as if they'd happened yesterday rather than ten years ago. Not just that horrid interview. Everything that followed it.

'You know he's widowed. Peter.' Max's words broke sharply into her unpleasant reverie.

'Yes, I heard. I am sorry.'

He gave a slight, mocking laugh. 'Of course you are.'

She turned on him again. 'I *am* sorry. Emily was my friend, and a lovely...' Her throat closed and she rose abruptly. His legs were still extended before him, blocking her passage along the veranda. It was utterly unladylike to step over them, but she didn't care.

As a maneuver it caught him by surprise and for a moment she stood with her legs straddling his, looking down at him. It was strangely satisfying to have him staring up at her in surprise, her skirts spread over his outstretched legs.

Fury, frustration and fear all coalesced to a sharp, bright point. She leaned forward, planting her hands on the armrests of his deckchair, her eyes locking with his, his sharp-hewn face inches away.

'Is that what this is about, Max Cavendish? Revenge? Or are you warning me off? I'll be damned if

I will allow you or anyone else to decide what I will and will not do. Or with whom.'

She shoved upright, holding his deep grey gaze as she very slowly brought her other leg over his. She gave her skirts a disdainful shake as if casting off whatever residue the contact with him might have left. Then she turned her back on him and left.

Max remained in the deckchair long after the door slammed behind her.

At least that encounter answered his question about whether she'd changed.

She'd been raw energy at nineteen, her mind as swift and unpredictable as a rabbit with a fox on its tail. The energy and intelligence were still there, but better controlled now. Sharper. At least until she let them loose.

Well, he'd wanted her to show the true colours under her cool exterior, and he'd succeeded. This was the real Mina Davenport. Ten years had only made her more dangerous.

He shifted his legs. For one mad moment as she'd leaned forward he'd thought…

His body had thought. His mind wasn't so stupid, but his body was, and it had clenched in readiness for…something. It was still buzzing at the emptiness of the moment. Even a slap would have done better than having that hellcat's skirts slipping along his legs, that tawny hair sliding forward over her shoulder, the sweet orange blossom scent of her closing in on him…

Anger was a particularly dangerous emotion—it liked to rouse the rest of them when it marched into battle. Anger mixed with Mina Davenport was even more dangerous.

He let out a long breath.

In little over a week they would reach London and poor Peter, aching from his loss of Emily and still bearing the scars of Mina's betrayal, would likely fall back under her spell faster than she flashed her claws.

'Mina, wait!'

Mina stopped as Septimus's voice carried down the long corridor, but she didn't turn. She'd hoped to escape onto the deck until she could breathe again. She was too angry to face anyone right now.

'I am sorry I took so long, but Eliza wished to...' Septimus came around her, waving a stack of papers, and stopped. 'What is wrong?'

'Your God-awful nephew is what is wrong,' she snapped.

'Oh.' The dismay on his face wavered.

'If you dare... If you *dare* laugh at me, Septimus Cavendish, I shall transform your diva into a shrieking harpy that will set Society on its ears in a way they've not been since Lady Abingdon brought her donkey to Almack's.'

'If you wish me to be serious, you must stop making me laugh, my dear. Come, we shall continue this in the lounge. You look like you could use something cool... Sorry, sorry, I shan't say another word.'

He took her arm and led her into the first-class lounge where a stained glass domed skylight danced with sunshine, casting rainbows on the brocade armchairs and mahogany tables. Potted palms with long pointy fronds between the islands provided privacy and the exotic sensation of an Egyptian oasis. Mina smiled despite herself at the whimsical thought of long-billed ibises bearing trays of champagne from table to table and perhaps a camel or two sipping cocktails beneath the palms.

There were more people here than had been on deck yesterday afternoon, but not many more, perhaps due to the early hour. Septimus led her to one of the tables and ordered cocktails with some outrageous name.

She considered protesting that it was far too early for spirits, but it felt as if the day had already been painfully long. Perhaps it was sensible to try and drown her fury, or at least pickle it. It was still bubbling and fizzing inside her, sending hot waves through her as her mind played through Max Cavendish's biting comments and her own outrageous behaviour.

What made it worse was that for those few moments when he'd first joined her he looked so...approachable, so much like the younger man who'd been kind to her and tolerant of her curiosity. Who unlike Peter's mother and even Peter himself had for some strange reason appreciated her odd sense of humour.

So approachable that within a few days of her arrival at Fairweather she'd forced herself into the role of his secretary and was soon treating him rather like the older brother she'd always wished she'd had.

Well, that had been just one more layer of her stupidity that had peeled away when the truth came to light and she'd escaped England. Just another loss to mourn on the SS *Speedwell* and her long, long voyage to nowhere in particular.

'You're angry at me.'

'I'm angry at myself.'

'Was Max very rude? He has that tendency when he's upset.'

'He has that tendency when he breathes.'

Septimus laughed out loud. 'To be fair, he thinks you're a schemer, Mina. That you left Peter to elope with some wealthy American or Brazilian or something.'

She wanted to snarl, 'Do I look wealthy to you?'

'What *did* happen, then?'

'That is none of your concern, or your ill-mannered, fat-headed nephew's.' She slammed her hand on the papers. 'Now, if you have no intention of working, I shall return to my room.'

He gave a faint chuckle and picked up her hand by her forefinger, setting it aside with care.

'Here is the schedule I have been considering...'

Chapter Four

'Come here, Mina Davenport.'

The voice—imperial and commanding—carried easily across the deck and snapped Mina out of her unpleasant thoughts.

It was only when she turned that she realised she wasn't being addressed by one of her New York employers, but by Anne Seymour Garfunkel. The girl occupied a deckchair under the promenade awning, half hidden by a rather unwieldy book and half by a plaid blanket. Only her eyes were visible under an olive-green felt cap, but they met Mina's for a moment before switching to a point above her left shoulder. Mina smiled, inexplicably warmed by that brief show of trust. She went to sit on the empty deckchair by the girl.

'Hello, Anne. What are you reading?'

'*Modern Marine Engineering* by Nicholas Procter Burg. Max Cavendish gave it to me. It has illustrations.'

She held it up for Mina to see. It did indeed have illustrations—an detailed diagram covered the whole page, under the heading of Details of Screw Engines.

'The book is old, but I like screw engines,' Anne continued. 'And back then people still believed paddle engines were the best solution for ocean crossings.'

'Back when?'

'1867.'

'Ah. A long time ago.' Mina didn't point out she had been older than Anne 'back then'. 'Do you understand all this, Anne?'

The girl frowned. 'Of course. These are engines.'

'Yes, but...' Mina realised she was asking the wrong questions. 'Do you like engines?'

'Engines are wonderful,' the girl said with a passion Mina hadn't heard in her voice before. 'There has never been anything like them. Ever. Not like this, not so many or so large, and so powerful. One day I shall design an engine.'

'A...a screw engine?' Mina glanced at the title.

'No. Something entirely different. Something better. That is why I must read all this. All that is right and all that is wrong. If I were a boy, Father would take me down to the engine rooms with Max. I heard Max owns fourteen per cent of this ship.'

'He does?'

'Yes. And of other ships, too, but I don't know how much.'

'Which fourteen per cent?' Mina asked, despite herself. 'The bilge?'

'Fourteen per cent of the company stock,' Anne explained kindly, and then, suddenly, she smiled. 'Was that a jest?'

'A poor one.'

'I cannot tell. Jests. It worries Mama.'

Mina's throat constricted and she wanted to touch the girl's hand, but something held her back.

'She need not worry,' she said. 'You are wonderful, whether you understand jests or not. I have never met anyone like you, and I have met many people of all kinds.'

Anne's eyes widened. 'That might be good or bad or nothing at all. We are all different. Like snowflakes.'

'You are quite right, but this is a good different. Very good. I am happy I met you.'

Anne's hands tightened on her book of engines. For a moment neither spoke.

'I am as well, Mina Davenport. Ships are good places to meet people because they cannot leave. I must find Nurse now or she shall be upset with me.' She took her book and blanket. 'Will you be here tomorrow? On the deck at three o'clock?'

Mina considered her schedule. She would have to make a few adjustments with Septimus.

'Yes. Or if I am late you may come to my room to fetch me, if you prefer?'

Anne hesitated. 'That is a very grown-up thing to do. To fetch someone.'

'It is indeed. But only if you wish.'

'I would like to try. If I do not like it, I shall come here. To this chair.'

'Very well. I shall come as well.'

Again Anne stretched her mouth. It wasn't quite a smile, but the expression in her eyes was far more telling. Mina remained there after the girl left, strangely soothed by that short encounter. It shouldn't have mattered in the grand scheme of things, but it did.

Mina was just rising from the chair when Max appeared. He saw her and stopped in the entrance to the deck. In light of her determination to avoid him, it wasn't wise to extend an olive branch. Especially after he'd been such a feckless bastard that morning, but somehow the words left that weaker part of her before she could slam shut the gates.

'Anne was just here. Reading your book. It was kind of you to give it to her.'

He gave a quick, almost uncomfortable shrug. She waited for him to move away, but he looked past her and spoke.

'I found her dozing over a book of sermons. She was clearly bored so I brought her the book.'

'Which you had on hand just by chance.'

'It is always in my library.'

'In your...' She thought of the state room, the intimate, restrained décor, the books... The truth finally sank in. 'Do you mean that those state rooms are yours? As in *always* yours?'

He shrugged. 'I often travel between England and New York.'

'Is that part of the fourteen per cent you own in the *Aquitania*?'

He frowned. 'How do you know that?'

'Anne. She is very envious. She wants to see the engines for herself, but her father will not allow her. You should convince him.'

He crossed his arms. 'Is that an order, Mina?'

'I am in no position to order anything, Mr Cavendish.'

'You never were, and yet I distinctly remember that you ordered. Often and vociferously.'

'I was young. And misguided.'

'You were…determined.'

She remembered that. The force of her conviction. The sense of knowing what was right. It seemed so long ago and so hopelessly naive. She hugged her coat about her and he frowned.

'Are you cold?' he asked.

'No. Merely feeling my age.'

His smile bloomed, warm and with the slumbering heat that had always set the young women around Fairweather plotting.

'That is unkind, Minnie. I'm six years your senior.'

'Is that all?' She'd not meant it as an insult and

when his brows rose she hurried on. 'I didn't mean... I thought...'

'Yes, I gather. That I was older. A veritable fossil. That I dandled Septimus on my knee.'

'No, merely that you two shared a governess.'

'I doubt it. I don't share.'

He spoke so lightly it took her a moment to register his meaning and she couldn't help smiling.

'You used to do that to annoy Lady Ashworth.'

'Do what?'

'Make an oblique statement that sounded perfectly innocuous, and yet she knew you were laughing at her.'

'Just laughing, not at her. My aunt doesn't have much of a sense of humour. Which was why she found you exhausting.'

'Goodness, yes. I was never as smooth as you at hiding my amusement. Another reason I daresay she was so delighted to be rid of me.'

The warmth and the smile disappeared from his face.

'She was not so shallow. After you left she hurt for her son and didn't know how to help him. None of us did.'

In a flash Mina turned a hot, painful red, her breath barely reaching her lungs. Everything came back—guilt, pain, confusion.

'Excuse me.' She pressed past him and almost tripped on the raised threshold of the doorway. He caught her, his muscles tensing as her hip pressed against his thigh, the warmth of his arm around her waist reminding her she'd not bothered with her corset that morning.

'Careful.' His voice was pitched somewhere below the rumble of the engines. 'My aunt always wondered how someone who rode and danced as gracefully as you could trip on imaginary cracks in the paving.'

The anger was gone again from his voice and she looked up. The sun was slipping low in the sky and reflected fire in the icy grey of his narrowed eyes. He finally let her go and she steadied herself against the door-jamb.

'I always wondered the same,' she muttered, grateful for the cold hard metal against her palm.

'Did you? It is no mystery. It usually happened when you were daydreaming. Then the world could collapse about you and you wouldn't have noticed.'

He hesitated, as if regretting his words, but she hadn't the energy to look for the offense.

'I never daydreamed when it mattered,' she muttered, brushing her hands on her worn coat. But she knew it was true—back then she'd thought she was so mature, but she'd often escaped into daydreams during the long days at Fairweather while Peter was out on estate business. Not always, though. Not when helping Max with his work. Not when Peter and Max were showing her around the estate. Then she was fully there. That in itself should have told her something.

She thought suddenly of riding out across the fields

with him and Peter, the three of them racing each other. Even weak from illness Max had outstripped them and she'd always wondered why Peter wasn't envious either of Max or of Peter's older brother Lucas, both of whom were taller and stronger than he.

But that was precisely why she'd been drawn to Peter in the first place. He was so at ease with himself and so generous to others. She'd wanted to be more like him and felt guilty when she fell far short, and guiltier when she'd caught herself watching Max's body move so effortlessly as he rode his temperamental stallion, Caliban.

That was when she'd begun to worry that her father might be right, that she would end up just like her mother...

'I must go to Eliza. She will have finished her voice exercises and we have a great deal to do before she makes her appearance at dinner.'

'Is she nervous?' he asked, moving a little away.

'Naturally. Part of her allure in New York was that she did not make public appearances off stage. This will be one of her first encounters with Society.'

'You and Septimus will be there to guide her through it.'

She looked down at her school-mistressy dress and thought of the exquisite gowns that would likely make an appearance in the lounge for dinner. Even her best gown was a dowdy dark blue taffeta affair which she wore when bringing the Vandermoot children down for tea three times a week. No, she would not be there. She still had *some* pride.

'Septimus will. Not I. My role is to provide guidance behind the scenes.'

'I think Septimus is expecting rather more than that.'

'Well, it wouldn't be the first time I fell short of expectations, would it?'

She stalked off before he could respond, kicking herself for slipping back into snappishness. She should have been content they'd pulled back from overt antagonism to mere wariness, but she could feel the weight of a depression that she had not felt in a long while. Just walking down the corridor felt beyond her. She wished she could slip into a daydream right now and not leave it until this was all behind her.

Chapter Five

Eliza and Mrs Oakes were already drinking tea after their voice exercises when Mina joined them, producing *Aquitania*'s ornately printed passenger list in order to coach Eliza on the social hierarchy of their fellow saloon class passengers. Eliza seemed far more buoyant than yesterday, asking questions and making careful notes in the margins of the list. But her skin was still pale, with an almost alabaster shimmer.

Very well, thought Mina, they would turn that fragility to their advantage.

'That's enough pedigrees for the moment, Eliza. Now it is time to inspect your wardrobe. We must decide what you shall wear tonight.'

'Something grand?' Mrs Oakes asked, laying down her knitting with a glimmer of a smile in her dark eyes.

'Definitely grand. But also…regal. *La Serena* shall make An Entrance.'

Eliza's smile wavered a little, but her eyes were bright with excitement as she hurried to the closets hidden by ornate sliding panels that covered the wall of the parlour.

'Septimus purchased a new wardrobe for me as soon as I signed the contract and it was delivered directly to the ship. I hadn't a chance to more than peek before I fell ill and then I completely forgot about it. Goodness, look at these colours. I want to try them all!'

'Extravagance,' Mrs Oakes said sternly in her telegraphic manner, but she smiled as she ran experienced fingers over the exquisite fabrics. Eliza opened the last closet and pulled out the corner of a gown of deep dusky rose that shimmered like phosphorescence on the waves.

'Oh, look how lovely!'

'That is from Lady Mina's trunks,' Mrs Oakes admonished. Mina shook her head, thinking rather sadly of her dark blue gown.

'I'm afraid you're mistaken, Mrs Oakes. All my clothes are in the wardrobe in my cabin.'

'No, Lady Mina. Two of the trunks had your name on them. Thought you knew. I set them all out in this closet. Not enough room in your cabin.'

'But...there must be some mistake.'

Eliza took out the rose gown, unfurling it like a shimmering waterfall.

'No mistake, Mina dear. This is definitely your size. I used to work in wardrobe with my mother before I became a singer and I can tell a size merely by looking.' She held up the gown next to Mina. 'Oh, and the colour is simply *perfect* for you. It is like old rose, and that silvery gleam with your dark gold hair... Mr Septimus has the most wonderful eye. *Do* try it on.'

She shoved it at Mina and turned back to her own closets. Mina took the gown instinctively, its buttery silk almost melting through her fingers.

She could not... She *ought* not...

The gown clung to her fingers, its colour something from an old French portrait, decadent and lush... Seduction in silk form.

She damned well would. She was not strong enough to look this gift horse in the mouth.

'They're late,' Septimus said, as tense as if an audience of hundreds was beginning to shift impatiently before an empty stage.

'Perhaps she's having second thoughts,' Max said, swirling his whisky as Sep took a glass of champagne from the waiter's tray.

'Nonsense, she was feeling much better today.'

'I meant Mina. Not your Serena.'

'Of course Mina shall come—she's no shirker.'

Max thought of that telling glance down at her plain dress.

'She told me she wouldn't come down to dinner,' he informed Septimus. 'I think she doesn't have anything suitable to wear.'

'Poppycock. Ten pounds says she comes.'

Max didn't bother to respond to his uncle's characteristic buoyancy. But neither did he turn down the wager.

The steward had just approached to lead them to the captain's table when there was a slight buzz near the doorway.

'Ah, yes,' murmured Septimus as Eliza entered. She wore a silk gown of cobalt blue that shimmered as if she'd drawn the night sky in with her. Folds of lace embroidered with silver roses wrapped themselves about her skirts like climbing ivy. Similar roses were woven into her dusky hair and a silver choker studded with pearls mirrored the gleam of her dark eyes. It was an entrance worthy of a larger stage than the *Aquitania*'s dining room, but the audience was as enchanted as any theatre crowd.

Mina entered half a step behind Eliza, her dress far more modest than the singer's. It was almost ascetic in its lines and the colour was hard to describe, something between pink and grey with a sheen of mother of pearl. It reminded him of the gowns in his grandmother's portraits, with fabric flowing over a natural female form rather than imprisoning it.

'You owe me ten pounds,' Sep said with unveiled smugness. 'I knew Parisian fashions would be perfect for Mina's silhouette. Dashed good luck I could convince the modiste to rustle up that wardrobe sight unseen at the last minute. Worth every penny.'

'You bought Mina clothes without a fitting?' Max asked as he watched the way the fabric clung to her.

Definitely not the debutante dresses she'd worn at nineteen with those ridiculous crinolines and bustles that seemed to swallow whatever chair one sat upon.

'Of course I did,' Septimus responded. 'A lifetime dealing with costumes has trained me well. Damn me, but I have good taste, don't I? And so does she, choosing that contrast between them. Dawn and dusk. Masterly!'

'I salute you, Uncle,' Max said as they watched the two women's progress. 'You always did know how to create a show.'

'I merely set the stage, boy. It is up to them to light it up.'

La Serena walked with an easy confidence and a light smile towards them, but her chin was a trifle too high, and halfway across the lounge she cast a quick glance back at Mina. Mina didn't quite smile, but there was the faintest reassuring curve to her mouth and a dip of her eyelids.

Max noted the creasing of his uncle's brow. They both knew the wily mavens of Society would note those telltale signs of insecurity faster than gossip travelled. Septimus caught Max's gaze and gave a tiny shrug.

'She is young yet—she will learn.'

'It is hardly of any concern to me, Uncle. Except to feel sorry for that poor girl.'

'Which one?'

'Mina is hardly a girl.'

'No. She most certainly is not. Her figure is all woman.'

Septimus didn't wait for Max's response, but moved forward to greet his protégée, hands extended.

'My dear *La Serena*. You put all the night stars to shame.'

Eliza flushed brightly and gave a faint laugh, but her bravado was clearly failing and Mina stepped into the breach.

'Then she has only the moon to envy, Mr Cavendish?'

'Quite the opposite! The moon will likely hide her face to avoid comparison. You shall wreak havoc on the tides themselves, *La Serena*.'

Mina's mouth quivered out of its flat line and even Eliza appeared to find that compliment absurdly overblown. She relaxed, her laugh far more natural, but tensed again as Septimus turned to Max.

'My dear, I never did have the chance to introduce you to Max, as the fellow was fiendishly late boarding in New York. Almost made us miss the tide.' He laughed. 'This is my nephew, or at least one of them. Max Cavendish. Max, this is the incomparable *La Serena*, Miss Eliza Serena.'

Max smiled and extended his hand, and Eliza placed her hand in his and blushed.

'And this is Lady Mina Davenport,' Septimus continued. 'But you two have already met, haven't you?'

'Yes, we have,' they both said in unison.

Since Septimus knew very well they had, his question was not only unnecessary, but smelled to high heaven of Sep's mischief and by the look Mina shot his uncle, she thought the same. Septimus, unperturbed, turned to hail the captain as he approached and within moments their little group had swelled to include half a dozen more guests eager to meet *La Serena*.

The poor girl answered questions in a soft voice that gave no clue as to its potential, but she contributed little to the conversation. Max wondered if it was that she had nothing to say or whether this rising star of the New York Opera was simply shy. If that was the case, he pitied the poor girl. Shyness was definitely not part of Septimus's plans.

When the conversation excluded her at one point her shoulders sank in relief. Her eyes just happened to rise to his and he smiled reassuringly, which was a mistake, because her faint flush turned red-hot and her gaze sank again.

Mina's gaze moved between them and she shot him a look that could have sunk a whole fleet of ocean liners. She then turned her shoulder to him and engaged the captain in an innocuous discussion of the entertainments planned for the voyage, gently weaving Eliza back into the conversation.

He felt an absurd urge to justify himself, but instead he moved back into the shadows of the row of palms, cursing Mina roundly in the privacy of his mind. She'd always had a shrewish side when thwarted, and it seemed the years had only made it worse. Ten years ago she'd all but browbeaten him into accepting her services as his secretary during their first encounter at Fairweather.

Knowing what he knew now, if he could only go back to that day she'd barged into the library and do things differently, he would send her packing right away. But he'd been all of twenty-five, still miserably weak after a brutal bout of influenza he'd contracted in Argentina and which had done its best to make his voyage back to England his last one. He'd not been alert or intelligent enough to perceive Peter's nineteen-year-old betrothed as a threat, merely a slightly amusing annoyance.

That had been his first mistake. The first in a long chain of mistakes.

Chapter Six

Ten years earlier, Fairweather Hall, Hampshire, July 1870

'Don't mind me. I've just come for my book.'

A woman's voice broke through the haze that too often plagued Max's mind since his illness and he looked up from the letter he was trying, and failing, to compose.

He'd not paid much attention to Peter's new fiancée when they'd been introduced yesterday afternoon and the last thing he'd expected was for her to barge into the library while he was trying to work. Everyone knew this was his domain while he was at Fairweather. The sooner this girl understood that, the better. He directed his coldest glare at her, but Lady Wilhelmina Davenport didn't even look at him and proceeded to prowl about, picking up and discarding cushions from the sofas and mumbling as she went.

'I'm quite certain I left it here on one of the sofas…'

'Next time leave it on a table in plain sight,' he said sharply and tried to fix his attention back on his letter. It had been weeks since he'd fallen ill and he still felt he was stumbling about in a fog-bound bog. He couldn't even seem to hold the pen without his hand cramping and the ink spluttering. He cursed under his breath and sat there for a moment, his fist around the pen, breathing heavily.

The silence alerted him that his problems had just expanded to include the unwanted scrutiny of Peter's annoying fiancée. She'd found her book and was clasping it to her plump bosom, watching him with a critical frown in her deep grey eyes.

'Couldn't you find anyone to help you, or are you being stubborn for the sake of it?' she demanded in the same abrupt tones. 'Here.' She pulled a chair to the other side of the desk and plucked the pen from his hand. 'Now, tell me what you wish to write.'

He stared at the girl, frustration and outrage creating a fireball inside him, burning past the pinching iciness in his limbs and shoving its way between him and the wish to just lay his head on the desk and surrender.

The girl rapped the tail of the pen on the blotter.

'Well? I'm waiting.'

He wanted to tell her to go to hell, but instead he began dictating.

His body might be disintegrating, but his voice was still at his command and he reeled out the letter with brutal speed, tossing in all the technical terms he could think of. It was utterly petty of him, but he watched her face with vindictive expectation, waiting for her to flounder in bewilderment.

When he finally concluded with a snapped 'Yours, Max Cavendish', she laughed, her eyes glinting up at him.

'Do you know, *Max Cavendish*, that if you'd been nice and polite I probably would have misspelled a word or two merely to help you feel superior, or perhaps dropped an *n* from tonnage. But your being nasty has put me on my mettle. What you need is some tea, with plenty of sugar.'

She pressed the bell and he woke from his stupor.

'What I need is to be left alone to finish my work.'

She planted her chin on one hand, and waved the other towards the wastepaper basket overflowing with his failed earlier drafts.

'The only thing you seem to be finishing is your cousin's writing paper.'

He drew a calming breath. Patience. This was Peter's fiancée. It wouldn't do to toss her bodily from the room. Not that he had the strength anyway.

'Lady Wilhelmina...'

'Mina. Wilhelmina is an awful name. I sound like one of the nastier characters from Wagner's operas.'

Patience.

'Mina. I appreciate your help, but I would really rather be alone.'

The door opened and Lady Wilhelmina—Mina—smiled at the footman.

'Tea for two, please, and lots of cake, or whatever you have that might sweeten this ill-tempered curmudgeon.'

The footman's eyes widened slightly, but he bowed his way out.

'I don't want tea or cakes. I want to be left *alone*.'

'From what Peter told me, you have been alone in here all week, against doctor's orders and your aunt's exhortations, and it isn't doing you much good. You can't even hold a pen straight for a full minute.'

Max discarded patience and manners in one fell swoop.

'Go *away*.'

'Make me.'

For a moment such a wave of fury caught him he had half risen from his seat to do just that, but his damned legs shook and he sank back, hot and cold and frustrated as all hell. He waited for her victorious comment, but she merely pulled the top book from a stack at the edge of the desk. A frown created two sharp lines between her brows as she read, and her mouth was pursed, like a child concentrating.

'How old are you?' he asked abruptly after his temper had calmed a little and she glanced up, marking her spot with her finger.

'Nineteen. Why?'

'You don't act nineteen. More like nine or ninety.'

'Either way that's older than you've been acting, Max Cavendish,' she said outrageously.

Before he could even formulate an answer the door opened again and Henry the footman entered with a tray. She patted the desk and after a moment's hesitation Henry set the tray down at the corner, careful not to upset the stack of books, and left.

'Here,' said Lady Wilhelmina as she pushed the plate of cake towards him. The smell wafted up and a flush of pale heat washed over him; that clenching, clammy sensation that kept coming and going. He hated it. He shook his head. She broke off a corner.

'Just this and I shall stop bothering you.'

He took it, his hand shaking. He forced himself to eat it, and even managed to drink some of the tea, cursing her in silence all the while. He set down the cup carefully, all his concentration on keeping his hand steady.

'I hate this.' The words were out of him before he could stop them and she leaned forward and rested her hand on his. It was warm, almost velvety on his tingling skin, as if his hand had fallen asleep. The gesture was both demeaning and comforting. He was too tired to even resent her any longer.

'I daresay you do,' she said. 'But I would wager that in a month you'll have forgotten what this feels like and probably think yourself invincible once more and go out into a rainstorm without your mackintosh and scorn anyone who wears a muffler.'

He couldn't help it, he smiled. 'Are you always so opinionated, Lady... Mina?'

'Yes. And Lady Mina is acceptable, but Mina is better. As you can tell, I'm not very ladylike. My father and mother despair of me, though quite frankly neither of them are very lordly or ladylike, no matter what they think of themselves.'

'Strange. Peter said you are known as a shining beacon of the *ton*.'

'I'm an excellent actress, that is all. Playing the supercilious ice princess in London keeps Mama and Father happy and allows me to do as I wish when I'm not dancing attendance on Society. Don't you ever act?'

'Not if I can help it.'

'Well, that's the benefit of privilege. You don't have to act. You're a man and wealthy and a Cavendish and handsome and you can do as you please. It is very annoying.'

He felt an unaccustomed blush heat his cheeks at the casual compliment, but he laughed again at this strange conversation. She shoved another corner of cake at him and this time he ate it without wanting to choke. He wasn't accustomed to sweet tea, but he drank it nonetheless and when she poured more he felt it easier not to protest. Protests only seemed to stoke her crusading zeal.

His whole career as an engineer was constructed on understanding and harnessing forces, and he knew that at least for the moment this particular force exceeded his own.

He wondered if Peter had any idea what he was taking on. And how the devil his strong-minded Aunt Almeria would get along with her equally stubborn daughter-in-law-to-be.

Perhaps that was why he'd accepted Mina's offer to act as his secretary that summer. He'd told himself it wouldn't only fill the gap until his own secretary arrived, but also keep Mina busy and out from under his aunt's feet while Peter was out on estate matters. A perfect solution for them all.

He'd never been so utterly wrong about anything in his life.

Chapter Seven

'Halloo! Max!' Septimus waved his hand in front of Max's face. 'Don't forget about the ten guineas you owe me.'

Max shook off the dark remnants of his memories and directed a quelling look at his uncle.

'Don't be so smug. You may have been right about Mina appearing, but you'll soon hit the impenetrable wall of her will.'

'You sound like you are looking forward to it. Smugly.'

Max couldn't help laughing and Septimus nudged his chin in Mina's direction.

'She's handling Eliza well, isn't she?'

'She isn't handling her at all. She's too busy flirting with Barrett.'

'Well, that's just it. Lead by example. She's staying within sight and earshot of Eliza, weaving her into the conversation when need be, but mostly just showing her how it is done.'

Max had to admit it was true. He'd always been rather amazed that Mina could be so irreverent in private and yet become as smooth as any of the vaunted Cavendish diplomats when forced into a social setting. He'd never quite been certain which persona to believe. In the end he'd realised they were both a lie.

'There, look,' Septimus continued. 'She's just drawn Eliza into the conversation. I'd wager once she sees the wheels are greased she'll slip away... Ah, there. Told you so.'

Max rolled his eyes, but Septimus was gesturing to Mina and didn't notice. She hesitated but approached, her chin rising a notch.

'Yes, master?'

Septimus grinned and handed her a glass of champagne from the tray of a passing steward.

'Barrett was a good choice. Opera lover.'

'And very wealthy. Perhaps he'll offer for her and you'll be short one opera singer by the time we dock.'

Max smiled as Septimus frowned and rushed towards his investment.

'Now you've ruined it,' Max said lightly. 'A budding romance blighted.'

'Eliza would eat him for breakfast, in any case.'

'She seems far more likely to hide under the table, frankly.'

'She is still intimidated by Society, but once she finds her feet, you'll see that all that sweetness is merely a coating for a core of steel. She's suffered great hardship in her life. She is no frail flower.'

'Isn't she? She certainly seems to wilt every time I so much as say good morning to her.'

'That's because you're intimidating.'

'Nonsense.'

'And what is more, you enjoy it. There is a good reason why you didn't follow the Cavendish path and become a diplomat. You like engines far more than people.'

'You make me sound like an ogre. *You* were certainly never intimidated by me.'

'Well, I had the felicity of meeting you at your worst. It is hard to be intimidated by someone who is too weak to rise from his chair. I spent a whole week thinking you were shorter than Peter. By the time you stood up and I realised you towered over him by four inches I had discovered a whole host of your flaws, so intimidation was never on the table.'

She was trying to rile him, but it had the opposite effect. He tried to clamp down on his smile, but failed. It was damnable, but she was reminding him why they became friends all those years ago.

'Have you ever been intimidated, Minnie?'

'Yes. By your aunt.'

'Ah, yes. I remember that. I never quite understood why, though.'

'Didn't you? Wouldn't you find it uncomfortable if

the woman who was to be your mother-in-law thoroughly disliked you?'

'Uncomfortable, yes. But not necessarily intimidated. That implies she had an advantage over you, when in fact it was quite the other way around.'

Her eyes narrowed and she seemed to go inside herself to consider his words. He waited, watching tiny shifts in expression flit across her face as she thought. That too was familiar.

He'd never been quite able to decide if she was beautiful. Sometimes he thought she was and sometimes not, and there didn't seem to be rhyme or reason to why. She was as complex and shifting as the most elaborate engine, except that he'd always been able to decipher an engine's blueprint.

'You're right,' she said at last. 'How peculiar. It always seemed as if she could see right through me.'

'Perhaps she could.'

Her eyes focused again and rose to his. 'Of course. I forgot my role. The scheming hussy trying to pull the wool over everyone's eyes.'

He wanted to agree with that. After all, that had been his conclusion that horrible day she finally ripped off her mask—that she had tricked them all finely and used them to further her greedy schemes. The shock that day had been so extreme he'd had to believe she was every bit as black as she appeared. But now, with that defiant tilt to her chin and the mocking smile on her rose-tinged lips, his certainty was crumbling at the edges.

'I think you wanted her to like you.'

'Your aunt? Don't be ridiculous. Why on earth would I? Just because you adored the ground she trod on, doesn't mean—'

'Do you know that your most mocking comments were always the least convincing, Minnie?'

Her eyelids fluttered and she turned her face away a little, as if watching the crowd.

'You used to do that when you felt your back was to the wall for some reason,' he continued. 'I always felt you were defending some hidden truth when you lashed out.'

'I'm not some engine to be dismantled for your inspection, Max. If you're bored, go flirt with someone.'

'That's no antidote to boredom. And you are merely proving my point. You said you felt my aunt saw through you—to what? To the truth of what you were planning to do to Peter?'

She began to move away, but he clasped her arm lightly, moving with her as if it was natural. His fingers settled on the soft warmth of her inner elbow where her pulse beat fast and hard against his fingers. Immediately his own shot up to match it, forcing a wave of heat through him like steam through a pipe. It was so fast and definite he had to concentrate to keep his breathing level.

Damn, damn, *damn*...

'Let me go,' she hissed.

He knew he had to. That he had to nip this strange conflagration in the bud. It was just old memories, all that talk of the past... It meant nothing.

'Good evening, Mr Cavendish.'

They both turned in unison to face an attractive woman dressed in a Hunter's green evening dress.

'Good Evening, Mrs Garfunkel,' Max replied, years of breeding draining the emotions from his voice.

'Do pray introduce me, Mr Cavendish. I believe you must be Miss Davenport?'

Max made the introductions, a little reluctantly, feeling the tension in Mina's arm.

'Pray excuse my being so forward,' Mrs Garfunkel continued, a faint flush spreading over her porcelain-pale cheeks. 'But I feel I ought to apologise for my daughter. I understood from Nurse that she was making a nuisance of herself on deck.'

'Oh, no. It was no such thing,' Mina said hurriedly. 'I was quite happy to speak with her.'

Mrs Garfunkel's smile twisted slightly, as if well accustomed to politely evasive answers when it came to her daughter.

'That is kind of you, but I shall of course make it clear to her not to importune you—'

'Mrs Garfunkel,' Mina interrupted again, her tone flatter now. 'I assure you, I am quite sincere. In fact, I admit to being in awe of your daughter. I have rarely met a child as bright for her age, and as a former teacher, I have met quite a few. Don't you agree, Mr Cavendish?' She turned towards Max, a sharp challenge in her eyes.

He smiled at Mrs Garfunkel. 'I agree with Miss Davenport that your daughter is exceptionally intelligent. I hope you didn't mind my giving her a book to read?'

Mrs Garfunkel appeared a little stymied by their responses, but then she smiled, her shoulders lowering a little.

'Was that your book? Arthur was most…surprised.'

'Miss Garfunkel expressed an interest in engines when Miss Davenport and I met her on deck the other day. I thought she might enjoy it.'

Mrs Garfunkel laughed.

'She did, indeed. She fell asleep reading it. It is usually quite hard for her to… But you cannot be interested in such matters. In any case, thank you for your patience. However, if she does become a bother, you must tell me. I do try to explain to her…' She paused again and Mina shifted forward a little, softening once more.

'If you don't mind, she might appreciate more books like the one Mr Cavendish gave her.'

'I have quite a few more in my rooms,' Max offered. 'I'm only too happy to share them. It is rare to meet someone other than engineers who actually enjoys what most people would find painfully dull.'

Mrs Garfunkel cast a quick glance in the direction of her husband.

'I am not certain… Our doctor said it is best not to encourage her inclinations.'

Mina's mouth went flat and Max tensed. He knew that look. But then it was gone.

'What do *you* think, Mrs Garfunkel?' she asked, her voice low and almost seductive. Mrs Garfunkel's hands twisted into one another.

'I think…the book made her so happy. That is rare. But Arthur and Doctor Innes think she must learn the scriptures before she is allowed to read anything else. The better to balance the mind.'

Max watched with amusement as Mina drew a long breath and he interceded before her patience snapped once more.

'If they have a taste for scripture, I suggest a line from Proverbs: "A merry heart doeth good like a medicine, but a broken spirit drieth the bones." Though I doubt your doctor would agree about the curative powers of happiness.'

'Well, I do,' Mrs Garfunkel said resolutely, eyeing her husband from across the room. 'I think I shall have a word with Arthur.'

They watched her cut through the crowd, doing a fair impersonation of a shark through a school of herring.

'Mr Garfunkel might not thank you for that,' Mina murmured. 'Does your business depend on him?'

'The other way around.'

'Oh. Good.'

'Good? I would think you would be happy to see me go under. Especially after our earlier conversation.'

She flushed and he cursed his pettiness.

'I apologise for that, Minnie. I should have held my tongue.'

'It makes no odds to me. I'm not surprised you think me vindictive as well as duplicitous.'

'That is not what I think…' He took a deep breath. 'I honestly don't know what to think when it comes to you. You've always been able to surprise me.'

She hesitated and seemed on the verge of saying something, but then she shrugged and he knew the moment had passed.

'I was merely pleased he was in your debt rather than the other way around, because that way he will wish to placate you and might even allow Anne to take a book from you.'

'I see. Though you might have had the courtesy of asking me first. You were very generous with my belongings.'

'I might, but I didn't.' Her chin rose again, but her eyes were laughing now and the dimple reappeared.

'You never did ask before borrowing my books, Mina.'

'You never did tell me you minded.'

'I didn't.'

'Well, then.'

'Well, then.'

Well, he'd forgotten that, too. Sometimes it was impossible not to smile around Mina. Even his aunt had sometimes succumbed, utterly against her will.

'On one condition,' he added and her eyes narrowed in suspicion.

'Which is?'

'That you help me choose. I don't see why you should take all the credit while I do all the work, Minnie.'

'I don't see why not. You had no problem when I did all the work and you took all the credit ten years ago, Maxie. Ah, we are being summoned to dinner. Good. Winning arguments always makes me hungry.'

With a smile and a nod, she sailed off. Max watched her go, amusement and annoyance battling for supremacy.

Chapter Eight

'Ah, nothing like a brisk walk the morning after a successful show,' Septimus announced, slapping his hands down on the railing beside Mina. It took her a moment to identify the theme of his waistcoat. The garish green and mustard-coloured parrots rising out of flowering bushes like pheasants at a shoot were probably a tribute to the *Magic Flute*.

He took a deep draw of sea air as he surveyed the ocean, like a potentate standing on the balcony above his cheering minions. Mina smiled at the image of a school of fish suddenly rising on their tails out of the waves, mouths agape in adoration.

What would it be like to be so incurably optimistic about life as Septimus Cavendish? Probably quite pleasant.

'Eliza is still asleep, but she did say she enjoyed herself last night. I think she did very well, don't you?'

'She far exceeded my expectations, Mina dear. Especially after her rocky beginning. You've done a marvelous job with her in such a short time.'

'I cannot take credit. She is a naturally nice person. People want to like her.'

'So they do, which is part of the problem. I don't want people to merely like her. I want them to adore her, and that is a whole different kettle of fish. But we shall work on that once she is a little more comfortable. Oh, and I wished to tell you that was an inspired choice of gown for her. I knew I could trust you.'

'How do you know it was my choice?'

'I presume she wanted to wear the primrose yellow.'

Mina laughed, remembering her almost argument with Eliza yesterday.

'True. She felt the blue too somber. Luckily Mrs Oakes agreed with me or we might have had our first falling out.'

'You stick to your guns, then, girl. The yellow will do for after a performance when I want her to be *éclatante*. The blue was perfect to convey presence and poise. It left them curious and wanting more. And contrasting it with your decadent rose colour... That, my dear, was a master stroke.'

Mina took a deep breath.

'Which reminds me. Those clothes. I appreciate the finery but you have wasted your money. There are far too many gowns for our short journey.'

'Well, of course, my dear. Most of them are for London.'

'I don't need a parade of evening gowns to tutor

Eliza. This isn't a pantomime. She can employ her imagination.'

He leaned his elbow on the railing, a look of surprise on his handsome face.

'But you shall need them the moment the invitations start pouring in to meet *La Serena*. And I plan for them to be pouring in immediately. In fact, we shall mostly likely have to commission more clothes once we reach London, but I believe we have enough to support us through the first week or so.'

'But... You *cannot* mean that I should accompany her *into* Society. My role is merely to prepare her...'

'No, no, I could have hired a governess or some old Society maven to do that. And there would have been plenty of hostesses only too willing to parade her about to their friends like a plumed parakeet. But I wanted someone to stand by her through all those endless evenings. Steer her through the shoals. You know—like one of those little boats that comes out to guide the ships into port.'

Mina leaned on the railing as well, her breath not quite filling her lungs.

'That is not what I understood at all. I cannot. That is impossible.'

'Nonsense. I saw you at Fairweather. You could always talk with anyone, duchess to scullery maid. That's what Eliza Serena needs to see... In action, not in theory. And she needs someone with her when she enters the pit of vipers that is the *ton*; someone savvy but perfectly respectable. That's you.'

Perfectly respectable.

She looked away, trying to anchor herself. Around them people were strolling or basking in the sun, their chatter above the rush of water, the scent of the sea. Cheery and bright.

She had to tell him the truth. What difference did it make?

Except it did. This was no time for sentimentality. She knew how the world worked. Being Lord Bascombe's daughter was her only reliable asset in a world that revered status. It was what had convinced the wealthy women of New York to hire her to teach their children, not her intellectual skills.

Returning to England was already putting her at risk. The moment she set foot in England the secret might find a way to bubble upwards, like noxious gas out of a swamp. Closing her eyes to that possibility would not make it go away.

No, she could not tell Septimus the truth. Yet she had to tell him something; explain why it was impossible…

A horde of children rushed by, interrupting her tumbled thoughts. Septimus clucked his tongue and took her elbow lightly.

'Come, it's too noisy to talk privately here. We'll go to our parlour. Max is spending the morning with the ship's engineers, looking at plans for some new four-stroke whatnot or something so he'll be down there for hours.'

* * *

Max's state rooms were just as lovely as she remembered. Now she wondered how she hadn't noticed the shelves of engineering books. Or how familiar the earthy colours of the furnishings and the clear, sharp lines of the drawings were. She'd seen it before, after all, in Max's study at Fairweather. No wonder it had felt so...comfortable.

'Come, sit,' Septimus said abruptly. 'You need a brandy.'

'It's barely noon.'

'Brandy has nothing to do with the time of day. It has to do with a time of need.'

She didn't argue. Septimus usually had his own way. In that sense he was like Max, though they both reached their ends by rather different routes. She took the glass he extended her and spoke the words that had been plaguing her from the moment he'd made his offer.

'For the life of me I cannot fathom why you hired me, Septimus.'

'Why? Because I knew you could help Eliza, of course.'

'But you must have known... You *do* know what happened between Peter and me.'

'Well, of course I do. There was very little else discussed behind Peter's back for several weeks after you jilted him.'

She hadn't thought she could feel worse. Apparently she could.

'Then why employ me? Why are you even being nice to me? Or is this some convoluted plot to punish me?'

He chuckled. 'Now *that* would be operatic in the best Greek tradition. My dear girl, I may make my living from histrionics, but I am too old to be impressed by them. Besides, what was there to punish?'

'I jilted Peter.'

'High drama indeed!'

'You find this amusing?'

'Hardly amusing, but look at it from my perspective. Here were two children—because that was what you were, no matter what you might have thought at the time—who thought they were in love, then something went wrong and you turned tail and ran. Now, had you merely run home to Mama, there would have been a hue and cry for a few weeks and then everyone would have been suitably bored and gone about their business. After a while you and Peter would have crawled out of your blue devils and probably pursued perfectly happy lives with other people. The only thing adding piquancy to your tale was that instead of hiding at Bascombe until the hullabaloo quieted down, you hopped on a boat for destinations unknown. But even that fell flat after a while. Now, if a severed head had surfaced, or perhaps a plot to subvert Parliament... Well, *then* we would have had a toasty little scandal. But I'm afraid as things stood, your tale was eclipsed within a fortnight by Lord Pulteney marrying his scullery maid.'

She didn't know whether to laugh or cry at Septimus's version of her life.

'Well, perhaps you are right and the scandal is rather tame as far as Society is concerned, but you know they will be all too happy to fan that measly flame, especially if I were to return to London in the company of a Cavendish.'

'Well, naturally, but it will be much more smoke than fire. And those tend to run out of fuel and fizzle. The way forward, my dear,' he continued, tucking his thumbs into his vest pockets, 'is bravado. If you hang your head, they will hand it to you on a platter. If you are Lady Mina Davenport and look down your pretty little nose at them and hint you have led a most fascinating life, they shall be as entranced as I.'

'Perhaps. Until they tire of me.'

'Perhaps. But until then you will have helped Eliza find her feet and her aplomb.'

'Mr Cavendish...'

'Call me Sep. I cannot see why you will not at least make an effort.'

'It has nothing to do with effort...'

'Are you truly so worried about what a few narrow-minded people might say? It is not like you to cry craven.'

She laughed. 'I cried craven ten years ago.'

'Well, you aren't nineteen any longer, and from the

abridged version you told me of your progress around the globe it strikes me you've rarely cried craven since. You'll have to provide me with far better arguments if you wish to convince me I shouldn't employ you.'

'No, she doesn't.'

With a sense of fatality, Mina turned. Max was standing in the doorway, wiping his hands on a towel. As was the case the last time he'd found her on the veranda he wore no coat or waistcoat. There were dark streaks across the white linen of his shirt in a clear pattern where he'd probably leaned on a greased mechanism.

'Max, my boy. I thought you would be occupied for at least another couple hours.'

'I'm sorry to disappoint you. And Mina doesn't have to convince you of anything. She is free to act as she wishes. You don't always know best, Sep.'

'Well, she certainly doesn't need *you* arguing her case,' Septimus replied, showing a flash of annoyance for the first time.

'I'm well aware of that. But at the moment you're her employer which means you have an advantage over her. Don't abuse it. Not on my territory at least.'

Septimus straightened, fists on hips, but he still stood several inches below his nephew, and with significantly less force of frame and manner. It was more a theatrical statement than a challenge, and some of Mina's nervousness faded into amusement. It didn't survive Max's next comment.

'Let sleeping dogs lie, Sep. Mina can help Eliza during the voyage and then return to New York. I don't understand why you are so obsessed with introducing that girl to Society in any case. She'll do just as well without putting her through a damned mangle.'

'Oh, now you're a theatrical expert, too?'

'No, but I don't think the risks of having Mina accompany her into Society are worth the benefits.'

'What risks? A few mean-minded gossips?'

'He means Peter,' Mina said coolly and Max finally turned to her. She had been wrong about his calm—he was as furious as she was.

'Yes, I mean Peter. I don't wish to see him hurt again.'

'Neither do I.'

'Unfortunately I have no reason to believe you. Even if I did, it may not be up to you.'

She snorted. 'I think I shall leave you two strong, clever men to continue this edifying discourse on what I should or should not do. You don't really need me here.' She moved towards the doorway but Max remained where he was and she cast him a sharp look. 'You're developing quite a habit of blocking doorways, Max Cavendish. Kindly rid yourself of it.'

Laughter shimmered over his face and was gone, but he didn't budge. Behind her Sep gave a lengthy sigh.

'There really is no point in arguing. After all, you have already contractually agreed to act as her Social companion in London, Mina.'

Mina turned sharply. 'I did no such thing.'

'Did too. Signed and sealed. It is right there in your employment contract.'

'It most certainly was *not* in there. There was only one page and I read it all.'

'That was the *last* page. I didn't want to burden you with the details.'

'Do you mean to say you showed me only one page of my contract?'

'It was a good summary of the most salient of the points. Not all of them, though.'

'Well, then I don't have to honour what I didn't agree to.'

'Legally you do. You signed it, even if you didn't read it.'

'I didn't read it because you didn't give it to me!'

'You could claim that in a court of law, but solicitors are expensive, you know. Barristers even more so.'

'Why on earth would I need to claim that in court?'

'Well, to sue me to pay your wages.'

Her mouth fell open. 'Are you threatening to withhold my wages?'

'Well, you're telling me you won't honour your contract…'

'You slimy, maggot-ridden bastard! You're *blackmailing* me.' She strode towards him, bubbling with anger.

'No, no, merely trying to convince you…'

'Well, you sure as hell aren't about to convince me by threatening me, Septimus Cavendish.'

He clicked his tongue. 'Sometimes you sound thoroughly American, Mina dear. It is clearly time you came home.'

'I don't *have* a home,' she all but yelled. 'And what home I had you convinced me to leave under false pretenses and now you...' Her voice cracked and she turned back to the doorway, but stopped as Max still didn't budge. 'If you make me push past you, I'll use a great deal of elbow. Move.'

Max did move, though not enough for her to pass by without brushing against him. She was about to make good on her threat when Septimus spoke.

'Why don't we draw straws?'

His voice was bright again, his brief show of temper having fizzled like a doused match.

'Straws?' she and Max asked in unison.

'Yes, you know. As in: short straw—I pay you and you board the first boat back to New York. Middling straw—you act as companion for *La Serena*'s social coming out. And long straw—you stay in London, but take no active role in social engagements. You could be an *éminence grise*, you know, behind the curtains as it were. *Whoooo*.' The latter sound might have meant to be ghostly, but came out slightly celebratory.

'Why does *my* choice get the short straw?' Mina demanded, not knowing whether to laugh or resort to violence. Max didn't seem to share her indecision.

'Why don't we just cut to the chase and toss you overboard, Sep?'

'Because you love me, nephew. Come now, where's your sporting sense?'

'Where's your sense of decency?'

'I'm a Cavendish. We aren't required to possess any. The Cavendish motto is *Factum Fortuna*, after all. We have always made our own rules and our own fortune. You two stay here. I'll go find some straws.'

He had no compunction pushing past Max, who was too busy glaring at Mina to notice.

'You cannot mean to take part in this,' he demanded, quite as if she'd penned this farce herself. She tried to meet outrage with outrage, but it just wasn't there. It was too absurd.

She shrugged. 'I'd forgotten how exhausting he is. A pity you cannot find a way to harness his energy to your engines—imagine how much you could save in coal.'

This time the amusement that flickered over his face stayed. She continued before his smile eroded her defences far more effectively than his attacks.

'You want to get your way, Maxie? You convince him to play fair and honour the contract I signed, not some bogus addendum. I was hired to act as companion on the voyage to England. That was exceedingly clear. I might consider adding a week to support her in London while she becomes accustomed to her new situation. Then Septimus pays me in full and I go on my way.'

'Where?'

'That is none of your concern. So if you wanna keep yer nose on yer face, you'll keep it out of mine, see?' She used the heaviest New York accent she could think of and this time laughter finally won over his control. He leaned on the door jamb and crossed his arms.

'You should go on the stage yourself, Minnie.'

'Maybe I will. Maybe Septimus could find me a role in Drury Lane. There's a solution to all our problems.'

The smile faded. 'You won't like the life.'

'Couldn't be much worse than governess to the gilded brats of New York.'

'Septimus said you'd also been a schoolteacher and a nurse and a few other things.'

'So?'

He shook his head. 'So nothing. You've led an interesting life. I'm just wondering how it all came about. What did happen ten years ago, Mina? Who *did* you run off with?'

'A tinker, a tailor, and a candlestick maker.'

'All three? How enterprising. Rather tiring, though. Who, Minnie? Was it Attwood? Where did you meet him?'

He noted the shock on her face, his own hardening as he moved forward. She backed away, not out of fear, just utter shock.

'So it *was* Attwood, then,' Max said, his voice low,

hard. 'But he was headed to Brazil, not San Francisco. What happened? Did you realise you didn't want to live in the backwaters of a mining town in Brazil after all? Did you meet him in London before you met Peter?'

He'd backed her against the veranda railing and planted his hands on either side of her. He was far too close; she could see the faint shadow of blue in his eyes, the darkness of stubble outlining his jaw. She looked away, her eyes catching on a smudge of engine oil on his cheek, just below the too-sharp rise of his cheekbone. She curled her fingers into her palm against the need to rub it off.

'Don't crowd me, Max,' she managed, her voice raw. 'You'll get grease on my dress.'

He glanced down at his shirt, but remained where he was.

'You didn't seem to mind getting greasy when you were clambering around the undercarriages of trains in Swindon ten years ago. You were as grimy as a coal trimmer by the end of the day.'

Her eyes widened at the memory of when she and Peter had gone with Max to visit the new Great Western Railway's locomotive repair facilities. Peter hadn't cared much for the warehouses filled with steam-huffing engines and dismantled machinery, but she'd loved it. She'd wandered about this artificial world in utter awe, not caring about niceties like clean clothes and neat hair. They'd sat down for tea with the engineers and railway officers in a large hall and dined on tea and bread and butter. It had been one of her happiest days while at Fairweather. Before everything became muddled and eventually exploded.

'Well, that was then, this is now. You may be able to afford new shirts every Monday and Friday, but I can't.'

'Don't try to change the subject, Mina. Were you and Attwood lovers before you met Peter? Did your father forbid you to marry him? Was that why you accepted Peter's proposal? God damn it, just tell me!'

She almost laughed at the absurdity of the accusation, but her mind fastened instead on another question. 'How on earth did you know who was on the ship I sailed on?'

'There is such a thing as a passenger list. He and a João Murinho were the only men on board the SS *Speedwell* who you could feasibly have eloped with. But Murinho had only spent one month in England, all of it in York and Manchester. Not a likely candidate.'

'But how did you even know *I* was on that ship? I didn't use our real names when I bought passage.'

'It was hardly a challenge. When you disappeared from the carriage in Liverpool your father assumed you'd run back to Peter so he descended on Fairweather demanding your return. Peter insisted on helping search for you so we returned with Bascombe to Liverpool and spoke to the harbour master who described a very fashionable and very stubborn young woman who bought passage for herself and her weeping mother on the *Speedwell*. So, it *was* Attwood. What happened? Did the reality of the elopement not match the fantasy?'

She laughed. Poor Timothy Attwood, reciting poetry to her mother on the fish- and tar-scented deck.

'I'd never met Mr Attwood before in my life. I wasn't interested in him or João Murinho and they weren't interested in me. They had enough on their hands with Mama. But at least they kept her entertained until Rio, the poor dears.'

His frown created two sharp lines between his brows, his skeptical gaze moving over her, gauging.

'Then why did you sail? Were you on your way to meet someone?'

'I don't owe you any answers. Don't think you can intimidate me, mister.' She poked his chest with her finger. Working with engines must be quite strenuous because his chest was as hard as a rock and it probably hurt her finger more than it hurt him. She considered poking him again, this time in the stomach. That had to be softer than his chest.

He bent his hands, moving closer so there was just a shiver of a breeze between their legs. She ought to have been a little worried, cornered by a very large, muscled and suspicious man, but she wasn't at all. She felt...exhilarated.

Not good.

It wasn't smart to be enjoying this game of cat and mouse, or rather, cat and dog. But she was.

This felt familiar, almost comforting. Ten years ago she'd revelled in the challenge of testing her wits against his. So had he. At least at the beginning. Towards the end of her sojourn at Fairweather he'd seemed to tire of it, retreating back behind his battlements, shutting her out.

The breeze rose, fluttering her skirts between his legs. He moved forward a little more, his legs slightly apart, his hands curving around the railing as his head bent towards her.

'You don't *owe* me answers, Mina. But tell me anyway.'

His voice, honey warm and soft, drew her gaze back to his. He had the Cavendish eyes—a deep velvety grey with a silvery sun around the pupil and just the faintest hint of blue. They showed so much of what he was thinking when he let them. And they could smile without a muscle on his face moving—just…light up.

Her eyes escaped that light, falling to his mouth which was no better because it was far too beautiful—sharp cut, like a marble masterpiece. But she knew it was nothing like marble. It was silk soft and firm and warm…

No.

She was damned if she would fall into the trap of being swayed by the deep, honeyed voice he'd employed when he wanted something. Just—no.

'Why did you leave Peter?' His voice kept going lower, approaching the deep thrumming of the engines.

'*You* told me why, Max. He wasn't wealthy enough.'

He shook his head. 'Don't play games. I didn't pay much attention at the time, but I heard you had far wealthier suitors before you accepted Peter. Bascombe made certain of that.'

'He did indeed. Perhaps I chose Peter as an act of rebellion?'

A burst of wind wrapped her skirts about his legs and whipped her hair about her face. A tendril caught on her lips and she raised her hand to draw it away, but he got there first. His fingers brushed against her mouth, drawing the hair gently to the side and resting very lightly on her cheek. His gaze held hers for a moment, then lowered to settle on her mouth. A wave of shock ran through her, tightening her skin like a corset drawn far too tight. She needed desperately to draw air, and against her will she felt her lips part.

His own indrawn breath was sharp, like a burn. He moved closer, his legs pressing her skirts against her.

'No. Not a rebellion. I was there when Peter brought you to Fairweather. You aren't that good an actress. So, what happened, Mina?'

'You know what happened, Max. You were there when I jilted Peter. Or do you need me to refresh your memory?'

'Hardly. Your unveiling of your true character was

very…memorable.' There was no trace of seductive warmth in his voice now. She should have known it was merely another of his devices.

'I'm flattered, Maxie. I hadn't realised I'd made such a strong impression on you. It's nice to have one's skills appreciated.'

'Actually, your skills were off that day. A little too Lady Macbeth trying to scrub Peter out like a damned spot. I was even so naive as to wonder if your guilt at coming between Peter and Emily had convinced you to test the depth of Peter's commitment to you.'

'Goodness, that is twistier than one of your uncle's operas,' she scoffed.

'True, but I was still labouring under the misapprehension that you weren't a conniving, greedy fraud. Luckily, you settled that point when I was foolish enough to follow you to Bascombe Hall.'

She shrugged, absurdly hurt though she had no reason to be—she'd earned his contempt fairly.

Some people rose to greater moral heights under adversity. Not her. That day…she'd been vicious. She'd been bad enough during that scene in the village, but a hundredfold worse when Max had come to Bascombe Hall later that afternoon to confront her over jilting Peter.

'Why *did* you leave him, Mina?'

His voice had recovered that soothing, coaxing tone. But she knew it for the trap it was.

She extended her finger again. This time laying

it gently on his chest. She'd played this game before once. She could do it again.

'You're the big, smart, capable man. You tell me, Max…'

She drew a line down his chest as she let out his name on a long breath. The wind was colder now, but she was flushed inside and out with her daring. He must have been clenching every muscle in his body because even his abdomen was hard. With the last sibilant hiss of his name she reached his waistband and her bravado faltered. She could feel her skin as if a hot wind was flaying it, like the thick summer winds in the valleys outside San Francisco, the kind that baked you and left you panting.

This is not a good idea, Mina, a sensible voice was calling out through the closet door where she'd shoved it head first.

His hand settled on hers, holding it against his waist. Without pressure, but firmly. She could feel his heartbeat, or hers. Probably hers—it felt swift, hard, like the rhythmic pounding of the engines beneath them. His voice was still deep, but a little breathless when he spoke.

'I think… I think perhaps your father forced you. I just don't know how.'

She tried not to react, but her fingers curled into his shirt, against his skin. He drew in another sharp breath and a flush of stifling heat spread through her, her own muscles bracing to repel it.

'You shall have to be more specific than that, Mr Cavendish. I don't award points for wide shots.'

'But it is true?'

He let go her hand, both of his curving about her waist as he moved even closer, his thumbs shifting the fabric of her dress softly against her skin, just a gentle, rhythmic sweep. In contrast, the rhythm of her breathing was completely awry.

'Is it true, Mina?'

'No points yet, Mr Cavendish. Toss your dice again.'

'I don't want to play games, Mina. All I want is the truth.' His voice was as tempting as his hands, but she managed to shake her head.

'No. You want weapons.' She steeled herself and shifted forward, one leg following her skirts between his legs. She knew, without a doubt, that this was a mistake but, by God, it felt good. It felt powerful. Alive.

'You want ammunition, Max. Don't you? Something to hold over me. You're caught in time, still treating me like a child, someone to be easily indulged or rebuffed. Managed. I'm not manageable, Max.'

She slid her leg even deeper, bending it to rub against the inside of his thigh. Under his tanned skin she saw the heat flush over his cheekbones and felt it in her cheeks as well, felt it everywhere. In the tightening of her breasts, the warming, softening of the inside of her thighs.

'The Mina you knew is long, long gone. If you want

something from me, you shall have to do a better job negotiating.'

His legs clamped on hers, hard, holding her there as his hand slipped down to cup her backside and pull her against him, forcing her to rise on tiptoes.

'You were never easy, Mina. But by all means, let us negotiate.' He bent, brushing his mouth over her cheek, utterly surprising her until he whispered in her ear. 'Go ahead, make your demands. I'm listening.'

The only thing she could think of demanding was utterly, utterly wrong. His lips were warm against her, her lungs filling with his scent, the coolness of the tall pines of the Presidio and a deeper scent—warm and earthy.

She couldn't think or move. Every thought that tried to form fizzled in the red-hot steam that was pumping through her. It was too strong. Foreign. Frightening. The heat between her legs shimmered like liquid electricity, building...

'Tell me what you want, Mina.' He spoke the words against her throat, his voice raw, his breath searing her from within.

Turn back the clock...

The words were clear in the haze of lust that engulfed her. Clear and cold.

Turn back the clock...

He drew away abruptly and she realised she'd said the words aloud. He took another step back, shoving his hands through his hair the way he did when he faced a problem he couldn't unravel.

'I wouldn't do that even if I could, Minnie. You play the cards you draw.' His voice was now as icy and biting as a Chicago winter.

She swallowed and nodded.

You play the cards you draw.

She gave a little nod of acceptance and walked past him and out of the state room.

Ten years ago she'd chosen precisely how to play the cards that life had dealt her.

That day... That confrontation had haunted her for years. Not just jilting Peter, but also what happened afterwards with Max. Even now the memory was as pristine and clear and coldly painful as an Alpine spring.

It was disingenuous to indulge in fantasies now. She'd not just jilted Peter, she'd burnt her bridges with him and Max and England with wild abandon.

There was no coming back from the choices she had made that fateful day ten years ago.

Chapter Nine

Ten years earlier, Bascombe Hall, July 1870

Mina sat on her bed and watched the chaos in her room at Bascombe Hall without seeing any of it. The hurrying maids, the footmen bringing and removing trunks and bandboxes... And her mother—standing in the middle of the now-cluttered room like Dido amidst the ruins of Carthage—dispensing orders to all and sundry in a chirrupy voice that made it clear she refused to see her daughter's predicament as anything but an opportunity.

Mina watched and said nothing. There was nothing to say. Nothing to feel. Just...nothing.

For a moment she tried to recall Peter's face as he'd stood before her in the village square while she'd publicly jilted him. Had it only been an hour ago? It already felt far away...submerged. So were her feelings. Poor Peter. He'd been upset, confused... But it was hard to remember his expression now. The dark shadow of Max loomed over Peter's shoulder, obscuring him. Max had remained on his horse. Watching it all. Like it was a penny play. A farce.

She shut her eyes, sinking her fingers into the coverlet of her bed. No, not her bed, not any longer. That was over.

Another wave of queasy cold rumbled through her and she wondered what her mother would do if she was sick all over the carpet.

It was tempting.

'Lady Mina.' Footman George stood in the doorway.

'What?' she replied listlessly.

'There's a Mr Cavendish here to see you, Lady Mina. In the library.'

'Mr Cavendish? I thought you told him it was over, Wilhelmina,' her mother snapped.

'I did, Mama. In no uncertain terms. I don't know why he came.'

'Oh, send him away, George.'

Mina was tempted to let George do just that. But that wasn't fair. If Peter wanted one last confrontation, she owed him that. She rose.

'No. I shall do it.'

Downstairs she paused before the library door, breathed deeply a few times, raised her chin, and entered.

And froze.

Not Peter's pleasant, caring, confused face.

Max.

An uncomfortable sensation of the ground being tugged out from under her was followed by a surge of relief—he'd seen through her. Of course he had. In a way he knew her better than Peter did. He had come to demand the truth. Perhaps this was what she had been waiting for.

This thought, childish and vain, lasted only a minute.

'What the devil are you doing?' Max demanded before she even closed the door. He was still wearing his riding gear and was still as coldly furious as when he'd watched her jilt Peter. 'You cannot mean to marry Sir Godfrey Renfrew. He's old enough to be your father. Has the Bascombe greed so completely possessed you that you've taken leave of your senses?'

Perhaps if he'd been kind, she might have succumbed to the need to tell him. But the mention of Bascombe tipped the scales with ease. All her training, her bravado, rushed back to protect her from her own folly.

'Thirty-eight is a perfectly reasonable age for a husband,' she replied. 'And only a person with more money than he knows what to do with would treat the wish to be wealthy as a mental aberration.'

'Peter is hardly poor,' he objected.

'Peter is a younger brother living on whatever allowance his brother allows him. All he has to his name is a modest house and some farmland on the edge of the Cavendish estate. Sir Godfrey could buy him out a hundredfold and not even notice he'd done so.'

'Then why become engaged to Peter in the first place, damn you?'

She shrugged, cold inside and out now. She thought of her mother upstairs, packing and planning a grand wedding for her in Sir Godfrey's estate in Cumbria. Of Lord Bascombe in his study, counting the gold he'd receive on delivery of the last Bascombe bride.

Neither of them gave a damn that she was an illegitimate fraud. That her whole life was a lie. She shouldn't either, but she did. It was hot acid, burning a hole inside her, emptying her out.

She straightened her back and channeled her mother, moving to the mantelpiece where only three figurines remained, too cheap to sell. Three china dogs with tails in the air, tongues lolling. Chester, Beef, and Grumpet. She'd played with them as a child, content with them and the village children as company long before she'd realised something was rotten within the Bascombe household.

'Answer me, damn it,' Max snarled behind her and she turned.

'Why did I become engaged to Peter? Because he is young and handsome and I thought he was far wealthier than he is. Everyone is always going on about how wealthy the Cavendishes are. How was I to know he only inherited a few measly acres of farmland and that he actually meant to farm them himself? It was very disappointing. Still, it served its purpose. Sir Godfrey hadn't come up to scratch while I was in London, but now I was out of reach he told Papa he had to have me. Enough to offer to settle five thousand pounds on me for my use alone. Imagine how many dresses I could buy with that! And in truth, though I've had a grand time at Fairweather, I don't really wish to become a farmer's wife, living off the charity of his older brother and under the shadow of a mother-in-law who looks down on me. I can do better. As Sir Godfrey's offer has just proven.'

He shook his head, as if chasing something away. She could almost hear his sharp, analytical mind trying to arrange these revelations with his previous convictions. Part of her wanted him to fling it all back at her, call it out for the lie it was. All she needed was a tiny sign of kindness...

When he moved towards her she almost hoped...

'Five thousand pounds. That is a rather impressive amount for the lesser of the Bascombe girls. Don't you think it would be fair for Peter to receive a measure of that as recompense for helping you land your big fat fish before being discarded like last season's gowns?'

He'd crowded her back as he spoke until her backside bumped into the edge of a table. Still he didn't stop coming. With a swift motion he raised her and deposited her on the table.

'Five thousand pounds, Minnie. You do realise that as your husband, Renfrew will still own that money?

That you might end up with less than you might have had with Peter? That once he has you in his drafty old castle he can, and probably will, do whatever he wishes? Are you so naive you believe otherwise?'

She placed her hand flat on his chest, pushing, but he didn't budge.

'I'm not a fool, Max. And I won't be staying at his drafty castle. We shall move to London and I shall continue as before. No man will tell me what to do, legal hold or not. Don't think you can change my mind with threats.'

'Change your mind? I wouldn't allow you to marry Peter now if you begged,' he bit out, so close now his thighs brushed her knees. 'You don't know how grateful I am you found a greater fool than Peter willing to pay for the dubious privilege of bedding you. In fact, I'll even send you a generous wedding gift to show my gratitude. What would you like, sweetheart? A diamond necklace? Or would you prefer it directly in coin so you can count it out with the rest?'

Every word was a razor scoring her skin, but if she'd learned one thing in her dealings with the man she'd believed to be her father, it was never to show weakness when your back was to the wall.

'Diamonds will do just fine, Max. I'll wear them to bed and think how grateful I am to you Cavendishes while my new husband is enjoying the delightful privilege of bedding me.'

He fell silent, his pulse slamming against her palm.

His face was pale and hard, so close she could see the silver flecks in the eyes that were glaring at her with hatred.

How to kill a friendship in two minutes.

She slipped deep inside herself, leaving her bravado holding the fort while she crawled into the cellars and tried not to think, not to feel. She couldn't afford any of that, not yet. Not for a long time, probably. From her tiny cubbyhole she watched his gaze drop, move over her face, pause on her mouth. Her lips parted of their own accord.

'Is that how you see your life, Mina?' he asked softly, one hand reaching up to rub his thumb gently over the bow of her lower lip. 'Back in London armed with Renfrew's riches so you can play queen in that slimy, incestuous little pond you call Society? How long are you planning to wait until you cuckold your husband?'

'I'm not planning to wait at all.' She laughed at the absurd image he painted of her.

Shock widened his eyes.

'I take my hat off to you, Mina Davenport,' he said, his voice hoarse. 'I thought I was a decent judge of character, but you had me well and truly fooled.'

She was far gone now, fueled equal parts by anger and despair. If she hadn't been, she would have thought better of doing what she did.

She patted his cheek gently, lowering her voice to

the seductive purr she'd heard her mother employ so many, many times with so many, many men.

'It wasn't that hard, Max dear. You're clever with engines and stocks, but you're only twenty-five, after all. You still have a way to go when it comes to women. When you're older, you and Peter shall thank me for broadening your horizons.'

She trailed her fingers down the taut line of his cheek and he caught her wrist, holding her hand before she could withdraw it. The anger was back now, flaming. She'd never seen him so angry and it felt good that she could push him. With all her choices being stripped from her, she took comfort in that. At least she still had some power in a world gone mad.

Her life as she knew it had just ended. She was taking nothing to her new life but some jewels she wasn't even certain weren't paste, her favourite books and three china dogs.

Common sense and propriety weren't relevant in her world any longer.

Still, the kiss took her by surprise. It wasn't really a kiss, just the faint brush of his lips on hers as he spoke, his words scalding her.

'Why don't I thank you now, Mina? Take an advance on that diamond necklace.' His teeth grazed her lower lip, his hands resting lightly on her waist and sliding up, shifting her dress over her ribs, against her breast. It stopped there, his thumb just brushing the curve as his lips did the same to hers, a soft drugging motion, like weeping willow leaves caressing a pond's surface.

His touch was so gentle compared to his words, but it didn't feel at all gentle. Her nerves were being wrung like sheets through a mangle, sending a confusion of signals through her body. Her freed hand touched his cheek again, the hard line of his cheekbone, the roughness along his jaw. His hair was warm silk slipping through the sensitive skin between her fingers. She'd noticed his hair often, a brown so dark it was black unless he stood directly in sunlight. Without thought she leaned forward, fitting her mouth against his.

'Max...' She didn't even realise she'd breathed his name against his mouth, until he shuddered. Before she could even register the fear that he might pull away, he made a hard sound of surrender, his lips parting against hers as he tasted her. Slowly at first, lingering on her lower lip, shaping it with his mouth and tongue and teeth as if he was bringing it into creation. Her body shivered, urgent, demanding she move, but she was afraid to. There was something so...poignant, like a slow waking from a dream, wishing she could stay in it but watching it fade away.

Another shudder ran through him, like a horse shaking off a harness. She felt it through every point of contact between them—his hands as they moved in her hair, his legs where they pressed against hers. She was afraid he was pulling away and she tightened her hold further, her lips parting, telling him she wanted more.

He brought her closer even as he deepened the kiss, his tongue caressing hers in rhythm with his hands. They were shaping her, bringing her skin to life like a candle lighting the dark. When he cupped her breast, his thumb just brushing her nipple, a small explosion detonated inside her, frightening and exhilarating. A single word kept rushing through her mind. *This, this, this…*

With another groan, between delight and defeat, he parted her legs and fitted himself between them, straining her skirts against her thighs. His erection pulsed hotly against the echoing heat between her legs and something close to agony twisted through her and crashed back into an even more urgent drumming in her core. His kiss deepened, his tongue teasing hers, his teeth pressing into the soft heat of her inner lip as he suckled it, setting off burst after burst of confused need.

She didn't know what to do, where to be—her hands tried to encompass him, moving over the hard planes of his back as if she could pull herself inside him. But it wasn't enough.

She was one big pulse, one goal. This. Her body felt like a hard shell was melting away, setting her free. It didn't matter that this was wrong, it didn't matter that he was furious, that Mina Davenport no longer existed. The world was reduced to This.

She'd had no idea, no inkling, that there could be This.

'Max,' she said his name again, a mix of wonder and need.

And he stopped. He was breathing heavily and too fast, she could feel his heartbeat where her hand had somehow slipped under his shirt without her even realizing, clinging to the warm silk of his skin. Her hips were still pressed against his erection, meeting pulse with pulse and heat with heat.

She wanted…

His hand peeled away from her breast, he raised his head and she tensed, preparing herself.

He stepped back, his voice unsteady when he made his Parthian shot.

'I think I'll keep that diamond necklace, sweetheart. Maybe I'll use it to come and bid on your offer once you've learned a few more tricks.'

She remained perched on the desk even when the door slammed behind him, clinging to the edges like a bird to a branch, the shaking growing and growing until it finally quieted.

Peter had kissed her several times since their betrothal, sometimes with a guilty glance over his shoulder, as if expecting his mother to pounce out at them from behind the sofa. And she'd been kissed far more expertly than Peter by several of her London beaus. Still, at no point had she understood why her mother had been willing to risk so much, so often, for something that gave Mina far less pleasure than reading a good book.

Her mother's response to this observation had been predictably annoying. A very smug: 'Once a man kisses you properly, Minnie dear, you'll see why a good kiss is worth quite a few risks.'

Mina hadn't thought much of that answer.

Now, her lips stubbornly pulsing and hot from Max's kiss, she'd had to admit her mother had been right.

Not that it mattered.

Nothing much mattered any longer. Her life as she knew it was over and she had no idea of the one that was to come.

Chapter Ten

Present day, The SS Aquitania, *July 1880*

The three knocks on the cabin door were much louder than Anne Garfunkel's usual tentative raps. It was also ten minutes before three o'clock, and Anne was nothing if not rigidly punctual.

Mina had no wish to see anyone and debated ignoring whoever it was, but as a glorified servant she had little choice. She opened the door warily, a little surprised to see it was indeed Anne, and even more surprised to see the girl appeared to be bouncing on the balls of her feet, a panicked expression contorting her face.

'Anne! Has something happened?' Mina asked in alarm, her own morose thoughts and memories shoved into the background.

'Wearegoingtotheengineroom!'

'We are what? Slow down, please, Anne.'

Anne took a deep breath and punctuated each word with a bounce.

'Mother said Max Cavendish told Father to take me to see the engines. We must go *now*!'

Well. Max was nothing if not swift to action. Mina felt a jolt of envy and resentment. With books and engines, Max was making Anne far happier than Mina ever could.

Not that it was a contest, to be fair.

'That is wonderful. But you hardly need me along.'

'But you *must* come,' Anne stated, still bouncing. 'You must see the engines, too. You might *never* have another chance. They don't let just *anyone* down there, you know.'

Of course, only Magic Max had the power to grant wishes.

She followed, knowing she was being petty. Again. She hated being petty.

When they reached Anne's rooms, Mr Garfunkel looked like he shared Mina's negative opinion of Max at the moment, and he said little as they followed a steward into the bowels of the ship.

Mina's resentment faded the deeper they went. It was a whole other world down here. More and more was laid bare, unhidden by panelling and wallpaper and carpets. Everything was humming and pulsing: the steel stairs and railings, the bare pipes bracketed to the walls, even their voices. They seemed to be moving ever downwards and inwards, drawn on towards the pulsing core of the world. A faint sense of claustrophobia tightened around Mina's chest—she was certain she could never find her way out of here alone. She might remain here forever, wandering the narrow passageways, trapped in the iron innards...

'Max Cavendish!' Anne cried as they entered yet another room, her voice high with delight. Max stood by a long table with three other men, bending over sheets of paper covered with diagrams. He turned and smiled at Anne as she rushed towards the table as a child might run towards the sea.

Mina felt it, too—like that moment when her feet touched the water—cold but exhilarating, alive. It was a bad sign.

Max made the introductions and they set out towards the engine room while Anne commandeered the conversation, raising her high voice above the roar and thump of the engines. Mina followed along, quite content to try and understand what vertical engines were and how something as nebulous and intangible as changing volumes of steam heating and cooling could move a ship the size of a town.

She was as awed as Anne by the scale of the ship's engines—rows of massive metal machines stood high, shoulder to shoulder, their arm-like rods and pistons rising and falling in an unrelenting rhythm of motion and sound. It was like being inside a living beast and watching the working of its heart, the huff and hiss of its lungs, the rumbling of its entrails as the boilers digested mountains of coal being fed by soot-dusted trimmers.

She followed at the tail of the tour as they left the worst of the noise of the engine room behind, stopping to lean over the railings to get a better look as the engineers explained how the pistons were connected to the shaft that ran all the way through the hidden belly of the ship to turn the single screw propeller.

'Careful. I thought you were too fastidious to get grease on your dress,' Max said behind her. She straightened and cast him a laughing look over her shoulder, too delighted with the tour to take offense.

'Oh, I'm always willing to get dirty for a good cause.'

'Are you.' His eyes narrowed, his lids shielding his expression. She could see nothing there, but after all those unwelcome memories had surfaced so vividly her breath turned shallow and she turned away, gesturing towards the engines.

'There was nothing like that on the *Speedwell*. There was a paddle engine, but the shaft broke just two weeks out at sea, and besides, everything was covered in years of soot and grime.'

'You went to see the engines?'

'I was on the ship for two months. I explored every corner of it. Boredom does wonders for one's curiosity.'

'I don't remember you ever needing boredom to spark your curiosity. It seemed to be fed by some eternal source of power, defying all laws of conservation of energy.'

'I know you don't mean it as such, but I shall take that as a compliment.'

'It is. It must have been hard, being confined to a dilapidated ship for two months.'

'It was hardest for my mother. She was ill for the first two weeks, too.'

'Seasickness or nerves?'

'Both. She missed…home.'

'Did you?'

His tone changed, losing its lightness again, and she tensed. She should have found a more neutral topic of discussion. She was saved from answering by Anne who marched over, her brows drawn into an awful frown.

'Max Cavendish agrees with me, don't you?'

Max shoved his hands deeper into his pockets and cast an inquiring look at the engineers.

'I don't know, Anne. What is it I am supposed to agree with?'

'That quadruple-expansion engines are the future for shipping. You do agree, don't you? Mr McDermott says they are too expensive.'

'I only meant they were expensive to replace in existing ships, Miss Anne,' Mr McDermott said with a rueful smile.

'But their cost would be offset by the savings in coal consumption,' Anne stated, her tone worthy of a civil servant on a cost-cutting crusade. 'Mr MacPherson just said that coal for a single voyage from New York to Liverpool can cost more than ten thousand dollars. And there is always the tonnage and the stokers and furnaces to take into account. Is that not true, Max Cavendish?'

'That's a fine point, Anne,' Max replied with admirable control over his countenance. The other engineers weren't as successful at hiding their surprise and amusement. 'I agree they are a good idea for future steamships, but by no means the only one. Engines have transformed so much in recent years, I'm hopeful someone will conceive of an engine none of us even imagined yet. Perhaps even you yourself might invent something completely new.'

Anne's eyes lit with a dreamy, inward look. 'I want to construct a ship with engines so fine it wouldn't need masts at all. Just like your navy's HMS *Devastation*.'

'That's an excellent ambition. But navy ships have different challenges than ocean liners. So you must think of the problems sails solve for today's large ocean liners and find new ways to solve them.'

Anne's hands fisted and she gave a slight nod, rather like a knight accepting her quest. The chief engineer, Mr Moffat, grinned at Max, and at a gentle tip of Max's head, began quizzing the girl about compound engines. Mr Garfunkel stood by, hands on hip, his expression now equal parts surprise and pride.

For the first time since she'd boarded the *Aquitania*, Mina managed to separate herself from her mistakes and remember why she'd felt so comfortable with Max ten years ago.

True kindness was rare.

It was no surprise Max's had impacted her so strongly. She'd not even realised how much she'd come to depend on his kindness at Fairweather until it had been withdrawn.

She'd always felt that it was she who had come to his rescue as he recovered from his illness, but now she wondered if he'd seen how lost she'd been and thrown tasks at her to keep her from sinking, like branches tossed to a drowning person.

She was probably exaggerating. No doubt all he'd wanted was to keep her occupied and out from under his aunt's feet.

But that was not his motive with Anne. He was enjoying this. It was evident in his face as he watched Anne's exuberant pleasure in being part of this world, if only for a while.

He turned towards Mina and she smiled, without thought. His own smile faded, and she wished she hadn't ruined the moment again. She gestured towards Mr Garfunkel.

'That is the look of a man realizing for the first time that his daughter is leagues more intelligent than he. Is it petty for me to be so pleased by the sight?'

He laughed. 'Since you made this happen, I think you are allowed to gloat a little.'

'I cannot take that credit. You gave her the book that set this whole thing in motion, and you made today possible. You do realise she will remember this day even when she is old and grey and dandling her grandchildren on her knee? This is kind of you, Max.'

He opened his mouth to speak and shook his head. 'Come. It is too loud here.'

Chapter Eleven

The metal stairs hummed beneath Mina's feet as they left the engine rooms and passed through a maze of stairs and corridors. Soon she was utterly lost, so it was a complete surprise when Max opened another door and the wind barreled through—chill and damp and wonderful. She gave a surprised laugh and he motioned her forward onto a deck criss-crossed with ropes riding up to the foremast and damp with the spray that burst in exuberant puffs against the prow.

'I was certain we were heading aft,' she said above the roar of wind and water, hugging her arms about her.

'Aft? I'd forgotten how hopeless with directions you are. It took you weeks to find your way around Fairweather without ending up in the pantry or the coal cellar.'

'Well, there were corridors heading every which way and stairs in the most absurd locations.'

'That's right, blame the house, not your abysmal sense of orientation.'

She laughed. 'No, you're quite right. The fault is in me, not in the stars.'

'In this case only?'

She cast him a sharp look, gathering her armour around her.

'I'd best find my way back. It is cold out here. Unless you brought me here on purpose for me to become lost on the ship like Hansel and Gretel in the forest.'

'Don't be ridiculous. You couldn't go five minutes on a ship without stumbling into someone.'

'Not here. It looks empty.'

'Passengers aren't allowed on the forecastle and the sailors are probably preparing the passenger decks for the storm. It will hit any moment by the look of those waves.'

There was exhilaration in his voice, his eyes intent on the monstrous swells moving towards them like hulking mountain ogres. The clouds were so dark their low-hanging bellies were almost green. They seemed to be sinking towards the ocean, as if at any moment the two forms of water would meet and swallow up the world. It was an ominous sight. And beautiful.

Mina stepped out of the partial shelter of the doorway, pressing into the wind.

'Careful.' Max caught her arm, but didn't stop her. They walked unsteadily over the shifting deck towards the bulwark as the wind grew stronger and sharper, unravelling her hair from its pins and cutting through her dress as if it were as porous as a fishing net.

There was none of the protection afforded by the promenade decks here—they were completely exposed to the elements.

It was *wonderful*.

She raised her face to catch the mist of spray that rose each time the prow struck a new swell.

'Careful,' he cautioned again. 'I hadn't realised the storm was here already. The swells are far bigger than they were an hour ago.'

She shivered and he slipped off his coat and draped it over her with the same casual ease as he might toss it over a chair. It was long and far too large, but surprisingly light. And warm. She resisted the urge to snuggle into it. The tension in his eyes faded into amusement once more.

'You look like a resentful turtle,' he called above the roaring and crashing elements.

'That's still better than a complacent ass,' she called back and his smile widened. In his shirt sleeves and with the wind tugging at his thick dark air he looked younger, lighter. Like a pirate well pleased with his haul. Her protective shell crumbled further. It used to serve her so well, but it was failing her when she needed it most.

She crossed the remaining yards to the bulwarks. Up front the motion of the ship was more pronounced and she could feel the bow quiver as it slammed into the swells. The last time she'd stood like this had been on the *Speedwell* as it plowed into a brutal storm off the Pacific coast of Mexico, wondering if after all those weeks of boredom and agony the world might finally be rid of her. Strangely she didn't think that now. She didn't believe in fate, but it seemed inevitable that she reach London, for better or for much worse.

'The next one looks big, you'd best move back.' He spoke directly behind her, his hand curving into his coat in search of her arm. She shook her head and tightened her hold on the bulwarks as she stared at the great mountain of greenish water coming at them.

'It cannot reach us, we are too far too high, aren't we?' she called out and he shook his head.

'Not usually, but these swells are high and even at our length we'll tip into the valleys and the force of...' He broke off. 'We're about to find out. Hold on.'

She could almost feel the bow being sucked free of the water as the swell rode under them, like a horse about to buck. Max braced his hand on the railing, his other arm slipping about her waist, pulling her against him just as the ship's centre of gravity shifted, the bow lowering with such speed that Mina felt her body remain suspended for a second. Fear coursed through her and without thinking she caught Max's arm where it was wrapped around her.

'We're about to get very wet,' Max called above the roar of the water just as the prow struck the crest of the following swell with a slap that shook the hull. Water erupted into the sky, like a sheet being drawn between them and the world. They were not at the most forward point of the bow so she had time to see the foam leap over the spit and make its way towards them. It was like a bucket of cold salt water flung at her face, hard.

She gave an exhilarated shout, releasing her hold on the railing for a moment to wipe the sea and wet hair from her face but didn't let go of his arm where it still held her snug against him. She should have been terrified at the sheer force of the elements, but she wasn't at all.

'That was amazing!' she cried and felt rather than heard his laughter.

'Madwoman! Another?'

'Another. I am already soaked anyway.'

He shifted her just before the vessel pitched forward again so that she stood between his braced hands, but with his side to the worst of the wave. He kept one arm about her and without thinking she threaded her fingers through his, pressing his hand to her waist under the sheltering coat. This time she was ready for the explosion, but still her hand tightened on his as the spray rose high, a great cloud of water like the paintings of the red sea crossing. She laughed again, leaning her head back against Max's shoulder as it came crashing down on them.

It was terrifying and wonderful and she was shivering with cold, but mostly with excitement and she didn't want it to end. She hadn't felt so alive in years.

She turned her head to look up at him just as lightning snaked in three directions on the cloud-dark horizon. It shot a silver halo around him, flashes of light shivering in each trickle of seawater running down his face.

He looked like a god, Neptune or Zeus, conjured out of the elements just for her. A crack of thunder as harsh as a gunshot was followed by a herd of charging horses. It was so close she felt it shudder through their bodies and then the sky broke above them. Curtains of rain blanked out the world, even the rising waves were nothing more than frothy blurs.

Max pulled her away and they half ran, half slipped on the deck, laughing like children. He had to pull hard at the door to open it into the wind, his muscles bunching under his wet shirt.

Inside, they stood for a moment in a small passage between the outer and inner doors, a two-yard bubble of muted rumbles. Even the pitching of the ship was subdued here, as if she'd imagined the whole of it, but her ears were still rushing with the sounds they'd left behind and the shadow of that flash of lightning played on her eyelids when she blinked the rainwater away.

He leaned against the bulkhead, his hair pitch black and glossy with streaming water as he shoved it back from his face, his eyes still alight. She couldn't seem to stop laughing, even as her teeth began chattering from the cold. She unpeeled the soaked coat from her shoulders and it almost sank to the floor under its own weight. She held the soggy mess up with two hands.

'Thank you for the kind use of your coat, sir.'

He took the coat and hung it from one of the metal pegs that held coils of ropes along the wall, but his gaze was on her, the laughter fading.

'I'm afraid it didn't do much good. You're soaked through.'

She glanced down at her plain cotton dress. The lavender fabric had darkened and was clinging to her like a second skin. She should have delayed Anne long enough to put on her corset, she realised. This dress was definitely not meant to be worn in the rain. Especially not in the cold rain.

She crossed her arms over her chest, taking a step back.

'So are you,' she replied. His pristine linen shirt was molded to his shoulders and arms, revealing their every contour. He seemed far too large and far too alive in the small space with its cold metal walls and floor and the water pooling at their feet.

'You have goose bumps.' He brushed a hand over her arm. It was far warmer than hers and so gentle her heart contracted in a painful jerk.

She shrugged and tried to laugh.

'It looks like you missed the perfect opportunity to toss me overboard, Max Cavendish. I doubt anyone would have noticed.'

* * *

Max drew his hand back as if she'd slapped him and fury as great as the exploding universe outside ripped through him without warning.

He planted his hands on the metal wall behind her, caging her in. Her lips parted in surprise, sea and rainwater still running down her cheeks and pearling on her lashes.

'That was a joke, Max,' she said breathlessly, her hands rising in a gesture of appeasement.

'A *joke*.'

'Max…' Her tongue darted out, licking the raindrops away. 'I didn't mean it. I'm sorry.'

He shook his head. He hated this. He hated sharp-tongued Mina who kept prodding and pushing and then confounding him by stripping back her veils to show glimpses of what she'd been and lost—her happiness, her pleasure in life…

He wanted her off the ship, out of their lives. He couldn't trust her.

He couldn't trust himself.

He started pushing away from the wall, but instead his hands came to rest on her shoulders. Her dress was cold and did nothing to hide the rounded curves of her breasts and the pressure of her taut nipples against the wet cotton.

His whole body warmed from the inside, like cognac pouring through him, paving the way.

If he unpeeled that dress her skin would be cold and

damp, but after the first shock of contact the warmth would return, caught between their bodies.

Oh, hell, hell, *hell*.

It was happening again, only so much worse. He didn't want this, but there was no purchase, no place to press back against it. It was like the water washing over him and he couldn't stop it.

A long shudder, like the deep extended rumbles of thunder, rippled through her. She was breathing fast and he had no idea if it was anticipation or fear. He forced himself to release her, set an inch of cold air between them. But the breaking of contact didn't alleviate the agony. The lashing rain, his cold shirt gripping his shoulders, it was all part of that anger that caught him—the buzzing, burning electricity thudding through him, looking for outlet. It wanted to close that current against her body.

She laid her hand on his chest, just above his heart. It burned.

'I'm sorry. That was cruel.'

'It was.'

She hesitated and then rose on tiptoe, her hands pressing against his shoulders. She touched her cold rain-covered lips to his cheek.

'I'm sorry, Max.'

There was real regret there, but it only made the fire burn hotter.

He caught her head, not hard, but holding her there, her lips on his skin until they warmed and softened and parted a little wider. He turned his head that inch, pausing when her lips just brushed the corner of his mouth, absorbing the shock, the welling of pleasure. Then he finished the motion, his mouth settling gently on hers.

Her breath was warm against his lips even as a raindrop slipped between them. He touched the coolness with his tongue, tracing the shivering line of her lower lip, heat and chill chasing each other through his body at the contact.

Part of his mind knew this was wrong, stupid and dangerous. Mostly dangerous.

It was a futile warning and he tossed it to hell with the rest of his intelligence as he fitted his lips against hers, brushing, testing. He'd been carrying her flavour with him for far too long, waiting to taste her again. The embrace on the verandah hadn't been anywhere near enough.

She melted against him with a whimper and the shock of cold, sodden fabric pressed between them did nothing to stop the surge of heat that barreled through him. It only made it worse. He wanted to burn it away.

Oh, God, this was bad.

The thought had barely formed in his mind when the inner door opened. They drew apart like two guilty children caught raiding the pantry. A sailor stopped, eyes wide at the sight of them.

'The rain…' Mina blurted out. 'It was quite…sudden.'

'You oughtn't to be on the forecastle, miss. It's dangerous, especially when there's a storm.'

'That's what I told her,' Max said without a smidgen of shame. 'We'd best head back to our cabin before the storm gets any worse. Good luck.'

The sailor nodded in puzzlement as Max led Mina into the corridor. She was shivering and he had to resist the urge to put his arm around her. The madness of the moment was already fading and he was left with a corroding sense of depression that once again he'd allowed lust to overcome good sense.

They reached Eliza's state room and without a word or a glance back at him Mina slipped inside and closed the door.

He stood for a moment in the corridor, dripping rain and seawater, his coat a sodden weight on his arm.

Chapter Twelve

'Where the devil is Max?' Septimus demanded as he surveyed the saloon that evening.

It was not as full as the previous nights. Though the storm had passed as swiftly as it appeared, quite a few of the passengers had succumbed to the pitching and rolling and remained in their cabins.

Eliza hadn't been among them this time, but after a quick review of his potential audience Septimus decided to postpone Eliza's 'impromptu' and 'unrehearsed' debut on the *Aquitania*.

'He was here a moment ago,' Septimus continued testily as Mina remained silent. 'The dancing will begin soon and I want him to dance with Eliza.'

Mina scanned the room as well. The musicians that had accompanied the meal with stomach-soothing tunes were picking up their tempo and the waiters were propping open the doors connecting the lounge to the veranda, allowing the cooler air to circulate among the dancers.

'He was talking with Mrs Sturgis-Wells earlier and she has also disappeared,' Mina replied. 'That might account for his absence.'

It was catty of her, but she was in a catty mood. Mina would, in general, applaud a wealthy widow like Mrs Sturgis-Wells enjoying her freedom. However, this was not a general case, but a very particular one.

The closer they came to England the more she was reverting to young Mina—making foolish mistakes, losing her temper, allowing uncontrolled and sometimes ugly emotions to bubble to the surface...

'Don't be foolish,' Septimus said with a scowl. 'Far more likely he's scuttled off to his room to read. Damned typical of him—charming Eliza one moment and disappearing just when the gel is getting comfortable around him and I need him to smooth the way. It's a dashed annoying habit of his. If I didn't know any better, I'd say he's enjoying getting all those women hot and bothered and then wandering off.'

Mina unfurled her fan, more than a little hot and bothered herself. She'd noticed the same about Max and Eliza. He'd been quite gentle and charming with her, though more in the style he employed towards Anne than his gallantry towards Mrs Sturgis-Wells. Unfortunately, that combination appeared to have a greater effect on Eliza than the dazzled adoration heaped on her by the likes of Mr Barrett.

'Do you...do you think that is wise, Septimus?

There is always the possibility she might become a little more than…comfortable.'

Septimus caressed his jaw thoughtfully. 'Now that you mention it, unrequited love could add some depth to Carmen…'

'Septimus!' Mina snapped her fan shut and he blinked.

'I say! Do that again, Mina. What a marvelous gesture!'

'You are an unfeeling, slimy sewer rat, Septimus,' she hissed.

'Steady on, steady on.' Septimus raised his hands in surrender. 'You merely made me think of Carmen's story, what happened in her younger life that made her so defensive. Tragedy doesn't come from nowhere, you know. The best tragedies happen to people who have already experienced loss. That's why I never found *Romeo and Juliet* convincing—those two tiresome children hadn't really earned the right to a grand gesture—'

'I'm in no mood for your literary lectures,' Mina interrupted. 'Eliza isn't a fictional character.'

'You needn't worry. I'm not some evil ogre, you know,' he said in that damned soothing tone the Cavendishes had perfected through years of diplomatic endeavours.

Mina unfurled her fan again to hide the sudden swell of tears in her eyes. She was becoming as unstable as the weather. 'We'd best go see to her. The dancing is about to begin.'

He patted her arm. 'I'll go. Barrett is hovering hopefully in the wings. Why don't you...ah...take a turn in the fresh air.'

With that euphemism for 'get control of your emotions' he sauntered off to secure Eliza's dance partner.

Mina remained standing by the veranda door.

She was as bad as Septimus. It hadn't been concern for Eliza that had sparked her fury. She might have no clear notion what she felt for Max other than this damnable attraction that had been lying dormant in her ever since Fairweather. But she did know what she felt about anything developing between him and Eliza.

She *hated* it.

She shivered, as if she could shake off the truth like a dog shook off water.

She inched backwards and slipped into the darkness of the shadows.

'Hiding?'

She yelped in surprise. 'Max! You scared me.'

'So I gather. Are you escaping your importuning suitors?'

'I have no suitors and if anyone did importune me, I'd importune him right back. Which reminds me— Septimus is looking for you. You were supposed to dance the first dance with Eliza.'

'I know. Which is why I came out here.'

He leaned against the railing, the haze of light from

the saloon outlining him with pale gold and catching in his eyes like a cat's.

She ought to return inside. After today's events she ought to steer clear of Max for her own peace of mind. And body.

But jealousy was a sneaky beast and had her crawling out on a branch before she could consider.

'Don't you like Eliza? I thought you were becoming better acquainted.' Mina hoped her tone was as airy and insouciant as any bored socialite's.

'She's a nice person,' Max replied, 'which is impressive given her success, but whatever Septimus is planning, I'm not interested.'

'Whatever...' Her mind ran dry for a moment and the branch cracked under her. 'Do you mean he wishes you to marry her?'

He laughed out loud. 'God, no, he's not such a fool. Septimus is all about show. He wants Eliza to be the most desired woman in London and all he wants from me is to play the part of one of her conquests. The reality of it doesn't concern him at all.'

'Of course, how foolish of me. A Cavendish would never consider sullying himself by marrying a lowborn singer.'

He pushed away from the railing. 'Don't twist what I said to suit your temper, Mina. My point was that I would never marry a woman with whom I share neither interest nor sentiment. Life is too short to lock yourself in a cage without a damned good reason.'

She flushed. How did she always manage to put her foot wrong?

'I apologise.' It wasn't very gracious, but he leaned back and shrugged.

'It suits you to think the worst of me.'

'I think that glove is thoroughly on the other hand, Max Cavendish.'

'Perhaps,' he said at last, and left the word hanging.

For a moment they stood between the sweetness of a Viennese waltz and the rush and hiss of the ocean against the hull.

Say good evening *and slip back inside, Mina. Don't give him the satisfaction of seeing how hurt you are.* She turned towards the lounge just as he spoke.

'I suggest a truce. For the remainder of this voyage.'

She turned back. 'A truce?'

'Yes. I admit I shot the first volley. That was ill-judged of me. Ten years is far too long to bear a grudge. No matter what the cause.'

The shift in the conversation was so severe she felt slightly dazed. She moved deeper into the shadows, leaning her hand on the railing. It was cold and damp, reminding her of what had happened on deck that afternoon. She couldn't keep track of the many different facets of Max Cavendish. It was like walking across a rolling deck; she kept going one way and the world another.

'I keep having to remind myself you were only nineteen, Mina,' Max continued in the same reasonable tones. 'When I think of some of the asinine things I did at nineteen... Let's just say I'm lucky they didn't have consequences. I had no right to expect more from you. My only excuse is that I did...' He scuffed something on the deck with the tip of his shoe. 'If anything I expected far too much of you.'

'Telling me you absolve me because you realise I was an immature idiot isn't the best way to convince me to agree to a truce.'

'Not an idiot, just human. Even had you run off with both a tinker and a tailor, it was far better you do that before the wedding than for you and Peter to discover how ill-matched you were.'

She could feel his gaze on her, those almost lazily hooded eyes watching for the tiniest reaction. She did her best to smile.

'Thank you for that. And now I think we had best return to the others.'

He frowned.

'I've upset you.'

'No, no. It's only... It's been a long day. And yes, I would like to... The truce...'

Her sentences were falling apart as well. She felt the same surge of dizziness, just as when she'd first come aboard and had to adjust to a floating world that was moving to a new rhythm.

'Mina? Are you unwell?'

She shook her head. 'I'm merely tired.' Her voice

settled into a croak. 'I think I shall go to my room now...'

'You're crying.' He sounded so shocked, she couldn't help laughing. But she pulled out her handkerchief and moved a step deeper into the shadows.

'Nonsense. I haven't cried in years. I doubt I would remember how.'

'Well, you're crying now. I didn't mean to say that about you and... Peter.'

It's not Peter—it's the world. Everything.
You.

But she could hardly say that. She didn't even know what it meant. She'd stopped making sense the moment Septimus corralled her at the tea shop outside the museum.

His hand closed on her arm, very gently. 'Come.'

She hesitated when they reached the corridor.

'Isn't it to the right?'

'This is a shortcut.'

'Oh.'

She should have known better, but she suspected nothing until he unlocked a narrow door and they stepped onto a veranda.

She recognised those deckchairs.

'I can access my veranda from the stewards' corridor.' Max said. 'It gives me a little privacy. Sit down and I'll fetch some whisky so we can officially seal our truce.'

'I don't think...'

'Good. There's a blanket on the chair if you're chilly.'

He was gone, leaving her in darkness.

A sensible woman would walk out.

Instead, Mina wrapped the cashmere blanket around her. It smelled of distant pines and warmth. *Parfum de Max*.

Oh, this was so stupid.

Loneliness was a dreadful, dreadful thing and the cause of so many mistakes.

He returned bearing a tray with a decanter, a bowl of chocolates and a small oil lamp whose flame shivered and danced.

'What the whisky won't do, the chocolates might,' he said as he pushed the bowl towards her. They too glistened and shimmered in the light, beckoning her. There were so *many* of them.

'There's an insult tucked into that, but I don't care.'

She tried to decide which one deserved her attention first. She struck lucky—a rounded bonbon was filled with hazelnut cream as fluffy as a dream.

Oh, God, she'd forgotten chocolate could be so... so everything that was best in the world. She never spent her money on anything so decadent, but perhaps she should. It made her eyes tear up so she took her whisky and tried to burn the taste away, but it just added earthy heat into the mix.

'Is there any chance you could go away and leave me alone here for an hour with these treasures?'

He sank more deeply into his deckchair and shook his head, his smile warming her even more than the whisky.

'I'm afraid I come with the décor.'

'Pity.'

'That comment isn't conducive to truce making, Minnie.'

'I disagree. A truce has no substance in the absence of war.'

'True. I meant to say peace, then.'

'No you meant a truce—a temporary cessation of hostilities. You are a stickler for correct definitions. I remember you were always correcting your poor solicitor's correspondence.'

'What a tedious fellow you must have thought me.'

'No, I didn't mind. Everyone in London talked about everyone in London, but you talked about the world and science and books and...life. And I never had to watch my words with you.'

Why was she telling him this? It must be the whisky. Dangerous thing, whisky. Especially when she'd already had wine with dinner.

She sighed and took another chocolate. It was creamy inside as well, but tart and...*oh...*

'Strawberries!'

She closed her eyes. It was almost too sweet. Her mouth watered, crying over the beauty of it. From now on she would spend more of her wages on fripperies like chocolates. And strawberries.

'Good?' His voice was deep, far below the sound of the sea.

She nodded. 'I can't remember the last time I tasted a strawberry.'

'We picked some in the woods at Fairweather, remember?' Max said.

'Yes.' She remembered. Parting the serrated leaves of the wild plants by the stream to reveal the blood-red berries. They'd been smaller and harder than their hothouse cousins; so tart and sweet they made her mouth weep then, too. 'I remember arguing with you about who should eat more of them.'

He laughed and linked his hands behind his head, looking up at the stars.

'Yes. You kept treating me as if I was just about to kick the bucket. It was damned annoying.'

'And you kept trying to prove you were invincible, which was even more annoying. The second week I was there you insisted on riding that ill-tempered stallion of yours into Winchester and nearly finished the job the influenza began. No wonder Peter and Lady Ashworth fretted so about you overtaxing yourself.'

He glanced across at her. 'Was that why you assigned yourself to act as secretary-cum-guard?'

'No, I did that because it allowed me to escape those horrid sessions discussing good works and county gossip with Lady Ashworth and her cronies. But I wouldn't have persisted if I hadn't enjoyed myself. As you've noted, I have a mile-wide selfish streak.'

'Did I say that? I don't remember thinking that, at least not until...' He broke off.

'Until I revealed my true nature.' She mimicked a waiter removing the cover from a dish with a flourish. Max smiled, but his assessing look was back. She held out her glass.

'More whisky.'

His hand brushed hers as he took the glass and she curled her tingling fingers into the softness of the blanket. The lamplight was flickering on his face and he looked so beautiful like that, his smile caressed by the light, his eyes shot with gold from the lamp.

More whisky wasn't wise, but she didn't wish to leave yet. She was becoming quite comfortable with the idea of a truce. She didn't want to fight Max. She wanted something quite, quite different.

He poured her a decidedly more modest measure of whisky and she took it, careful not to graze his fingers again.

'Thank you.'

He gave the bowl of chocolates a little shove towards her.

'Take another.'

'Not yet, I want this taste to linger.' She looked away, searching for something safe to say. 'Do you often sit out here?'

'When the weather allows. Especially at night.'

He leaned towards her, but even as she tensed he merely turned off the lamp and they fell into darkness.

After a short moment the stars came into stark relief. Millions of them.

'Did you know people once believed stars were pinpricks in the fabric of the sky?' she murmured, 'And that their light was the celestial heavens shining through behind it?'

'Mmmm. People will always search for explanations and almost always be wrong. That's the beauty of it. Nothing is ever fixed. Not even the heavens.'

She smiled at the flickering universe above them. It didn't seem to mind its fallibility.

'That is one of your better qualities, Max. You were always willing to consider you might be wrong.'

'What on earth are you talking about? I can't count the number of times you told me how opinionated I was.'

'Well, yes, you are. But when it truly mattered, you listened. You didn't start and end on the assumption that you knew better.'

His chair creaked. 'A compliment. God save me.'

'Well, I must offer something in exchange for the chocolates. Compliments will have to do since I don't have anything else.'

His pause was longer this time. 'So long as it's sincere.'

'It is. I miss…'

'What do you miss?' He prompted as she fell silent. She ought to stay silent. She was already a little tipsy and the whisky was unravelling her brain into wisps of oaky smoke.

'I miss the first month I was at Fairweather. Everything was so…uncomplicated.'

'Only the first month?'

She frowned. Why had she said that? It was true, though. At some point halfway through her stay the balance had begun to shift.

'What changed, Minnie?'

'Changed?'

'Was it because Peter spent so much time out on the estate?' he prompted. 'Because he didn't pay enough attention to you? Were you angry? Or jealous?'

'Jealous?'

'Of him and Emily. One way or another we met her almost daily and it was obvious she was in love with him.'

A shaft of pain twisted through her. It was so wrong that someone as good as Emily should die so young. What a horrid place the world was.

'She was my friend.' Her voice cracked and she sipped some more whisky. 'We were at school together. I didn't even know she liked Peter until I came to Fairweather.'

'Yes, I know. That must have made it worse.'

'It did. I felt so guilty.'

'Guilty? Why would you feel guilty?'

'I stole him from her. If he hadn't come to London and met me… He might have married her without…

without everything that happened. You know that's true.'

'Probably. Yet she remained your friend even after the engagement.'

'Yes. Because she is... She was lovely.'

'So if it wasn't Emily, what *did* change?'

'What does it matter? It was so long ago. It makes no difference to anyone. Let it be. Please, Max. *Please.*'

The tears were beginning to burn again and she rubbed her eyes. She was suddenly so unbearably tired and the whisky wasn't working. She wished she could just sleep and sleep and wake up like Alice in Wonderland back in a world where everything was simple and good.

Chapter Thirteen

It makes no difference to anyone...

Max watched her rub her eyes like a weary child and a surge of compassion joined the dangerous mix he'd been carrying around with him since he'd discovered she was on board.

She looked even more exhausted and miserable now than she had on the saloon veranda.

He ought to do as she asked—let it be.

The whole logic of offering a truce was to defuse the conflict and put this whole episode behind him. Mina was no longer relevant to the Cavendish family. She hadn't been from the moment Peter wed Emily.

It makes no difference to anyone.

Except it did, damn her.

He didn't even understand why, but it did.

He didn't know what to make of her sleepy, whisky-induced admissions. He ought to feel guilty about prompting her while her defences were down, but he wasn't. The need to know the truth of what happened at Fairweather was an ulcer burning inside him. No matter how often he told himself it was in the past, that it made no difference to anything, he wanted... *needed* to know. He had to settle the battle between his mind and his instincts about Mina—they couldn't both be right.

This Mina, grudgingly handing out compliments in exchange for chocolates, could not be the manipulative temptress who'd callously rejected Peter for a richer prize or some previous suitor she'd regretted leaving. It could not be that simple. *She* wasn't that simple.

Which only made her leagues more dangerous. In a few days they would reach London and Peter would hear she was back and then... He had no idea what would happen then. It was like carrying a ship's hold full of explosives.

All he knew was that he could not allow himself to slip back into that pit again. His growing infatuation with her ten years ago could have done real damage to his relationships with his adoptive family. He'd not admitted it to himself at the time, but he'd gone to Bascombe that day on the mad hope that perhaps now she'd jilted Peter, she might... It had been too unforgivable to even admit to himself. It still had the power to fill him with shame.

He could not give her that power again. Not over him or over Peter.

Yet this was her third time on his veranda in as

many days, and this time he'd actually invited her. Or rather, tempted her here with the promise of a truce.

She was right about one thing—a truce was merely a function of war. It had no substance otherwise. Which meant it was time to remove his enemy from his veranda.

She gave a faint sigh, like a child settling into sleep, her head turned away from him and exposing the sweep of her neck. The darkness and starlight leached her skin and lips of colour and the impossibly intrusive, inquisitive eyes were shielded. But even stripped to her essence, she didn't look any less dangerous. Her pulse was visible in the dip above her collarbone, the engine working away, pumping heat and life. It was a matter of inches to lean forward and...

She shifted and the blanket slipped to the floor. He reached for it as she did, her hand briefly touching his before falling back to her lap and curling into the soft fabric like a child.

It was a slight contact, accidental, nothing in comparison to their embrace that afternoon, but it made his body clench, hard.

He ran through a long string of silent curses as he waited for the wave to crest and ease. She hadn't even woken, damn her.

'Mina...' His voice was hoarse and he cleared his throat and tried again. 'Mina. Wake up.'

Her eyes opened slowly and her mouth curved into a smile. He swallowed and held himself through another crest of heat. It was damnable she could do so much damage by doing next to nothing.

'You fell asleep. You ought to return to your cabin now. Take the blanket with you.'

'Oh... Oh! I'm so sorry... I'm not accustomed to whisky.' As she struggled to her feet, her voice was hoarser than his and even in the darkness he could see her flush as she tried to untangle herself from the blanket.

'No, keep the blanket. I have another.' Desperation gave an edge to his voice and she stopped, the blanket half open as if she was about to spread wings and sail off the veranda and through one of the pinprick holes to the celestial heavens. It caught the shimmer of the stars inside it, sliding down the silk curves of her gown as if she had transmuted starlight into liquid.

The third wave that struck him was stronger and wouldn't break. He took the edges of the blanket and brought them together, his hands just above hers. Her eyes were still dilated from sleep as she looked up at him.

'Minnie... What happened at Fairweather?'

Mina squeezed her eyes shut, hurt coiling through her. She untangled herself from the blanket, pushing him back.

'Should I be impressed you managed ten whole minutes without asking me, Max?'

'You should,' he replied sharply. 'You can't imagine I'm going to let it rest.'

'Why not?'

'Because. Why can't you just tell me the truth?'

'So you assume I'm a liar?'

'I assume,' he said carefully, 'that you lie when you think it necessary. You told Peter you were leaving him to marry Renfrew.'

'So?'

'That was a lie.'

'It was a possibility. I hadn't decided at that point whether I would or wouldn't.'

He shook his head. 'So you jilted Peter, unsure whether you would marry Renfrew, then halfway to your destination you decided not to and then jumped on a ship to the Americas. With your mother.'

She nodded. 'In a nutshell.'

'It makes no sense whatsoever. It sounds like the plot of one of those ridiculous novels.'

'I find most novels are based on a modicum of truth, however exaggerated.'

'So where is the exaggeration in your tale? I know your father wanted you to wed Renfrew. That much was real. When he came looking for you he was in a flat panic, and not because he was worried about your well-being, I'm sorry to say.'

'Of course not. He owed Renfrew a small fortune he'd borrowed in advance of my delivery. And Renfrew wasn't the only one he owed. My disappearance was the straw that broke the Bascombe camel's back.'

'Is that why you did it, then?'

She shrugged. 'That would certainly be a good plot for one of your uncle's operas. The ungrateful child and wicked jilt.'

'There are other possible tales.'

'Such as? Do edify me.'

'Such as your father had something he was threatening your mother with.'

'That is certainly a far more flattering tale. Dutiful child sacrifices her own happiness to save her mother from... What was he threatening her with?'

'Had your mother killed someone?'

Mina's mouth fell open. '*Killed* someone?'

'Evidently not.'

She couldn't hold back a gurgle of laughter as she strode past him and into the lounge. 'You have been spending too much time with Septimus. My mother was far too indolent for violence. Try again.'

He caught her arm, stopping her. 'This isn't a game, Minnie.'

'I'm not the one who's insisting on turning it into third-rate theatre fare. Next you shall say she conspired against the queen and had to escape transportation. Life is much more mundane.'

'It doesn't feel mundane at the moment,' he grumbled.

No. It didn't. Once again depression struck her and the words escaped her before she could stop them.

'Please, Max…please *stop*… I'm so *tired* of this. *You* offered a truce. You promised…'

Beneath them the ship quivered and hummed as she waited for his response. She ought not to have said anything. She ought…

He reached out, his fingers brushing over her cheek. It was wet. She blinked in surprise and two more tears spilled over. He let her go and stepped back.

'For the moment. I can't promise more than that, Minnie.'

She sighed and pulled away. At least he had the decency to be honest. Perhaps she ought… She moved swiftly towards the door, as if temptation was a physical presence, creeping up her legs like the cool sea air wafting in from the veranda.

It was time for the maid to return to her cinders.

Chapter Fourteen

It was no surprise her nightmare returned that night. It had plagued her often in the months after her escape from England. For a recurring nightmare it was quite boring. Just a shadow moving towards a distinctive tombstone in the Fairweather graveyard and the shimmer of pale flowers tucked between grass and stone. And pain—the kind that curled its fist around her lungs and heart and innards and squeezed and squeezed.

She'd only been to that graveyard once, but it had been enough to change everything.

Ten years earlier, Fairweather, the Cavendish family graveyard, July 1870

This was definitely not the way to the stream. She'd have remembered if there were pine trees. Mina cursed her rotten sense of direction once again. That and letting herself become distracted by her morose thoughts.

She ought to return to the house. That would mean

turning... Left? That would be west, no? Or was it north?

The determinedly grey sky was no help whatsoever. Even the lovely summer weather that blessed her first weeks at Fairweather had abandoned her. The past fortnight had been glum and grey and sullen. Like her.

How had everything gone so wrong? She'd entered the halls of Fairweather full of hope for a newer, happier life, but that dream had shifted away from her, fading... The last fortnight had been especially difficult—Peter spent most days out on estate matters for his brother and Max was closeted in the study and hadn't needed her secretarial services for days. She'd had nothing to do but read and try to evade Lady Ashworth's attempts to domesticate her. It was all wrong...

She stopped abruptly. She'd never seen the Cavendish graveyard. Unlike the one at Bascombe the grounds and headstones here were well tended. There was also a stone crypt flanked by two dark granite statues of angels with bowed heads, one with arms spread, as if displaying the wealth of a breakfast sideboard, and the other with hands clasped to its heart.

There was a third figure there as well. Not of stone, though he stood as still and dark as the angels. His hands were shoved deep in his pockets as he stood before a raised tomb. Mina stopped at the edge of the trees, her heart beating a little too fast.

Peter had told her a little about the accident that killed Max's parents and almost taken Max as well.

Before she'd met Max she'd found it strange that a boy who'd survived a brutal train crash would choose to become an engineer. She still didn't quite understand it. It didn't even seem to be a question of taming the mechanism that had ripped apart his life. She didn't know quite what it was. She didn't know quite what Max was.

As she watched, he pulled his hands from his pockets and pressed his palms to his eyes. A surge of shock, like touching a voltaic cell, coursed through her. It propelled her forward rather than back, which would have been wiser.

Max turned at the sound of her approach, his handsome face hardening, the sharp lines that bracketed his mouth going as straight as a knife's slash. She hesitated, stumbling a little on the mossy ground.

'Careful,' he said impatiently.

In the weeks since she'd begun working with him she'd come to recognise that tone—*stay away, I don't want to go there...* He never said as much, she wasn't even certain if he knew, but she was coming to know him as well as she knew Peter.

'What are you doing here? Lost again?' he continued in the same impatient tone, shoving his hands back into his pockets. They were fisted, tightening the fabric on his thighs. 'The house is that way.' He pointed his chin in the opposite direction from which she would have guessed.

She stood dumbly. She wanted to make him laugh

and chase away that pain. It made her feel raw, stripped to her own shaky essence and she didn't like that.

She ought to say something light, or something polite, or just do what he wished her to do and leave. But she couldn't. He was her friend and she didn't want to see him in pain, though she knew it wasn't the kind of pain to be chased away, but the kind one lived with. The best one could do was share it.

Her mind flickered through these thoughts and before she knew what she was about she slipped her hand through his arm.

'I'm sorry, Max.'

Surprise, almost shock, drove the taut anger away. He half turned back toward the grave, but he didn't shake off her hand. Her own shock began to dissipate and it seemed the most natural thing to stand there, holding his arm. His light coat was warm and soft, but she could feel his tension through the fabric. She wanted to slip her hand into his, but she hadn't lost her senses that far. Not yet.

'They would be fifty this year,' he said in the same curt tone. After a moment he added: 'My mother was three days older than my father.'

'Did she lord it over him?' she asked before she could consider whether levity was the best path to take. But he did laugh, his arm pressing her hand to his side for a second.

'She did. I have a memory of her telling him he

ought to learn to listen to his elders. Then she winked at me.'

'She sounds lovely.'

'They both were.' His voice betrayed him. 'They liked being together. They would have done better without being burdened with a child.'

'I doubt they thought that.'

He shot her a mocking look, but ignored her platitude.

'Oh, I knew they loved me, but they enjoyed being footloose and embracing everything the world offered a young and wealthy diplomat and his pretty wife. Luckily I was always welcome at Fairweather when they went off wherever. I had the best of both worlds.'

Mina tried to stop her hand tightening on his arm, but he looked down at her.

'You don't agree.'

'You deduce that from a reflexive movement of my hand?' she replied, trying for lightness.

He glanced down at her hand, laying his fingers very, very lightly on her knuckles. The same shock of awareness coursed through her, but this time along with an even harsher internal denial.

Please don't let this happen. Please.

'You can't help worrying, can you?' he said gently. 'Given two possible outcomes, you will always contemplate the worst one.'

'I think that's a sensible approach to life.'

'Caution isn't always sensible. Not if it stops you from going forward.'

'You are vastly exaggerating my response.'

'You're not feeling sorry for me?'

'I... Not for you, precisely. You're too arrogant and convinced of your own worth to waste my worries on as you are today. But if I wish to feel sorry for the boy that was sent to Fairweather while they were gallivanting about, I will. So there.'

He smiled. She smiled back, relieved to have found her way out of the pit without revealing too much. She wasn't even certain too much of what. She just knew there was something very wrong about being here with Max. That she'd crossed a line she had not even been aware existed. That even if she rushed back across it, it would always be there, scored into the ground like a crevasse formed after an earthquake—a new reality engraved on the map of her world.

She finally forced herself to withdraw her hand. She crossed her arms, hugging herself.

'Cold?' he asked and slipped off his coat and placed it over her shoulders. She murmured her thanks and didn't tell him that he was making it so much worse.

'I don't feel sorry for you at all,' she blurted out. 'In fact, I'm quite envious.'

'No need to tip the scales all the way to the other side,' he said, tucking his hands into his pockets once more, but he was smiling now, so she continued.

'I'm not. I'm merely remembering how frantic Peter

was when he received word from Fairweather that you'd arrived from Argentina and were very ill. He packed up in an hour and was on his way to the station. I remember thinking that my half-sisters would never come rushing to my deathbed. I don't even know if Mama would. Your aunt appears to dote on you far more than my own mother cares for me. So if anyone should feel sorry for anyone, I think I am far more to be pitied.'

'I think if I said I pitied you I'd likely end up with a black eye.'

'I wouldn't be so crude. A bruised shin, perhaps. More likely I might omit a choice zero or two from the next contract I transcribe for you.'

He laughed and reached out to adjust the collar of his coat where it had turned in over her shoulder. His fingers brushed the side of her neck and she shivered again, hugging the coat around her. His smile faded and he turned back to the grave.

'I don't pity you, Minnie,' he said at last. 'I think you are very lucky. Peter is a good man.'

She looked down at the mossy stones by her boots and took a deep breath.

'True. He is wonderful.'

There was another long silence again and this time she didn't look up. Caution forbade it.

'Then what is wrong?' he asked, his voice rougher, almost accusing.

Strange that only a few moments earlier she hadn't known the answer and now, somehow, she did.

A wave of panic washed over her. Was what her father so often said true? That she was just like her mother? Here she was, betrothed to a wonderful man—caring and warm and kind—and drawn to another. Was this how it began? Would her life now be an endless chain of passing from one infatuation to the next, like one of those insects that skimmed the surface of a fetid pond?

Her mother must have begun down this path at some point, too. Perhaps the first time the pull had come towards someone decent, like Max, and in time it no longer mattered whom... Perhaps this, right here, after losing her way in the woods, was her first step towards perdition...

'Mina?'

His voice was strained and she realised he'd asked her the same question again. She shook her head, but she needed to answer, for herself as well. Not the truth, but something that was still true.

'I think... I'm scared. I don't know if I can be the...the right wife for Peter. I thought, since he is the younger son... I never took into account that with Lord Ashworth always abroad on diplomatic missions, Peter was more the landlord or squire here than his brother. Peter is just like your aunt in that sense—he's as tied to this land as she is. He loves it and lives it even though it isn't his. And he expects the same from me. To fit in here and be gracious with everyone and…and all the things they do so naturally… I'm not *good* at it.'

It was all true as well, she realised. Completely separate from these horribly unwelcome feelings towards Max.

She finally looked at him and he drew a deep breath and his hands rose from his pockets, but he shoved them in again. He walked a little way towards the praying angel and picked up a pebble resting on the pedestal, weighing it in his palm.

'I don't think Peter wants you to be like Almeria, or even someone who loves this life as much as he does. If that was what he wanted, he would have married Emily, yet he chose you precisely for those differences. Still, if you wish I can have a word with Almeria—'

'No!' Mina said hurriedly. She brushed her hand over her forehead. It was cold, but she was hot, stifled. She slipped off Max's coat and handed it back. He took it automatically, still frowning.

'Please don't tell Lady Ashworth anything,' she pleaded. 'She might listen to you, but she will only dislike me more. I must do this on my own.'

'But you aren't on your own. That is the whole point. Haven't you told Peter any of this?'

'I have told him and he's wonderful about it, truly he is. He says he knows it's difficult right now, but that summer is always busy on the estate and come autumn we shall have more time to ourselves and when we are married we will move to Beech House and I won't have to see Lady Ashworth all the time and...' She stopped the headlong tumble of words and took a deep breath. 'I think... I think I'm a little tired and everything looks worse when one is tired. And it is natural to feel nervous, isn't it?'

Her laugh was off-key, but he said nothing, just began walking towards the house. She fell into step beside him in silence, wishing she hadn't said anything, not a word.

After that afternoon Max avoided her even more assiduously. She guessed she must have revealed something of her confused feelings towards him and he was being sensible. It hurt, but she knew it was for the best.

She'd tried to be rational after that day—telling herself it wasn't surprising that someone with her mother's tendencies might become infatuated with someone as attractive as Max. Half the women in the county went weak at the knees about him and Lord Ashworth, and not merely because of their wealth and looks and Cavendish name. Perhaps if Lord Ashworth had been in residence instead of on a Foreign Office mission to Paris, she might have become infatuated with him as well.

And infatuations didn't last, after all. She'd also learned that watching her mother tumble in and out of lust for years and years. They came and went faster than the seasons and so would this unfortunate attack and all the attacks that would likely follow. One should treat them like...like a bout of gout. Unfortunate, but with proper care and abstention it could be abated.

What mattered in the end was that she'd found a good, kind man like Peter who made her feel safe and cherished and didn't fly up into the boughs when she told him that she didn't like his mother very much. That alone made him a rare jewel, didn't it?

That solid foundation would remain with her long after Max went on his way around the world and she forgot she'd ever indulged in a childish *tendre* towards him.

Once she married Peter, everything would settle into place. Everything would be all right.

Perhaps it was a blessing that she'd never had a chance to put that leap of faith to the test.

A fortnight after her unwelcome revelation in the graveyard came another—this time not from her heart but from Lord Bascombe. He'd summoned Mina back to Bascombe Hall and ripped her and her mother's world to shreds, putting an end to her short engagement to Peter far more effectively than her inconstant heart. All her doubts and vacillations had gone up in a puff of irrelevance and within two days she'd been on a ship and on her way around the globe.

The groan of the ship that brought Mina back to the present. She pulled her blanket up about her chin and turned over to face the wall.

Two realisations settled inside her—as light and as incontrovertible as the night air.

First: time had proven she'd been very wrong in one assumption—she was not at all like her mother.

Second: however brutally delivered, she had to be grateful to Lord Bascombe. His greed had saved her from a lifetime of regret, and Peter from a lifetime of probable misery.

She couldn't mark the moment when she'd fallen out of love with Peter and into love with Max, but it hardly mattered. Lord Bascombe's intervention had wrenched her away mid-fall, and without even realizing it she'd remained suspended in that state all these years.

Until now.

Meeting Max again had cast her right back into that vertiginous plummet, as if she'd held her breath for all those long years.

She let her breath out, slow and hopeless. Her fantasy of making a modest life in London, perhaps finding some old friends who wouldn't shun her... It was folly. She would return to New York and let foolish fantasies fade. As they ought.

As for her contract... She would tell Septimus the truth. He would likely be only too happy to shove her onto the first ship back to New York once he realised the threat she posed to his star's reputation.

And that would be that.

Chapter Fifteen

Mina stared at the mahogany door of cabin 22. The gilded numbers winked merrily at her under the electric lights.

Once contemplated, the thought of telling Septimus the truth had haunted her all morning, taunting and tempting. It hovered over her like something between a guillotine's blade and a lover's kiss. The temptation to bare her neck to them was excruciatingly real.

Get it over with. Once and for all.

She raised her hand to knock just as the door swung open. Her heart, already pumping faster than the *Aquitania*'s engines, gave a hefty clunk, but it was only Septimus.

'Hullo, Mina. Looking for me?'

'I, uh, yes, yes I am.'

'Come in, then,' Septimus took her arm. 'I was about to go to the lounge for a relaxing beverage before our grand event tonight, but I shall make do with some of Max's excellent cognac right here. Is Eliza resting?'

Mina nodded, a little too energetically.

'Yes, yes, she is asleep. Mrs Oakes is knitting.'

He cast her a strange look and picked up the decanter of cognac.

'Good thing you came by. I've been thinking about how to approach London. We have three rehearsals with the singers before opening night. Then after the premiere we'll hold a ball at Cavendish House. I want to show her to Society hot on the back of her success and before the critics become blasé. And you shall be there to guide her through that horror and see she doesn't sink the ship before it's launched. Yes?'

'Septimus...'

'You disagree about holding a ball?' He handed her a glass with a finger of cognac and she took it, glad to have something to hold.

'No, no, I'm sure that's an excellent idea, but you know I cannot accompany her into Society.' She glanced around the room cautiously. 'Is Max not here?'

'No. Gone ashore. Has business with the shipbuilders in Queenstown.'

'Oh.'

Max had left.

Just like that.

Well, he was not accountable to her. He was nothing to her and she nothing to him. More fool she that her heart creaked with misery at the realisation he had departed before she could even see him one last time.

'It's good you came by,' Septimus said in a business-like manner. 'I've been meaning to speak with you. Not about Eliza this time. I wish to make you an offer.'

She was already teetering on the edge of a cliff and this sent a wall of freezing water over her—shock, disappointment, panic... Luckily she was too shocked to react because Septimus continued.

'You've done a stellar job with Eliza. When I saw you commandeering those three little monsters in New York like you were the queen yourself, I remembered how you used to twist everyone in London and at Fairweather around your finger and make them enjoy the contortion. I knew fate had dealt me a high card just when I needed it.'

'I'm not that girl any longer, Septimus.'

'No, you were instinctive then, raw. But now you think before you leap—'

'I don't leap.'

'That is debatable. I've seen you lose your temper rather spectacularly a few times these past days.'

She flushed and stopped herself from blaming Max. That was cowardly, even for her.

'I don't often... It is merely...'

'Yes, I know. Finding yourself back among those who knew the old Mina. It is bound to be unsettling. But you've transformed Eliza.'

'Nonsense. She is utterly herself.'

'Well, that's precisely my point. Because she wasn't herself when I met her in New York. Utterly natural when she sang, but as stilted as a child called before the headmistress the moment anyone other than the cast spoke to her. Somehow you helped her find the confidence to be herself. So, here's my offer—I want you to work with me. There's this French tenor I heard in Marseille a few months ago. Son of a fisherman. Sings in one of the smaller operas, but, *dieu*, what a voice. Zeus himself would set down his lightning bolts to listen.'

'If he can sing like a god, that should be enough.'

'It should, but it isn't. You know that. Look—you can read people,' he coaxed. 'I've watched you this week, Mina. You're like those little boats they send out to guide...'

'You've already used that analogy, Septimus. I'm flattered, but I am afraid that is impossible.'

'Why? Give me one good reason other than that foolish contretemps ten years ago and I'll let the issue rest.'

One good reason.

Here it was, here it was. The rope cut and the blade set free. Finally.

Her heartbeat picked up speed, as if a tiger had materialised out of the dark, its breath misting the back of her neck. Except this tiger was inside her, and it wanted out. It finally, finally wanted to roar.

She would tell Septimus and he was bound to tell Max... And then Max would realise how wrong he had been about her, how brave she had been, how...

Oh, child.

So that is why you want to tell.
How sad.
She shook her head. Defeated.

'It isn't a foolish contretemps. I made a mockery of Peter when I jilted him. I don't understand how you can be so unfaithful to him by even contemplating this.'

'Oho! There's a fine flight of fancy.' His mocking was not unkind, and he continued even more gently. 'I have a gothic mind, my dear. It tends to subtext. In other words, I prefer what is between the lines to what is in them.'

'I don't understand.'

'Well, let me clarify. Max told me the details of *how* you jilted Peter. In the village square.'

She closed her eyes. She didn't want that day dragged up yet again. Ever since her ill-fated meeting with Septimus at the museum that memory kept resurfacing in painfully vivid bursts—her brutal words, Peter's confusion and pain, and then later back at Bascombe—Max's shock and fury and then contempt. And then… No, she didn't want to relive it. It hurt.

'Yes. In the village square. And so?'

'Surely you must see that is a very operatic scene.'

'So it was. And I the villain.'

'That's just the point. I can't see it.'

She gave a bitter laugh. 'Then you had best consult your libretto, Mr Cavendish. It says so in black on white.'

'Indeed it does. We are in the second act. The gentle hero discovers his inamorata has feet of clay.'

'More like a mace of iron.'

He grinned. 'Yes. You dealt him quite a blow. The result? Within a year he marries the young woman who'd loved him all her life and who he himself had been quite sweet on before he went to the Great Decadent City and became ensnared by the Scheming Hussy. Now, saved from that fate when said hussy reveals her true face, he and his steadfast love live in blissful happiness. Until her tragic death, of course, but that part, as in most tales, happens after the curtain falls. But, you see, operas have more than two acts.'

'This isn't an opera!'

'Everything is an opera, my dear. Because that is all opera is—an exaggerated glimpse of life, a tool to unravel how this strange world we live in operates. That's why people relate to it. Humans live to certain rhythms and rules and opera merely plays these rules out on a stage.'

'Not everything goes according to the rules, Mr Cavendish. People break them as often and as fast as they can make them.'

'Yes, but there is always a rhythm. Always. Even in the breaking. Because there are only so many notes we can consistently maintain in our lives. And when I hear a note that is out of place, I cannot help but wonder what the true tune was.'

She didn't want a lecture about opera and life and rhythms. She wanted this over with.

'In this case the note out of place is that I lied to you, Mr Cavendish.'

'Did you?' He looked more interested than worried.

'I am not what I appear.'

'You aren't?'

'I'm afraid...' She drew a deep breath. 'I am afraid you have employed me under false pretenses.'

'Dear me. What are those pretenses?'

She took another deep breath and drew back the bolt on the tiger's cage.

'That I am the Earl of Bascombe's daughter.'

That did surprise him. He pushed away from the piano and for a second looked truly disconcerted.

'The devil you aren't. I met you at Fairweather. I'd not make that mistake. Max certainly wouldn't. He would have told me straight off I'd the wrong girl. Can't be true.'

'You met me at Fairweather, but I am not Lord Bascombe's daughter. My mother had an affair with another man.'

There, it was done. Finally.

She was breathing fast, but not with fear—with exhilaration. The tiger was out and prancing about this highly respectable lounge, peeing on the carpets.

For a moment Septimus stared at her, then slapped his palm on his thigh.

'Ha! I knew it.'

She jumped, her tautly drawn nerves jangling in alarm and even the tiger extracted its claws from its gleeful shredding of the leather armchairs.

'You knew I was illegitimate?'

'No, no, just that there *was* a subtext. Act three! Damn it, girl, you're not the villain, you're the tragic heroine. Sacrifices herself. Goes to live in an attic. Dies of consumption.'

A startled giggle burst out of her.

'I did live in an attic for a while after my mother went to Mexico. No consumption, though. I hope.'

'You know what I mean.'

Another giggle threatened to escape her, and she fought it down and took a bracing sip of her drink. Septimus Cavendish might not be serious, but the situation was.

'I didn't sacrifice myself. Lord Bascombe sacrificed me. The only reason he hadn't kicked us out long before was that he was an expert at selling his daughters to the highest bidder. When I refused, he told me the truth of my birth and that he would inform the Cavendishes what soiled goods they were thinking of adding to their sanctified family tree next to the Plantagenets. I told him he'd just ensured I couldn't marry anyone at all.'

'Damn, this gets better and better. Has a Joan of Arc flavour to it. No, no... Who's that gel in *Ivanhoe*?'

'Lady Rowena?' she asked, completely confused.

'No, no. Not the niminy-piminy virtuous one who

probably bored that sad fellow Ivanhoe to death with her piety. The other one who tells the Frenchie she'd rather jump out of a tower... Rebecca, that's it!'

'Mr Cavendish, this is not a story. This is my *life*.' Her voice wavered and he sobered.

'True. Sorry, Mina. Force of habit. Bascombe was a nasty piece of work. Damned good thing he wasn't your father, then.'

She was crumbling, but she giggled again, pressing her hand briefly to her eyes.

'*Damned* good thing,' she echoed. 'So you must see why I cannot do what you wish me to do.'

'Don't see it at all. Do you, Max?'

She twisted around and her glass went flying from her hands. It rolled tipsily along the carpet, coming to rest by the door to the corridor. Max picked it up.

His face showed nothing. Nothing but that blank look he managed so well.

She turned sharply to Septimus. *He* looked a little shamefaced.

'He won't tell. You can trust Max.'

She shoved to her feet and for a second the room went dark, a hot heavy thudding filling the world. Then it cleared, making room for fury. And hurt.

It made no sense. She'd *wanted* Max to know. It shouldn't make a difference that Septimus had known he was listening, had prodded her on... That Max had stood there without telling her, taking it all in...

It felt like they had stolen something from her. A beggar's crumb.

She tried to speak, but couldn't.

'Mina,' Septimus said, gently. He was standing close to her now, his hand touching her sleeve. She stepped back, the back of her leg catching painfully on the carved claws of the armchair.

'I'll work out my wages until the premiere, Mr Cavendish. And then I leave.'

'Mina…' he said again, but she held up her hand and he fell silent.

She wanted to say something truly grand, operatic… Make a grand exit and leave these two privileged men wallowing in remorse. But there was nothing in her. Nothing. She walked away, but even her exit was ruined because Max was still in the doorway and for a moment he didn't move.

Then, just as her pain and fury were gathering to a crescendo he stood back and she had no choice but to leave.

Slamming the door wasn't in the least satisfying.

'Oh good, we're sailing again,' Septimus said cheerfully over the reverberating slam of the door. 'I wouldn't put it past her to storm straight off the boat and keep walking if she could.'

Max finally woke from his shock. He turned on his uncle.

'You saw me in the doorway. Why didn't you tell her I was here?'

'Why didn't *you* tell her? Could have cried *halloo* at any point.'

'I didn't think of it.'

Not a good answer, but the truth. When he'd entered the state room and heard her voice he'd meant to come straight in, but by the time he reached the lounge door he'd stopped and just…listened.

'You *meant* for me to overhear.'

'Well, yes. Besides, she was just coming to the interesting part and I was damned if I was about to stop her mid-story. At least now you can stop badgering the poor girl into telling you the truth.'

'I wasn't badgering her.'

'Were too. Watching her, waiting for her to tear off her mask and reveal the evil hussy beneath. It was downright exhausting. I admit when I saw you there I thought here was a fine opportunity to finally drum it through your head she had no intention of playing your villainess. How was I to know she'd feel the need to make a confession? And *what* a confession!'

Yes, *what* a confession.

'Come to think of it, Max, why the devil didn't you just keep to the shadows?' Septimus continued. 'If you'd just listened from the corridor she'd never have known you were there. Not a smart move. Or actually, perhaps it was a masterly move on your part—now that she knows you know the truth, there's no chance I'll talk her around to staying. Was that why you did it?'

Max shook his head. Such a stratagem hadn't even occurred to him. Nothing much had occurred to him other than shock, followed by a cranking of inner machinery as the gears finally fell into rhythm, the wheels no longer grinding as they settled into their proper grooves.

Finally, the secret—so simple—was unveiled. Strange that it had never occurred to him. No, he'd been too set on his own operatic tale of betrayal and lovers and...

Wrong betrayer, wrong lovers.

What a colossal idiot.

'No,' he said at last. Septimus gave a slight smile.

'No, not your style. More mine. Lucas at a pinch. You should have stayed hidden. I daresay I made a hash of it, but you gave me a bit of a turn popping up like that.'

Yes, but he'd needed to see her face. See for himself if what she was saying was true or some other maneuver she was concocting...

But he'd known it was true. It was in her voice. And it had been in her face ten years ago.

Hell. Hell and damnation.

That day in the village, she'd been crossing the square in those long strides that made his aunt sigh with resignation. He thought she'd looked pale, but when Peter called to her she'd turned and laughed. He remembered that well. And then laughed again as she told Peter she couldn't marry him because she was leaving to marry Sir Godfrey Renfrew that very same day. As if it had all been a grand joke. As if expecting them to enjoy it with her.

'Well, that was unfortunate,' Septimus said as he refilled his glass. 'But we'll find a way to bring her around. Want some?'

'What the devil is wrong with you?' Max demanded, slamming the glass he was still holding on the sideboard. Septimus took that as an affirmative and filled it.

'Nothing that can be mended at this point in life, Max. I should have shooed you away, but that would have been a little obvious. Besides, I happen to think it's best she knows that we both know. And at least that will stop you making all those nasty swipes you've been enjoying at her expense. At least I hope it will. Rather childish of you, I thought. Holding a grudge all these years. Not in character. If Peter wishes to berate her, then that's his business. None of your affair as far as I can see.'

'My only concern in the matter is to protect Peter.'

'Well, that shouldn't concern you either now you know she's not the Jezebel you thought her. The problem is, now she will be even more determined to return to New York. We haven't long to soothe her feathers and convince her the best thing is for her to stay with Eliza.'

'This isn't a case of soothing the feathers of some

spoilt *prima donna*. This…' He had no clear idea what this was. He took the glass and drained it and headed for the door. 'Just make sure you pay her well for putting her through this torture.'

Chapter Sixteen

Max wasn't surprised Mina wasn't in her cabin. Mrs Oakes, eyeing him with grave suspicion, could only confirm she hadn't even come that way.

He tried to think like her. Striding off as she had used to do at Fairweather when she wished to be alone... Adding to that her shaky sense of direction... She could be anywhere.

Septimus was right—it was damned lucky they'd weighed anchor. Mina was perfectly capable of disappearing again.

He stopped halfway down the corridor, struck by the enormity of what she'd revealed.

Not the truth about her parentage, but that at nineteen, an age when the most audacious thing most young women her class ever did was steal a kiss in the garden, she'd discovered her identity was based on betrayal and a lie. And then she'd escaped her father... No, escaped the man who'd planned to sell her to a pox-ridden reprobate, secured passage on a ship, and set off round the world with nothing but a few guineas in her purse.

Because she would not bow to her fate, nor would she force it on Peter.

What a damnable mess.

He wished Peter had never gone to London that summer. Never met Mina Davenport. Never brought her back to Fairweather.

No, that wasn't fair. Peter wasn't to blame for Max's sins. Or his stupidity.

He headed towards the deck, cursing himself as he went.

He should have known something was horribly wrong the day she'd jilted Peter. No—he *had* known something was wrong, but he'd preferred to believe she was as vicious as she'd painted herself. How could he have allowed himself to believe that?

Because you wanted to, came the sly response. *If she was vicious and greedy and debauched like her father and mother, you could be rid of her. You wouldn't have to watch the woman you'd come to desire*—to need—*marrying your cousin, becoming a part of your family, and forcing you out of it…*

That day she'd laughingly cast off Peter in the village square—it had been a fantasy played out before him. He could remember every moment—her odd expression as she stood stock still in the square, watching them approach, the shock as he caught her words…

And then the overwhelming, choking relief that she was jilting Peter.

At least until he'd registered her mention of Sir Godfrey.

He still should have known. The Mina who coaxed him through his convalescence, who held his arm with such concern in the graveyard, who defied Almeria but was hurt by her dislike, who worked with him on his business affairs with more conscientious diligence than any secretary he'd ever had, who greeted Peter with relief and pleasure every time he returned after a long day's work…

She was many things, quite a few of them abrasive and imperfect, but she was not vicious, or greedy, or cruel.

He'd been willfully obtuse, he realised now. Had chosen to ignore how much he'd come to look forward to Mina's entrance to his study every morning once Peter left on estate matters. He'd attributed this pleasure to his improving health and clearing mind, to the progress in his business affairs made possible through her clever efficiency. He enjoyed her company, her humour, the way she gave no quarter and showed him not an iota of respect without him earning it fairly.

Not once did he question why he was annoyed when she ran off each afternoon the moment Peter returned. Or why his temper shortened with his aunt at her cool treatment of her soon-to-be daughter-in-law.

He should at least have had an inkling when he kept

delaying his search for a new secretary. Until Peter had made a laughing comment during dinner one day that Mina was spending more time with Max than with him. There had been no acrimony in Peter's words, but they had struck Max like a blow. That had been the first beam of light piercing his fog. He'd sent out a request to an agency in London the next day. Without even telling Mina. That had been another sign ignored.

But when the truth of his folly finally struck him, it hadn't come in the guise of anything so grand as a bolt of lightning. Not witnessing her dancing in the moonlight, enveloped in a flowing ball gown, or laughing with Peter's friends at a local assembly. It had come almost trivially—in the same place he usually saw her—in his study, dressed in a plain white morning dress.

She'd been going through his correspondence and had come across another letter from the employment agency with a new candidate for secretary. He'd kept waiting for her to say something, but until that day she'd made no comment whatsoever about his unannounced plan to replace her, merely handing the letters to him in silence and continuing with her work, perhaps a little more subdued than before.

But that day she'd tossed the latest on the desk with a flick of her wrist and it skittered across, almost slipping into his lap.

'Another applicant for my job. He appears more qualified than the previous ones.'

Her voice was sharp and he glanced up at her. The

mulish rigidity of her face gave her what Peter called her Ice Queen look. Peter always tried to tease her out of it, especially when it was sparked by a conflict with Almeria, but guilt and the rotting unease that had been plaguing Max more and more left him in no mood to accommodate her ill temper.

'You do realise you are not employed by me, Mina. You are Peter's fiancée. This was never "your job".'

'I am fully aware of that. Jobs are rewarded by wages. And appreciation. Usually.'

'You know full well I appreciate your help. And as for wages…'

She waved a hand, the ice melting in a sudden flush of colour rising over her cheeks.

'I shouldn't have said anything. I told myself I wouldn't. Of course you need a proper secretary. Ignore me.'

She bent back over the mail, tucking a tangle of tawny hair behind her ear and picking up her pen.

After a month in the country she'd begun to put less and less effort into her appearance. Not that she looked any less pretty, merely less…*soignée*. Her hair was gathered loosely into a knot, the warm brown tendrils curling over her cheeks. When she was deep in concentration she would wind them about her finger and release them into bouncing corkscrews that made his fingers tingle and tauten, as if he'd created them, not her.

He sat and watched her, his previous train of thought lost.

'What's wrong, Minnie?'

She looked up and for a brief moment there were no defences, no humour, no defiance. She looked… Lost?

'Has something happened to your family?' he prompted and her face sealed up again. She gave a dismissive snort and returned to her writing. He wasn't surprised. It hadn't taken him long to realise that her relations with her parents were not particularly warm.

He leaned forward, touching the edge of the sheet of paper she was writing on.

'Then what is wrong? Is it Peter?'

Her pen wavered and she cursed as a spot marred the end of the sentence.

'Look what you made me do. Now I must start over.'

She reached for another sheet, but he laid a hand on it. He felt strangely distant, rather like those first days after he'd recovered from his fever—as if everything could only be reached through several layers of mist.

'Did you argue?'

'Don't be silly. Peter is too nice to argue. May I have another sheet of paper? I want to finish this before the post goes out.'

'It can wait.'

'You were the one in a hurry to—'

'Minnie,' he interrupted, shifting his hand to cover hers as she reached for a new sheet of paper. She stilled and so did he.

A sharp, icy shaft struck through his chest and for a second he couldn't quite breathe.

It hurt, he thought with wonder. It actually hurt.

Her hand was warm under his and shaking. He watched himself gather it into his, his fingertips on her palm.

Inside him a kind of horror was filling and rising like a hot air balloon.

What are you doing? Are you mad? Let go, let go before...

Too late.

He finally withdrew his hand, carefully, but he couldn't stop his gaze moving over her, rearranging everything. His mind touched the curve of her cheek, the bow of her mouth, held tensely now, the vulnerable line of her neck. He could see her pulse in the hollow at the base of her throat and her scent... Faint, but as potent as an orchard of orange blossoms.

His mind was numb with shock, but his body was anything but numb. The clutch of lust tightened around him like a cruel vise. The desperation to reach out, touch, take... It was utterly wrong, but he couldn't stop it. He could only contain it, hold it tight inside as it rose and rose, like a beast awoken from long sleep, angry, confused...

It peaked and calmed a little. But it had already changed everything.

The switch was thrown, the train barrelling down the wrong track.

I'll have to leave Fairweather—the thought struck through him with another shaft of pain. *I can't bear to stay here and watch them...*

He held himself still until the pain diminished enough for him to bring cold sense to his aid.

This would go away. He'd been ill, vulnerable, and he'd come to depend on Mina. He liked her. At least when she wasn't annoying him. No, even then he liked her. More than liked her...

He pushed that thought away, too. Best not to rationalise, then. Ignoring was wiser. He *would* leave Fairweather, for a while. Go to London. Find a secretary there. Put some distance between him and in time...

He rose, very carefully. Her eyes followed him, turning pewter with the lamplight behind her.

'I didn't mean to be a nuisance. Are you angry at me?' she asked.

He shook his head. 'No. We shall finish this tomorrow.'

She hesitated and stood as well. Her mouth opened, but she said nothing and after a moment she left the study.

After that quiet catastrophe he'd begun making arrangements in earnest to remove to London, but in the end that hadn't been necessary. In the end she'd jilted Peter and run off, leaving chaos and confusion behind her.

Chapter Seventeen

A group of passengers came around the corner and he let out a long, controlled breath and continued down the corridor, managing a polite smile as they passed.

There was no point in dwelling on those memories, even if they remained stubbornly vivid. More vivid than most of the years that had come between then and now. Perhaps that was the nature of disasters. Like the accident that had almost killed him, some vicious moments were engraved in stone.

Perhaps if he'd been older and wiser he might have been able to help her that day he'd been so foolish as to come to Bascombe Hall to confront her about jilting Peter. Instead he'd…

There was no use crying over spilt milk. Besides, he doubted she would have told him the truth. It was Peter she might have told, and Max knew why she hadn't. Peter would have insisted on marrying her, whatever her paternity. She would have known that. So, Septimus was right—she'd sacrificed herself…

With that realisation, the truth finally sank home—she must have loved Peter far more than he'd realised. Was that why she'd agreed to Septimus's offer to return to England? Had the news that Emily was dead sparked a wish to see Peter again?

This was something he hadn't taken into account.

For a moment Max leaned his hand on the cold metal of the forecastle. Then he pushed away and continued his search.

He found her on the promenade deck with Anne. The girl was holding hard to the railing, her profile sharp and serious as she spoke. Mina's head was inclined, her lashes lowered. He could tell the precise moment she noted his approach though she neither looked up nor moved. Anne turned towards him.

'You went to Harland and Wolff in Queenstown, didn't you?' she accused. 'I wanted to see the shipyards, too.'

Mina had praised his patience, but it deserted him now.

'I must speak with Mina, Anne. Go read your book somewhere.'

'No,' said Mina. 'I don't wish to speak with you.'

'Too bad. Anne?'

Anne, looking surprisingly pleased with his brusqueness, nodded, tucked her book under her arm and walked off.

'That wasn't polite,' Mina snapped.

'Anne doesn't give a damn about polite. I want to talk with you.'

'And what you want is all that matters.'

He gave a short laugh at the absurdity of that statement and cast a quick look around. Most of the people on deck were watching Queenstown fall away, replaced by the rugged green and grey of the Irish coast. He took her arm and ushered her towards the seaward side.

'You should have told Peter. Then.'

She lowered her chin at his words, her defiance leaching away.

'No, I shouldn't have. He would have defied Society and his mother and fate and insisted on marrying me. You know he would have.'

'Of course he would have. That is the point.'

'Well, there you have it. I was already enough of a cuckoo in the Cavendish nest. I couldn't do that to him. He was so proud of your family. All those tales about knights and chivalry and serving under Richard the Lionheart... All I would have brought was a great big stain to the family tree.'

'You should have trusted him.'

She shrugged. 'Well, apparently I didn't. And it is all for the best, isn't it? He married Emily within the year and was happy with her. I knew he would be.'

'Were *you* happy?'

Her mouth quirked into a smile.

'I used to yearn for adventure and daydream about

being one of those people who explored the world. I never thought I would do anything about it any more than Peter thought he would be a knight errant. Well, now I have been halfway around the globe and back. That is something, isn't it?'

'It is extraordinary.' He watched her face—the shivers of thoughts reflecting in her eyes like passing shadows. 'What happened that day, Mina? How did you discover Bascombe wasn't your father?'

She looked out to sea.

'You may as well hear the whole of it, then perhaps you'll stop pestering me. That morning I received a summons to Bascombe Hall from my not-father. He'd come up from London and wanted to see me immediately. I presumed he wanted to harangue me again about becoming engaged to Peter without his approval, but I went because I didn't want him to come to Fairweather and worry Peter. I told Peter I was merely going to have tea with Mama and would be back that afternoon.'

'I remember that part of it. Peter was to meet you in the village. He was a little upset you didn't want him to come with you. He certainly didn't know your father was there. So what happened?'

'I went. Lord Bascombe was with my mother in his study and she was crying. The first thing he did when I entered was call me a slut's spawn and show me the letter he'd received from your cousin, Lord Ashworth.'

'Lucas? *Lucas* wrote to him?'

'In answer to a letter Lord Bascombe sent to him in Paris demanding a financial settlement if the Cavendish family wanted him to approve the match. Lord Ashworth wrote back that he had no intention of paying for the privilege of Peter marrying me and that if anything, he should be the one demanding a dowry. Lord Bascombe threw the letter in the fire and told me the truth. That my mother was a practiced slut and that I was probably nothing more than a stable hand's leavings conceived on a bale of hay, which might explain my disposition.'

She laughed, her eyes challenging Max to agree. He didn't answer and she shrugged and continued.

'My mother objected, saying that I had been conceived in all propriety on a bed and that my real father was probably one of two, or possibly three, reasonably respectable men. That didn't help. Bascombe struck her and she fell unconscious. He said he hoped she never recovered her wits because he would save a great deal of money if she finally died. And that if I didn't want her and my reputation dragged into the filth where we so obviously belonged, I would wed Sir Godfrey and keep him sweet so we could milk him for all he had.'

Her words came in a flat monotone. Max curbed his fury, careful not to move or do anything that might put a halt to this outpouring of the poison she'd been carrying about with her.

'I picked up a candlestick,' she continued, 'and told

him if he touched me or my mother I would kill him. I told him to leave my mother's home. He told me it wasn't her home. It wasn't even his anymore. He'd sold it that week to a wealthy merchant. My mother and I now had only the clothes on our backs. I said we would sell our jewelry and leave, and he laughed and said he'd exchanged them for paste eons ago. I told him I would take my mother to Peter's house. He said, "good luck convincing Lady Ashworth and her politically ambitious son to take in a doxy and her by-blow." Because unless I broke our betrothal that very day he would ride over and tell everyone the truth and be done with us. No one would marry me, not even a stable hand.'

'Peter would have.' The words came out of him, against his will, and she looked up, shoving a curl of hair away from her face.

'I knew that when I saw you both riding towards me in the village. I knew he would walk into that fire, not even because he loved me, but because he'd believe it was the right thing to do.' Her mouth wavered and she looked away again.

'It took forever until you two reached me. I could see you knew something was wrong. Then Peter dismounted with that worried frown… He was always so…kind. And I knew that even if I wanted someone else to bear the burden, it wasn't right. I had to do what Peter would have done if our positions had been reversed. He wouldn't have forced his burden on someone else, so how could I?'

She drew a deep, gulping breath, her hand pressed to her abdomen.

'So I told him I'd decided I didn't want to be a country squire's wife like his mother. I wanted someone urbane and wealthy like Sir Godfrey. He didn't say anything, just stood there... The more he was silent, the more my anger...everything...' She drew another deep breath. 'Then he asked me: Didn't I love him anymore? Like a little boy. All hurt. And I said... I said no, I didn't. Then he asked: Was I in love with someone else? And I said—yes, yes I was. And we just stood there, like two bumpkins. I knew you were watching us... Everyone was watching us, like we were on a stage. Or taking part in some village ritual. The annual jilting of the fools. I think I started laughing.'

'You did,' Max said, his throat so tight even those two words were painful. He regretted speaking. She looked up, her eyes sharply bright, tears coating her lower lids without spilling over.

'I'm so sorry. That was horrid.'

'You didn't do it on purpose. You were in shock, Minnie.'

She nodded slightly and pressed her fingertips to her eyes, the moisture spreading. 'Yes. I realise that now. None of it seemed real. Not even enough to understand what it meant. Then you both rode away and I stood there with everyone watching me. And that was that.'

'No. That wasn't that.'

'No. You're right. Then you came to Bascombe and

I was horrid to you, too. Vicious. I couldn't seem to stop. The closer I came to speaking the truth the more vicious I became. I was everything my... Everything Lord Bascombe said I was, everything my mother was. For all I know everything my real father was. That was the truth of me. I used to despise my mother for needing all those men. For being so empty that she couldn't fill herself with anything else... I wanted to destroy everything—her, him, all of you. Everything.' She turned her back on him. 'I wish you hadn't come that day. I was hateful.'

He closed his eyes briefly, trying to block out that memory. The truth made it a thousand times worse. His only defence against his part in what happened that day was that he'd believed her lies. He shouldn't have. He should have seen through them to the pain, the shock, the...terror. She'd been terrified. And he'd made it so much worse... He fought the burning ache in his throat. He had no right to pain. This wasn't his tragedy, it was hers.

'You were nineteen and you'd just had your whole world turned on its head. A lesser person would have collapsed, Minnie. You...fought. I can't think of anyone who would have done what you did.'

'I burned my bridges and ran away. That is hardly commendable.'

He sighed. He was learning not to press when she dragged up her drawbridge.

'We won't argue the point. Tell me instead what

happened when you left with Lord Bascombe that day. Were you still contemplating marrying Sir Godfrey?'

'*God*, no. He reminded me too much of Bascombe and I was pretty certain he had the pox. But I needed to think. And I needed transport. I'd saved some of my pin money, but I didn't want to waste it. I knew we must pass through Liverpool to reach Sir Godfrey's estate. When we stopped at a posting house there I told my mother I was leaving. I let her choose whether she wished to come with me or stay with Lord Bascombe. She decided to come.'

'She might have denounced you.'

'Not likely. I told her my only other plan was to tell everyone the truth about my birth. She preferred to try her luck in the Americas than be shamed and destitute in England. She was ever the optimist.'

'You planned all along to sail to San Francisco?'

'Not San Francisco. I had a school friend who married a man in Boston. It wasn't much, but it was something to cling to.'

'Then why sail to San Francisco?'

'Because I'm an idiot. It was the first ship I found that was sailing to the Americas. I was afraid Bascombe might find us before the tide turned and I was too panicked to ask questions about the distance between Boston and San Francisco.'

Her voice was steady, but her hands were shaking and he took them in his and brushed his thumbs gently over her skin in a pointless attempt to soothe what was unsoothable.

'Oh, Mina.'

'My lamentable sense of direction played me a fine trick, didn't it? I realised my mistake two days into our voyage. My mother was furious, but your Mr Attwood cheered her up nicely. He was completely smitten with her, which was most useful. She began to see the potential of a new, free life.'

'What happened to her?'

'The year we arrived in San Francisco she met a Mexican nobleman and left with him.'

'Why didn't you go with her?'

'I wasn't asked. She left me a note wishing me well. Not that I would have gone in any case. I'd begun teaching at a girls' school thanks to what Mrs Timms called my "proper lady's voice". I discovered I quite liked it. It was lucky my mother found someone to pamper her. My wages certainly weren't enough to provide her with the luxuries she was accustomed to. Selfish of me, I know.'

'Very.'

'Well, in fairness I must admit it *was* selfish. I was tired of her and she was tired of me and for the following three years I felt amazingly free. I had nothing to do but teach and read books and take walks along the bay. But then poor Mrs Timms fell ill and the school closed, so I found a position as governess in Chicago and then in New York.' She pressed her hands to her cheeks and gave a long sigh. 'It seems rather tame laid out like that. As if it happened to someone else.'

Her eyes flicked up to his and her smile was a flash of warmth and mischief pushing through the pain. His heart felt like a vise was closing on it, and not just because of guilt and regret.

'I should have known it was something very bad for you to act like that.'

'You aren't omniscient. Why should you have guessed? I was not your responsibility in any case.'

'No. But I should have known nonetheless. It was out of character.'

'I daresay your aunt didn't think so. She was right in the end, too. Peter was far happier with Emily than he would have been with me.'

He thought of Almeria's ill-hidden relief. The speed with which she had maneuvered Peter into proximity with Emily. A flash of fury struck through him.

'He was in love with you,' Max bit out and she shrugged again. He'd seen her do that so often. Especially when it mattered, when he came too close to her pain.

'Not very much, evidently,' she replied coolly. 'I don't wish to argue about this. You've finally won and had your way on this, Max. Now *please* let's not talk about it ever again. I am so *tired* of it. All I wish is to fulfil my contract and return to New York. This is too...complicated.'

Max didn't stop her as she walked away.

You've finally won.

It didn't feel like victory.

Because she was right—it was best she return to New York as soon as possible. Certainly before Peter came across her in his newly vulnerable state. No good could come of that encounter. Peter had proven that whatever his inclinations, he was far better suited to someone like Emily and hopefully, eventually, he would find another such gentle soul and wed her and be happy once again.

As for himself, he had no intention of falling down that same rabbit hole again. He was no longer twenty-five and vulnerable after a life-threatening illness. He'd cared for other women over the years and enjoyed their company and thankfully none of them had unsettled him like Mina. The attraction might still be there, but he'd passed through this before and he would do it again. In a few days she would be back on a ship to New York and they would all get on with their lives.

This was nothing more than an Atlantic squall—it might be brutal, but it too would pass and leave behind comfortably calm seas once more.

Chapter Eighteen

The passengers erupted into a roar of applause as the last star-spun note of 'Solveig's Song' faded into the sound of the waves.

Septimus had been right—unlike Eliza's reaction only a week ago, the young singer smiled and spoke animatedly with the men and women crowding around her. She might not be achieving the queenly demeanor Septimus hoped for, but her sweetness was working just as well, apparently.

After a few moments, Mina ceded her place to the crowd, shifting back towards a knot of potted palms. Septimus closed on her and Max followed. He didn't want Septimus making any more mischief.

'Mina, my girl!' Septimus's tones were a little too hearty. 'Did I tell you how exquisite you look in that shade of blue?'

Mina met this bluffness with the contempt it deserved.

'Don't play your games with me, you gelatinous

weevil. I'm here for Eliza, but that doesn't mean I have to listen to you trying to sell me snake oil.'

She strode off and Septimus barely waited until she was out of earshot before whistling.

'Good Lord, did you see that? She curled her lip at me. I do believe I am in love.'

'Don't be any more of a fool than you must, Sep. This isn't a game. You did real damage.'

Septimus sighed and patted Max's arm before letting it go.

'I know. I know. That was a mistake. Can you not talk to her and smooth it over?'

'Not on your behalf. Even if I wished to, she has no reason to trust me, either. I was there ten years ago, remember? I saw her at her worst. If nothing else she may never forgive me that.'

'Is there something else?'

'Is there what?'

'You said "if nothing else". That usually implies there *is* something else.'

Max felt an unwelcome flush creep up his cheeks.

'Why don't you do something novel, like apologise,' he shot back. 'Or better yet do as she told you and leave her be.'

'So she can return to New York and be a governess to more little piglets? Do you think so little of her?'

'Spare me your self-righteous blather, Sep. I know you. All you care about is the success of your projects.'

'Not *all* I care about. I happen to like Mina. Always have. Damn pity. But that's life. I've been thinking, see.'

'Oh, God help us,' Max moaned.

'I've been thinking,' Septimus persisted. 'That even when Eliza returns to New York I shall need someone like Mina to assist me. I mean, look at her.'

Max had been looking and it was doing him no good. She was speaking with Henry Barrett who was smiling at her like a shy fawn. Max knew she didn't give a damn about the young man, but every time she gifted him her sweet, mischievous smile, Max's guts clenched, completely beyond his control.

'She's only improved with age,' his uncle continued, clearly far more appreciative of her performance. 'How old was she when she was engaged to Peter? Eighteen? Twenty-one?'

'Ask her,' Max snapped. 'You should never have set this in motion, Sep.'

Septimus sighed, abandoning his bonhomie.

'I don't believe in avoiding life's truths, Max. I never thought you did, either. Surely you realise she and Peter must meet?'

The music wound on and on, like a tightening noose.

'This was what you intended all along. It was never about Eliza.'

Septimus pursed his lips and shrugged. 'I saw her and thought—what are the odds? I knew I had a choice. I could walk away and wonder at the strange twist of fate, or I could walk up to her and see… Well, you know what I chose.'

Max didn't bother answering and after a moment his uncle repeated in that same gentle, persuasive tone, 'You know they must meet, don't you, Max?'

A surge of illness rose through him at the thought of what might happen when Mina and Peter met again. Mire as thick and dark as the mud that squelched and sucked at him every time he'd tried to tear himself from the tangled wreckage of the train that had held him and his dead parents firmly in its grasp two dozen years ago.

I can't go through that again.

It was a childish, empty cry. He knew that. She wasn't his to lose. She never had been. In the end Septimus was right. It could not be stopped.

'Yes. I know they must meet.'

'One of us should go to Fairweather,' Septimus ventured and Max threw him a disdainful look.

'One of us.'

'Almeria would take it better coming from you…'

'Coward. Very well, I'll stop there on our way to London.'

Septimus sighed with relief. 'Thank you, Max. I won't lie—I don't envy you that task. Will you tell her the truth?'

'It isn't my tale to tell. Or yours. I will tell her Mina believed she had good reason to act as she did. That should be enough.'

'She won't be happy.'

'Too bad.'

Septimus gave a slight laugh. 'You won't dither there, will you? You promised to attend opening night.'

'Don't push your luck, Sep. I'm doing your dirty work, that should be enough. I'm off now. Enjoy the show.'

He left his uncle building castles in the air and retreated to the privacy of his veranda. He needed to think clearly and that wasn't about to happen if he stood there watching Mina prove his uncle's point.

He doubted he could think clearly at all until he finally saw her with Peter.

Perhaps he was worrying for no reason. She might have cared for Peter once, cared enough to sacrifice her own future to protect his, but ten years was a long time. Perhaps when she saw Peter again there would be nothing there but memories. Or perhaps time would roll back for her, just as it had for him, no matter how hard he fought.

He indulged in the fantasy of commandeering the ship, turning it around and sailing off...anywhere.

Foolish. It wouldn't change the fact that Mina had been forced to give Peter up.

'You know they must meet, don't you, Max?'

Yes, damn it to hell. That knowledge was a cursed knife lodged between his ribs, tearing at him with each damned breath.

He watched the faraway glisten of the Welsh coast.

There was the scent of land, the cool, damp swirl of English weather against his face and hands, the rush of water against the hull. It used to soothe him, the sensation of coming home.

Not this time.

Chapter Nineteen

London
Her Majesty's Theatre, Haymarket, London

Mina slipped into the Cavendish family's private box and settled onto the plush upholstered seats just as Eliza stepped onto the stage of Her Majesty's Theatre.

For a moment the singer stood there, a lone, slim figure at the heart of the empty theatre, utterly dwarfed by the forty-foot stage, the detailed set of a Spanish town square and the rising walls of a stone amphitheatre.

She wore a plain pink dress and her hair was tied back with a ribbon of the same colour. She looked like a girl who'd strayed onto the stage, dreaming of the day she might walk those boards in earnest. The image was even more pronounced when she clasped her hands before her as if in prayer.

But then she began to sing.

Goose bumps danced up Mina's arms as Eliza's

voice rose and rose, shedding layers as if the air was rarified up there.

'*L'amour est un oiseau rebelle...*'

Love was a rebellious bird indeed. Right now it felt like a vindictive vulture pecking at her innards.

Tomorrow *La Serena* would be launched. Both on stage and off. Which meant Mina had to make a decision. Thus far her arrival in London had gone unremarked by London Society, but she had a strong suspicion that this reprieve was temporary. The servants at Cavendish House knew precisely who she was and what she had done ten years ago. They weren't impolite, but there was a level of tension in her presence, like an audience waiting for the grand scene to finally occur.

Well, so was she.

Ever since her confession on the boat, Max had been unfailingly kind and considerate and...distant. In fact, he'd treated her precisely as he did Eliza. She could now better understand how tantalizing and infuriating that was, and she'd come close to kicking him a couple times on the train from Liverpool just to elicit an honest response from him.

Instead she'd kept her gaze on the passing landscape—the familiar rolling green fields dotted with puffy sheep, the clumps of cottages and verges of wildflowers. It was so achingly familiar Mina found it hard to breathe, as if the air itself was different, unsuited to her lungs.

When the train had stopped in London Max had calmly opened the door, bade them goodbye and left without a backward glance. Eliza hadn't Mina's scruples and had demanded to know where Max was going, but Septimus had merely said Max had another train to catch and beckoned for a porter.

Mina had occupied herself with their belongings, furious at herself for feeling so absurdly abandoned. She ought to have known that the moment his curiosity was satisfied, and his concerns assuaged, he would lose interest in the puzzle. Well, she refused to regret telling him and Septimus the truth. It had been the right thing to do and it made everything easier. She was at her worst when Max was around and she needed her wits about her to survive her return to London, however temporary.

Besides, she didn't want him there to witness what would likely be a disaster. She ought not to have agreed to Eliza's plea to be at her side during the ball that was to follow her debut, but part of Mina wanted that moment done and over with as well. For one last time she would step into a room full of London's so-called finest and she would take the full brunt of whatever they wished to throw at her.

'*L'amour…*' The notes soared upwards, sweet and light as a rainbow, along with a swish of Eliza's skirt as Carmen flirted with the imaginary crowd of men—half of which lusted for her and half of which reviled her.

Mina shivered slightly. Septimus's choice of Carmen had nothing to do with her, but imagining the crowd lashing out at a woman for being bold and different wasn't precisely calming as she contemplated what might occur in the Cavendish House ballroom on the morrow.

'She's a little off.' A voice intruded on her thoughts. 'Is it nerves or have you two been out late on the town?'

The seats creaked as a large form settled beside her and two expensive shoes appeared in her line of vision.

Max.

Her thoughts scattered and she gathered them and shoved them ruthlessly back into place. She could do nothing to stop her pulse from bolting, but she kept her voice as level as possible.

'She is not off. Her Carmen is perfect. If you are looking for Septimus he is behind the curtain on stage.'

'She is off. Must be nerves. And I'm not looking for Septimus. After a week at sea with him I'm quite happy to have a rest from my irrepressible uncle.'

'Then why are you here?'

'Curiosity. I want to know what to expect at tomorrow's debut. Besides, Cavendish House is in utter chaos with everyone preparing for Sep's ball.'

'It is Eliza's ball.'

He gave a low laugh. 'If you wish to think so.'

She finally turned to him, and confirmed what she'd already suspected.

'You're in a foul mood, Max. Take it to another box.'

'I prefer to share my foul moods.'

'I'll send over an usher.'

She rose, but he stretched out his leg, blocking her passage. She was tempted to step over it as she had on the *Aquitania*, but the memory of having his legs between hers again, of leaning in...

'Have you seen Peter yet?' he asked, his voice harder.

'What?'

'Don't be coy. He left Fairweather at dawn.'

Hurt coursed through her. So that was where Max had gone. She ought to have guessed he'd rush to shore up the Cavendish defences against her.

'No, I didn't see him,' she snapped. 'Now, let me pass.'

He rose, shrinking the box around them.

'It can't be a coincidence that Peter left without a word the morning after I told him you were in London.'

'I don't think you would break many bones if I pushed you out of the box, Max. Probably just an arm or a leg. But maybe that would be enough to keep you out of my way.'

Reluctant amusement softened his face for a moment.

'It would take more than a broken arm, little hellion. What are you planning to do, Mina?'

'I don't answer the same question twice, Maxie. You can report back to your precious aunt that her once almost-daughter-in-law hasn't sunk her talons into her precious baby again. At least not yet. Now move.'

He moved, forwards. She stumbled, barely managing to avoid ending up in an ignominious heap in one of the seats. He kept coming, pressing her back into the dark recess behind the thick velvet drapes until the wall stopped her. Her heart was racing, slipping out of its flimsy controls.

'Max, stop behaving like a troglodyte.' She tried to sound cool and dismissive, but her voice wavered. He wasn't merely in a foul mood, he was furious, she realised. He planted his hands on the wall on either side of her.

He was far too close. All the aching need she'd been carrying gathered into a hard, hot stone in her chest. She wanted so desperately to wrap her arms around him and tell him that it hurt when he still thought the worst of her after everything she'd revealed.

'How does a troglodyte behave, Minnie? Like this?' He bent, his mouth just touching the curve of her ear. An unbearable wave of sweetness coursed through her and she held utterly still as his lips brushed the sensitive skin below her ear, a light, almost chaste, caress. Her shoulder shuddered as he traced the soft bend above her collarbone, a wave of longing and denial sweeping over her.

She laid her hands on his chest. She could push him away. She knew all it would take was the slightest pressure, a clear message, and he would back away. Her fingers curled, nails pressed into the linen. Raked down.

'Hell...' The word squeezed out of him and he grabbed her waist, raising her onto the parapet that separated the boxes. Instinctively she clung to him, her arm around his nape. He sucked in his breath, his own arms tightening around her, bringing her even closer. The dark blue drapes stretched precariously under her behind, but her attention wasn't on the possible damage to Her Majesty's draperies. She turned her head, her lips against the soft skin beneath his ear, and breathed him in, filling her lungs, tasting his heat.

Oh God, she was lost.

'Max...'

With something between a curse and a growl, he sank his hand into her hair, pulling her head back. But instead of pushing her away, his lips found that same spot on her neck, as if he was punishing her, sending shivering cascades of agony down through her body.

His teeth grazed upwards and closed for a moment on the lobe of her ear, suckling the sensitive flesh and raising an answering throbbing between her thighs. Without thought, she slid forward and froze.

His eyes were a grey storm above her, his erection hot and hard just where another heart seemed to have come into life inside her—hot, pulsing, almost painful with need. Her legs were shaking with the need to move, to wrap around him, hold him as close as physically possible.

Behind them was a theatre as massive as an ocean liner, an audience of three tiers of empty boxes. At any moment, someone might appear—an usher, a cleaner, one of Septimus's minions checking the lighting. None of these threats broke through the mist of need. All she could think of was Max. Max wanting her.

He might hate her guts, but his body wanted her. Fed by anger, resentment, whatever... It didn't matter. He *wanted* her.

She finally let that realisation hit, and every muscle in her body contracted, shuddered, a moan rising out of her, her legs clamping hard on either side of his.

Her shudder spread to him, his hand tightening harshly on the pliant flesh of her behind, pulling her more deeply against him. A fireball burst outwards from their contact. Harsh, burning everything sensible in its way. The pressure of that pulsing heat against her had an immediate response in the matching throb between her legs. She moaned, shifting against him, wondering what to do.

'Don't move,' he muttered against her hair, his body as rigid as his cock.

'I can't. Not move,' she gasped. 'Besides, you moved first.'

'I know, damn it. This is madness.'

Yes. Madness. Any minute now he would realise just how mad this was and stop.

She didn't want to stop.

She turned her head, her lips moving from the soft

skin of his throat to the roughness of stubble along his jaw, stopping just at the corner of his parted lips. He was breathing as shallowly as she was.

It felt good. Powerful. Right now she didn't care if he wished her on the other side of the globe. The only thing that mattered was this moment. This man.

She buffed his lips with hers. They were as smooth as sun-warmed marble and at the moment just as immobile. Her hands mirrored the exploration of his lips, sliding down his back, under his coat, curling into the soft warmth of his expensive shirt. She tugged the fabric out of his trousers, her fingertips tracing the exposed skin of his abdomen. His body jerked against her.

She could feel the deep pull of his breath as he battled for control. She didn't want him in control again. She shifted her hands upwards and he gave an almost agonised groan.

'Damn it, Minnie. Stop it.'

'Stop what?' she murmured, leaning back to survey him. His shirt was half opened, his necktie crushed and dangling. She liked him unraveled like this. All he needed were some engine grease stains.

His hands tightened on her. 'We're in a damned theatre, Minnie. This is madness.'

'You're a grown man. If you want to stop, then stop. I'm not forcing you.'

It was a foolish challenge. She didn't want him to stop. Why couldn't she tell him that? Why bother with something as stupid as pride when she would soon enough be leaving and never see him again?

'No, you're not forcing me,' he grumbled, his gaze moving over her, lighting fires wherever his dark grey eyes settled. 'It just feels like it. I don't want to stop. This has been a long time coming, Minnie.'

Her body was on fire, but she couldn't help laughing. 'Is that a pun, Maxie?'

He blinked in confusion and then a thoroughly wicked grin spread across his face.

Lord help her, he was beautiful.

'You're a true original, Minnie.' His hands softened on her skin, his thumbs stroking the sensitive skin of her inner thighs. His movements were slow, almost soothing, but their effect was anything but that.

A door opened somewhere below and voices rose, carried up by the acoustics as a group of stage hands came on stage to work on the sets. She hadn't even noticed the singing had stopped.

He drew a long shuddering sigh and let her go, resting his shoulder against the wall. She turned her back to him, staring out over the empty chairs. Her breathing was shallow, almost painful, and her body was throbbing with something between fury and desperation.

She had not the faintest idea what Max wanted from her and she was terrified of asking. She moved towards the exit but he grasped her arm, stopping her.

'What will you do when Peter calls on you?'

She clenched her jaw hard, ill with disappointment, and forced herself to answer calmly.

'I doubt he will call on me, but if he does I shall tell him the truth. I think it's only fair now you and Septimus know.'

He drew a deep breath and nodded.

'Yes.'

'Now let me go, Max. Please.'

His hand tightened on hers for a moment and then let go. She was about to move towards the entrance when Septimus's voice carried up from the pit.

'Mina? Where the devil are you?'

She went to the rim of the box and he waved up at her. 'There you are. What were you doing? Dozing? Never mind, come down, girl. Everything up till now has merely been a skirmish—tomorrow the real battle begins.'

Mina nodded and turned back to Max, but the box was empty.

Chapter Twenty

Mina stood by the window, watching the murky grey and green world submerged in endless rain and wondering why on earth she'd thought it a good idea to return to England.

Damn Max for showing up like that at the theatre yesterday just to toss her emotions about again like a dinghy in a storm.

She could happily do without emotions at all. She'd done well enough without them for years and years.

Damn Max.

She let the heavy curtain fall into place and was just reaching for her book when a maid entered the parlour.

'Mr Cavendish to see you, Lady Mina.'

Mina's heart tried to leap out of her chest. She lassoed it and pinned it to the ground.

Tell him to go jump in the Thames.

She didn't say the words aloud, which was lucky, because the maid continued, her eyes wide with excitement: 'Mr Peter Cavendish. What shall I tell him, miss?'

Cold queasiness rippled through Mina's stomach, but there was nothing for it but to do precisely what she'd told Max she would do.

'Show him in, Susan.'

Peter looked exactly the same.

A little older, lines fanning out from his blue eyes, but the same. He still looked like a boy. How strange.

He took a step towards her, a tentative smile curving his mouth and giving his eyes a downward tilt, like a happy dog.

'Hello, Mina.'

She curved her mouth into a smile as well. She could do this.

'Peter. Hello. You haven't changed. You look…well.' She cringed inwardly at her words. 'I'm so sorry about Emily.'

She was certain that sounded wrong, too, but he merely nodded.

'So am I. I miss her.'

Her eyes and throat began to burn.

I will not cry. I will not.

He tugged his gloves between his hands, a nervous habit his mother used to scold him about. It was so familiar, and yet not.

This is Peter. The man you wished to marry and live with for the rest of your life. You should feel something.

But the only thing she felt was a fuzzy numbness,

like being wrapped in a quilt, except it wasn't cozy, merely stifling.

He finally looked up. 'This is strange.'

'Yes.'

'I was rather surprised to hear you are working for Uncle Septimus.'

'I am rather surprised to be working for him myself.'

'Yes, well… When I heard you were staying here, I thought… I felt I should come.'

'I daresay your mother wasn't happy about that.'

'God, no. Which was why I left early and didn't tell her.'

Again it struck her how nice he was. And that she felt nothing more than a faint, nostalgic affection for him. She let out her breath and smiled back. Somehow, she'd done right. Doing right wrongly was still right, wasn't it?

She sat on a claret-coloured sofa and he glanced at the chair opposite her.

'May I sit?'

'This is your home, Peter.'

'Well, to be fair it is Lucas's…' He drew the chair closer and took a deep breath. 'The truth is, Mina, that though I left Fairweather yesterday to come see you, I stayed the night at a hotel rather than come here directly. I needed to consider if seeing you was wise, but in the end I realised it was cowardly not to ask you the question that had been bothering me.'

She straightened.

'Which is?'

'I came because I was hoping to understand... I keep wondering what I did wrong all those years ago.'

Her eyes burned with those damned tears that never seemed far enough away any longer. She pulled out her handkerchief.

'Oh, Peter. You did nothing wrong. It was all my fault. Everything.'

The second telling of the truth was definitely easier. She'd expected to bawl and blubber, but the tears never came and the handkerchief's only use was to be twisted nervously about her fingers as she unfolded her sordid tale.

Well, most of it. She excluded Max's visit ten years ago and her horrid behaviour with him and everything that had happened on the ship. That would add nothing relevant, and she couldn't bear harming his love for Max.

'I'm so sorry, Peter. I acted atrociously and you have every right to hate me,' she said at last, a little too loudly. It woke him from his thoughts and he smiled.

'I don't hate you, Mina. You found yourself in an impossible situation...' He sighed again. 'You do know I would have wed you, regardless.'

'Of course. Which was why I had to be very clear I would not marry you.'

'By clear I gather you mean brutal to the point that I would despise you.'

'I was not so calculated. But I *was* angry. At fate, at

Lord Bascombe, at my mother, at you and your mother and Max… I wanted everyone to suffer.'

'With Max? What had he to do with it?' he asked, surprised, and she wished she'd kept quiet.

'Nothing, but I always felt he could see everything that was flawed in me and knew I was wrong for you.'

He shook his head. 'That isn't quite fair. Max respected you or he wouldn't have allowed you to help him with his work. He was always a private person, even as a boy. I admit I was a little jealous.'

Mina stiffened, but Peter was smiling. 'When I offered to assist him myself, he told me he was managing quite well. Then you came along and offered to help and he agreed without a peep of protest. It was a blow to my vanity.'

She relaxed and smiled.

'He knew how much you had on your plate already, Peter. And I think he agreed to my offer because he knew it would keep me out from under your mother's feet. Which it did.'

'Yes. I realised later how bored you must have been. You led such an eventful life in London and then… At the time I wondered if that was why you had fallen out of love with me. I should have done more…'

'Oh, Peter. Please let's just accept that it was for the best. You have two lovely children to show for it.'

His smile transformed his face. He fished in his coat pocket and extracted a small case, opening it to reveal a photograph of two dark-haired, light-eyed children.

He smiled at it with a look steeped in love and handed it to her. 'Amy and George.'

'Oh, my goodness, they look so much like Emily!'

'They do indeed. Amy in particular. She shares her disposition, too.'

'That is lucky. Heaven forfend she share your peevish disposition.'

Peter blinked and then gave a slight laugh. 'I'd forgotten that about you.'

'My awful humour?'

'No, that you could be flippant about the most serious issues.'

'Your poor mother hated that.'

'I'm afraid she never seemed to know where she stood with you. I would like to tell her the truth, Mina. She won't tell anyone else, my word on it.'

Mina gritted her teeth and nodded. She owed him that.

'Thank you, Minnie. And would you do me another favour? I would like you to meet Amy and George.'

'Do you think that wise, Peter?'

'I'm not concerned with wisdom, but in doing what is right. They owe their existence to your self-sacrifice and I want them to meet you.'

She untwisted her handkerchief and pressed it to her eyes. What a weepy willow she was becoming. It was damned annoying. She cleared her throat.

'Peter, pray don't make a martyr of me. I cared for you and trusted you to the extent of my limited abilities, but in truth I was very uncertain about marriage. There were times at Fairweather when I found it hard to breathe. Even before Lord Bascombe's arrival I was coming to realise we weren't quite right for each other.'

He gave a strange little humming snort, not quite a laugh.

'Too honest?' she asked.

'No, no, I'm actually relieved. I felt quite awful that I fell in love with Emily so soon. I had a romantic notion of wasting away for a while in the wilds of Scotland.'

She giggled at the image of Peter with a scraggly beard hiding in the mountains like a gold prospector in the Californian hills.

'You would have made a dreadful hermit. You would have been worrying about crop rotations at Fairweather and whether there were complications with the lambing. But at least I served a purpose. If you hadn't fancied yourself in love with me that season, you might well have succumbed to some other silly miss and then you and Emily might never have come together.'

Peter took her hand and raised it to his lips.

'That is a little extreme, but I am happy you are well, Minnie.'

'Peter!' The door swung open and Septimus strode in with his usual exuberance, followed more slowly by Max. Peter let go her hand and rose.

'Hello, Sep. Welcome back. Hello, Max.'

Septimus clapped Peter on the shoulder.

'Good to see you, my boy. You've come for the premiere, of course?'

'I... I wasn't planning to...'

'Nonsense, of course you must come. Where's that rascally brother of yours, by the way? We need him here for the ball.'

'As best I understand, Lucas is returning today from Paris, but I don't know...'

'Never mind. I've learned never to count on Lucas for my opening nights. But you must meet Eliza. Coming, Mina?'

Mina started forward obediently, but Max was at the door before her.

'You two go ahead. I would like a word with Mina first.'

Peter frowned, but Sep was already propelling him out the door. Max closed it and stood for a moment with his back to her. Her heartbeat shot ahead, like a cat with a dog nipping at its tail.

Max went to the sideboard, picked up a glass, set it down, went to stand by the window and gave the drapes a little tug.

'You told him.'

'I told you I would. It concerns him most, after all.'

'Yes. Of course.'

'He asked if he could tell Lady Ashworth. I said yes.'

He twitched the curtains back and gazed out into the gardens, as if checking for intruders.

'I don't know if that is wise. She might worry it will begin again.'

'Begin?'

'You and Peter.'

'That makes no sense. She must realise I could never marry at all now.'

She plopped down on the sofa and he looked over his shoulder at her.

'Why? Setting aside the fact that no one but us knows your secret, you are not even truly illegitimate. Your mother was married to Bascombe when you were conceived, which legally makes you his daughter, whatever your true paternity.'

'In the eyes of the law perhaps, but not in the eyes of Society. They might tolerate the illegitimate children of a royal duke, or even, within limits, an illegitimate child of someone from their favoured bloodlines like a Cavendish or a Davenport. But that doesn't apply to my mother. Lord Bascombe married her for her dowry, not her lineage, which was merely respectable. In any case, even if I did wish to marry, and even if I was willing to inflict my secret on some hapless fellow, I wouldn't inflict it on whatever children might come into that union. That would be selfish and an abuse of their innocent trust.'

'Isn't that a tad dramatic?'

'I don't think so. If I knew I was the daughter of a stable boy it would be a relief. But for all I know my real father might just as well have been a murderer or a fool or a madman. Which could account for quite a bit.'

He finally turned to face her fully. 'I take that back. We've passed "a tad" and entered the realm of penny dreadfuls. If we are discussing heritable traits, then given the gaping chasm between yours and your mother's characters, your father was evidently sane. Though I would infer he was also as stubborn as an ox. But whoever your father was, you, Minnie, are clearly your own person.'

She could do nothing about the stinging blush that spread up her face, but she waved away his words and continued, stubbornly, on her own track.

'And as for it being a secret... There is no such thing. I've already told three people and soon your aunt shall know as well. And though I never knew or asked, it is possible that my father told his real daughters the truth. They may not live in London at the moment, but they are part of its social fabric. Now I am back, it is probably a matter of time before my so-called secret becomes public knowledge.'

'You don't seem particularly bothered by that possibility.'

'Not anymore. It's a relief not to hide it as if I was a heretic escaping a papal inquisition. But I won't impose that decision on anyone else. It is as simple as that.'

He smiled, the friendship smile, but with an edge of sadness that seemed separate from her tale, more like something dear of his own fading away. As if he was watching *her* fade away.

Which she was. Perhaps he finally believed her. And now that she wasn't a threat... She wasn't truly anything at all.

She rose from the sofa, and unwound her handkerchief from her fingers.

She ought to say something. Something light. Cheerful. But nothing came other than the strangest sense of the floor sagging beneath her feet.

'Goodbye, Max.'

Chapter Twenty-One

Max waited until the door closed behind her before he set down the glass and sank onto the sofa she'd vacated.

Luckily he'd had a moment's preparation when Saunders informed them Peter was in the drawing room with Mina. But the sight of them holding hands... Mina with that sweet smile she always seemed to reserve for Peter...

It was becoming unbearable.

Mina could say what she wished, but if her father hadn't ripped her world apart that day, she would have wed Peter and that would have been that. The honorable thing to do would be to stand back and allow them to discover whether they still cared for one another.

He didn't feel honorable. He felt murderous.

If it had been anyone other than Peter, he would use every weapon in his arsenal to wipe that man from her memory. Even Lucas he would fight without restraint because Lucas was an equal.

But this was Peter.

He left the library and went up to his study. After a moment's hesitation he turned the key in the door. He didn't want to see anyone. He wanted...

He shrugged off his coat. Unfastened his waistcoat. Went to his desk and sat down.

He'd never felt emptier or more useless in his life.

In his rational mind he knew he had no reason to complain. That he had everything most people could dream of in life. He had wealth and power and an occupation that still fascinated him. There were boardrooms where his advice was sought, and bedrooms where women would happily welcome him. He'd never been greedy in life, and he knew he was lucky to have attained everything he'd ever wanted.

Except for one thing.

One person.

He sank his head into his hands. The pain welled inside, a cold hard steel sphere, pressing up and outward, leaving his lungs no room at all. It was physical—a harsh, probing pain, making his shoulders ache, his head pound.

The image kept rising to the surface no matter how much he tried to drown it. Mina with her hands in Peter's, smiling... Peter leaning forward to kiss them. Then the two of them drawing apart, Mina flushed with...

He must have been mad not to put her on the first boat to New York. He should have. Sent her back.

Gone with her. Anything but tell Peter she had returned. Now they would flow together again, close that ten-year gap.

Peter would bring Amy and George to meet her and they would love her, just as she made Anne Garfunkel love her, and made Eliza love her.

And made him love her.

Again.

'I can't do this,' he muttered into the darkness of his hands. If he had any resolve in him he would pack up and leave London. He'd done it before and it had worked. Almost. Not well enough, obviously. He'd thought he'd torn the damn thing out by the roots, but it had still been there, underground. Not even very deep.

Damn Peter.

Damn Sep. Damn him to hell and back.

He pressed the heels of his palms against his eyes, hard. It didn't stop the burning, but the pain helped.

'I don't want this.' His voice was hoarse, but he spoke the words aloud, to be absolutely clear to himself. 'I don't want to go through this again. I don't want to watch them again. I don't want any of this. I don't want her. I...'

Against the darkness he saw her, rain pouring down her face like a glass mask, her hair darkened, plastered against her cheek in dark swirls, her eyes narrowed but alight with joy and laughter at the storm, lightning cracking open the sky behind her.

He wanted her so much, so damn much.

He kept lying to himself and avoiding it and lying some more, but he'd wanted her from the moment he'd recognised her on the deck of the *Aquitania*. It had just...been there. As natural as seeing her again. As if he'd always known she must come back into his life.

Well, she was back and was ripping his innards to shreds all over again, except he wasn't twenty-five and he couldn't hide behind his childish defences of temper and contempt. He'd sure as hell tried and every time it fell apart and he was left...wanting her, watching her, waiting for something.

Waiting for her and Peter to get back together. That's why he'd gone to him. He had to know...

'Oh, God.' The words were wrenched out of him. It felt like his bones were being crushed. It made no sense that something that had no substance could hurt like this, but it did.

He sat there until it diminished, his breaths becoming less shallow. He waited some more, too tired to do anything else. Then he slowly pulled off his boots, poured a glass of whisky, and sat some more.

The knocking on his study door was loud, peremptory and familiar. At the second tattoo he snarled 'go away,' but he should have known it wouldn't work. The door opened and Lucas strode in, his dark hair still damp from the rain and his expression just as stormy.

'What's this Saunders is telling me? Is Lady Mina

Davenport actually staying here? Has Sep finally lost what little wits he had?'

Max curbed his reflexive anger. He'd responded no better a fortnight ago, after all.

'Hello, Lucas. How lovely to see you again after all this time.'

Lucas gave a sharp laugh at the rebuke and went to the sideboard.

'I'm not wasting my diplomatic skills on you, Max. I'm exhausted, parched and damned annoyed. And what the devil were you about letting Sep arrange a blasted ball here?'

Max sighed and held out his glass to be refilled as well. 'You try to stop him.'

Lucas gave an angry sigh and sank into an armchair by the fire.

'Fair enough. No point in wasting time on lost battles. But what the hell was he thinking bringing the enemy into the middle of our camp?'

'It's more complicated than that, Lucas.'

'I don't care. I damn well won't have her in my house. I know Sep can be quixotic, but I never thought him gullible. How did she get her talons into him? And more to the point, how could you allow it?'

'It's the other way around, Lucas. It's a long story, but the short of it is that we were wrong about her ten years ago.'

'That is a little too short, Max.'

'You'll have to trust me.'

Max held Lucas's gaze, and his cousin exhaled slowly.

'Since you're possibly the only person I fully trust on this fair earth, I daresay I must. I only hope you know what you are doing. Has Peter seen her yet?'

'Yes.'

'And? Were there...sparks?'

Max couldn't stop the image of Peter leaning forward, her hand in his, smiling at each other...

'Damn it, Max.' Lucas groaned. 'The boy has just lost his wife. This is the worst possible timing.'

'He's not a boy.'

'Peter will always be a boy. That's his charm. He's just like Father.'

'True.'

The pain was building in him again. A howl pressing upwards, echoing Lucas's demand: How had he let this happen? He could have stopped it. Played on her guilt. Insisted on putting her on the first ship back to New York. She would have gone.

It was his own selfishness that had stopped him. He'd wanted her to stay and he'd wanted to put to rest the damned fear of what would happen when she came face-to-face with Peter. To get it over with. That had been foolish beyond belief. Now it was too late.

'Hell,' Lucas cursed softly after a while. 'Does Mother know she's here?'

'Yes. I told her. I thought it best she and Peter hear it from me rather than gossip or the servants.'

'You're mighty cool about this, Max.'

Max gave a short laugh. 'She's in London. She was bound to see Peter. Anything else is denial.'

'So we take the fatalistic approach.'

Max shrugged.

'I didn't mean to lay the blame on you, Max,' Lucas said. 'I'm just worried. It's not been a full year even and Peter was always too damn nice for his own good. If she decides she regrets letting Peter go, he doesn't stand a chance.'

'Probably not. You never told me Bascombe sent you a letter asking for money in exchange for his approving the match.'

'Didn't I? I was in Paris at the time and Bismarck had just taken his first steps towards war with France. In the middle of that I received Bascombe's letter demanding five thousand pounds for the honour of Peter wedding a Bascombe. I knew he was hard up, but that was damned cheek and I told him so. Why? What had that letter to do with anything?'

'It convinced him to favour Renfrew's suit.'

'Renfrew? He went mad from the pox a few years back, didn't he? Do you mean to say that was why she ran away?'

'Not entirely. There were other reasons.'

'You're being damned mysterious.'

'I told you, it's complicated, and it's not my story to tell. The important thing is that she found herself in an impossible situation and decided the only way out was to escape. I'm asking you not to hold it against her.'

Lucas leaned back in his chair and stared at the ceiling.

'Since the end result is that Peter had Amy and George I'll trust you on this, Max. I'm still not happy about her meeting up with Peter, though.'

'Neither am I, believe me.'

Lucas cast him a quick glance. 'What is it, Max?'

'Nothing. I made a mistake.' The words lurched out of him, like a drunkard out of a public house.

'How bad?'

Max tried to smile. 'You don't have to sound so worried. It is mostly bad for me.'

'That is the definition of bad, Max. Is it related to the she-devil?'

Max shook his head. He wasn't in the mood to have anyone stick their fingers into an open wound, not even Lucas. He rose before his cousin saw more than he intended and Lucas followed suit, rubbing his nape wearily.

'Will you be attending the opera's premiere?'

'I promised Sep.' Max nodded. 'It's a damned pity he didn't follow in the Cavendish diplomatic tradition and put his substantial persuasive powers at the service of his country rather than his music.'

'True. He would have given Bismarck a run for his money. I'll avoid him until he leaves for the theatre or he'll have me toddling along as well, blast him.'

Chapter Twenty-Two

La Serena's entrance into the Cavendish House ballroom was everything Society could have hoped for.

She floated in on Septimus's arm, her claret-coloured silk gown even more exquisite than the pomegranate-red dress she had worn on stage as Carmen. She gleamed like a living ruby as she moved into the ballroom, her head high, her dark hair woven with a diamond tiara, and a single knuckle-sized amethyst in a delicate filigree choker about her neck. The crowd, many of whom had come directly from attending her premiere, fell back before her as before a queen.

But as her gaze met Max's he could see that under her assumed poise she was anything but calm—she looked both elated and terrified. He smiled reassuringly, but his attention was on the other woman by his uncle's side.

He wasn't surprised Sep had convinced Mina to attend the ball tonight after all. If she'd been having doubts, one look at Eliza would have convinced her she couldn't leave her charge alone in this pit of vipers, not when so much was at stake.

He felt Lucas stiffen beside him.

'Blast,' Lucas cursed under his breath. 'You didn't tell me she'd actually be attending the ball tonight.'

'I wasn't certain.'

'She always could act like a queen when she wished. You wouldn't think this was her first foray into Society after ten years of scandal and exile.'

Max turned to his cousin. 'She's your guest, Lucas. Whatever your personal feelings, you'd damned well better put them aside for this evening.'

Lucas's brows rose. 'You don't have to lecture me about form, Max. I know my duty.'

'Good. Now go and perform it.' Max strode towards the newcomers, furious at the lot of them and mostly at himself.

He greeted Eliza with a reassuring smile. Her hand was shaking slightly and he bent over it in a sign of overt gallantry he'd always been careful not to show her.

'I don't know why you made such a fuss,' he said in a low voice. 'I told you it would be a breeze.'

She burst into a trill of laughter, her hand clinging to his.

'May I return to New York now?' she asked, her smile a little truer.

'You will return in triumph. You didn't think about all this while you were singing, did you?'

'Not for a second.'

'Well, then. Imagine this is merely another opera. Without a second act twist. Or better yet, with Septimus as the villain.'

'Very amusing,' Septimus interjected, but twirled an imaginary mustache and leered. Eliza laughed again, her hand softening a further degree in Max's, and he let it go as Lucas approached them with the Marquess of Cranthorpe in tow.

Max finally allowed himself to turn to Mina. With her cool smile curving her lips and a dress of a blue so pale it looked like the sky reflected on a frozen lake she did look like an ice queen. She acted like one, too, not reacting by so much as a flicker to the awareness that entered Cranthorpe's gaze as she was introduced, nor to the dry note in Lucas's voice as he acknowledged her. In fact, she seemed to be precisely as Lucas had said—utterly unaware there was anything at all unusual about her reappearance on the social stage. But Max knew her and her calm didn't reassure him in the least.

As the night progressed his unease only grew.

Gossip was a strange, unpredictable beast. In the half hour since Eliza and Mina's entrance Max watched warily as the fetid ripples of rumor spread through the crowd. Eliza smiled and laughed and seemed to be genuinely enjoying her notoriety, but she kept Mina close by her, and even closer when Sep melted away and came to stand next to Max, beaming with pleasure as he surveyed the fruits of his labours. 'This is going well, isn't it? Told you there was no need for all that worrying. Come, let us find some champagne to celebrate.'

Max wished, for the umpteenth time, that it was good form to punch one's uncle in the face.

'Eliza is doing far better than I thought,' he admitted. 'Though it would be preferable if she didn't cling to Mina like that. She'll need to do this on her own, Sep.'

'Oh, she will, she will, never fear. She's adaptable, that girl. And Mina is doing beautifully as well. All that buzzing gossip is just rolling off her like water off a duck's back. She looks as unblushing as an ice queen. I wonder if she had Mrs Oakes put some grease-paint on her cheeks.'

'It's not rolling off her. She's hiding,' Max snapped and Septimus glanced at him and patted his shoulder awkwardly.

'She hides well, then. Don't fret. She's a strong 'un. And her appearing here at Cavendish House with all of us will put paid to old rumours. Why, if we welcome her back with open arms, why shouldn't they?'

The answer to that question came not half an hour later.

Just as noise rippled, so did silence. The pause in chatter began at the doorway and spread inwards, like a biting north wind.

It took a moment to recognise the guest that brought it with her. Lady Cartwright's resemblance to her father was still marked—she had Lord Bascombe's pale blue eyes and patrician nose, and the sharp lines that bracketed her mouth hinted she was no better tempered than her sire. But, unlike her father, she was known to be a highly virtuous woman and her husband was cut from the same prudish cloth. She entered on her husband's arm, her mouth a flat line of disapproval, her chin firmly aloft. Since neither she nor her husband were known to either enjoy balls or be patrons of the arts, it was clear the object of their appearance in Cavendish House was related to the news of Mina's presence.

Max's gaze shifted towards Mina. Despite her more modest inches she must have seen or heard someone mention the new arrival. Her chin was up, her face devoid of expression. Beside her Eliza was chattering happily with Septimus and the opera-loving Mr Fortescue.

Max moved towards them just as Lord and Lady Cartwright spotted her and shifted direction as well.

Mina watched as her not-actually-half-sister spotted her and changed direction, her hand tight on her husband's sleeve. The crowd melted before them as if they were enacting the parting of the Red Sea. It had been over a decade since she'd seen Emmeline, but she still recognised that expression. It did not bode well.

It was strange that now the moment she had feared had come she felt very little. Cold, empty, fatalistic. It had been bound to happen. Septimus had been too optimistic and now he would have to pay the price. She was only sorry for Eliza.

She shifted a little away from Eliza and waited for the inevitable. Lord and Lady Cartwright reached Septimus, who greeted them with some surprise, blinking rapidly as he introduced them to Eliza. Then he compounded his original blunder in ever employing her, by turning towards Mina, beckoning her to join them.

Oh, Septimus. She almost heard the words aloud in her head. Her once half-sister had clearly been waiting for that moment and the near silence of those around them only magnified her words.

'Well, we must be off, mustn't we, Cartwright. We are expected at Lady Mitchcombe's soirée. Farewell, Mr Cavendish.'

The two sailed out as they entered—serene and unimpeded. Noise flowed into their retreating wake, murmurs, whispers, titters. Septimus moved towards Mina, Peter a step behind him, Max approaching from the other side of the room. It had all been so fast. And so final.

Mina didn't wait for the Cavendish clan to close ranks—either for her or against her. She turned and left the ballroom.

Chapter Twenty-Three

Max moved deeper into the garden that swallowed the remnants of light from the house in a tapestry of dark on dark shadows.

Perhaps the footman was wrong about seeing Mina come this way... Perhaps he was wrong about Peter slipping out after her...

He turned as a pale shimmer became visible through the yew hedges that bordered the garden path. Not that he had any idea what he would do if he found her. Nor what he would do if he found her with Peter. He only knew what he wanted to do.

He came around the corner of the high hedge and stopped. So did the man moving stealthily towards him.

'Max! You scared the devil out of me.'

'Good. What the hell are you doing here, Peter?'

'Looking for Mina. Did you see what that woman did?'

'Of course I saw. So did everyone else. Which is

why you need to return to the ballroom right away, you fool. The last thing we need is for you two to be caught together alone in the garden.'

A frown marred Peter's boyish face. 'It isn't for you to tell me what to do, Max. I'm not a child.'

'Precisely. You should know better. She's been teetering on a knife's edge all evening and that damned woman just gave her a brutal shove. Don't you make her slip as well.'

'But we can't leave her outside here alone. She…'

'*She* is perfectly fine here alone,' interrupted Mina, materializing from a narrow path beside them. 'In fact, I came out here to get away from you lot, not to have you bring the gossip here with you! Go away!'

'Mina, I'm so sorry about…' Peter began, but broke off as she raised her hand imperiously.

'About what? Did *you* invite Lady Cartwright?'

'What? No, of course not, but…'

'But nothing. I don't need you to apologise for her or anyone else. I need you—*both* of you—to Leave. Me. Alone. Oh, for heaven's sake, not another one!'

'Damn it, Max,' Lucas expostulated as he strode towards them. 'We're trying to scotch rumours, not fan them into full blaze. First I see Peter scuttling off and now I find you here with her.'

Mina flicked open her fan. 'Well, it certainly will be interesting if on top of being snubbed by my so-called half-sister I am discovered with not one, not two, but with three of the Captivating Cavendish men. The gossip rags shall feast on that for a month at the least.'

'This isn't amusing, Lady Wilhelmina,' Lucas snapped.

She rounded on him. 'No? I saw you smirking quite contentedly in there, Lord Ashworth. Perhaps it was *you* who invited Lady Cartwright here in the first place to ensure my pretensions were nipped in the bud. A most impressive political maneuver.'

'I bloody well did not!' Lucas said explosively. 'Max!'

Max wondered what his cousin had seen on his face, but he shook off the moment of doubt and shook his head.

'No, it wasn't Lucas. And before you point the finger at me, Minnie, I had nothing to do with it, either.' He met her furious gaze. At least it was an improvement on the cold, blank look she'd worn in the ballroom. 'They could have and probably did hear from a dozen sources that you were staying at Cavendish House,' he continued. 'And they wouldn't have had any difficulty entering tonight. Septimus isn't discriminating when he has something to sell.'

'Ouch,' said his uncle behind him. 'Unkind, nephew. Though not wholly inaccurate. But I do promise you I didn't invite them either, Mina.'

She gave an indelicate snort. 'I know. You wouldn't do anything to eclipse your own story. Not unless it would help with the reviews.'

'Now, now. You're upset, my dear...' The snap of her teeth was audible, but Septimus ignored it and continued. 'But you needn't worry, no one likes the Cartwrights. We might even make this work in our favour...'

'Bloody hell, Septimus,' Max exploded.

'What?' Septimus demanded. 'Every crisis is an opportunity!'

Mina ran a hand over her face and sank onto a stone bench beside the path. Peter rushed to her side. 'Mina, pray don't cry. We...'

She shoved him away as he tried to put his arm around her, making him teeter on the edge of the bench. 'I am *not* crying, Peter Cavendish. I am contemplating murdering your uncle so I don't have to listen to his damned opera act philosophy of life any longer. Now would you all bloody well go away before I murder all four of you? I need to pack.'

'You're *not* running away again,' Max bit out.

'I damned well am,' Mina snarled up at him and shoved to her feet. 'As you pointed out from the beginning I was a fool to ever agree to come here. You should be delighted. That was what you wanted, isn't it?'

'You're being hasty...' Septimus began, and was cut off by Lucas.

'She's being sensible. Best thing for her is to return to New York.'

'For the Cavendishes, you mean, Lucas,' Max said coldly and Lucas shrugged.

'For *everyone*. There's no coming back from the storm brewing inside that ballroom. Speaking of which, we Cavendishes should return to the ballroom posthaste because God only knows what the devil is being said in there, and the four of us disappearing like this is bloody social suicide. Not just for all of us, but for your operatic protégée as well, Uncle.'

With that he stalked off.

'He's right about that part at least,' Septimus mused. 'I'd best return and see to Eliza. We'll have a nice chat over breakfast and fix this all up, Mina dear, don't you worry.'

Mina gave a strangled little laugh as he patted her on the arm and hurried off towards the house.

'We *will* fix this, Mina,' Peter said earnestly. 'I promise you.'

Mina brushed the dust of the bench from her skirt.

'No, you won't. There is nothing to fix, Peter. The only sensible Cavendish here appears to be your snake of a brother. As he said, there is no coming back from this, nor do I wish to come back from his. I doubt it will harm you lot much. Probably the opposite. You've provided the *ton* with some excellent entertainment tonight...'

'Devil take the *ton*,' Max snarled, the shreds of his temper slipping fast. 'You don't care about them. You never did. Are you really about to allow them to send you packing?'

Something shifted across her face, but then her eyes widened, fixing on something behind him and Peter, and she let out a very American curse.

'Oh, good Lord. It's Lady Murchison and Lady Upton,' Peter muttered as he noticed the two women who had appeared at the other end of the path. Even in the dim light from the ballroom, their silken gowns and exquisite tailoring gleamed as they approached.

'How delightful,' proclaimed Lady Murchison with a practised titter, her fan languidly raising and lowering the heavy curls arranged at her temples. 'See, Lady Upton? I told you the Cavendish gardens are worth a visit. I do believe the statues are from Rome, are they not, Mr Cavendish?'

Peter was staring at her like a hare caught in a lantern's glare, so Max forced himself to smile.

'These particular ones are from Capri, Lady Murchison.'

'Ah, Capri. How utterly *delightful*. Such a lovely setting for a midnight...tryst.'

Her gaze skimmed over Mina whose chin rose further. Max wished he could shove these busybodies into the hedges. Before he could act to defuse the situation Peter stepped forward.

'I agree it is a lovely setting, Lady Murchison, but not for a tryst—for a proposal...'

'Peter!' Mina interrupted in anguished tones.

Max had no clear recollection of the next few moments, which was probably for the best. If he had stopped to think he might have been too slow. He moved forward, taking Mina's hand. It was cold and shook a little as he pressed it against his arm.

'Never mind, Mina. I am certain Lady Murchison and Lady Upton can be trusted to keep the news of our engagement to themselves until we tell my aunt and place a formal announcement in the newspapers.'

He spoke lightly, though he was quite certain neither woman would keep the news to themselves for five minutes once they regained the ballroom.

Peter had made a strange choking sound, but thankfully remained silent and for a moment his audience of four merely stared at him. Then, finally, Lady Upton blinked.

'You and... You are *betrothed*?'

'We are. Lady Wilhelmina has been so kind as to accept my offer. My cousin was just congratulating us when you arrived. And now I think you should all return to the ballroom while Mina and I find Lord Ashworth and share the good news with him.'

He gave the two gossips his best smile and drew an unresisting Mina towards the house.

At least she was unresisting until they entered the conservatory where he was fairly certain they wouldn't be interrupted. Or overheard. He knew her well enough to know what was about to follow was best conducted without an audience.

The moment the door closed behind them she wrenched her arm from his grasp. He let her go and locked the door, leaning back against it as he watched his newly minted fiancée stride up and down the room like a caged tiger. He'd had no choice, but she'd not forgive him for this.

'Is all that exercise helping your temper, Minnie?'

She rounded on him.

'It's not my temper that needs help, but your senses. Have you gone stark staring mad, Max? What have you *done*?'

'Saved yours and Peter's hides amongst other things.'

He could swear he could almost see steam rising from her. Her face was flushed. Her eyes blazing. Full battle stations.

'There was nothing to save! How many times must I tell you I have no intention of marrying him. None. Never. Oh, damn you to hell and back, Max. Now it will take the devil's own luck to unravel this mess. Why on earth did you have to say that? It's preposterous!'

Max couldn't hear the noise of the ballroom from here, but he could well imagine the news rippling through the crowd. He really ought to find Lucas and Septimus and ensure they managed the scandal, but the truth was he was afraid to leave Mina. He wouldn't put it past her to disappear and board another ship to God only knew where.

Not this time. This time she would stay and face the music.

'It isn't in the least preposterous. There will be some gossip, but that seems to be par for the course wherever you go, Minnie. I think it's a rather elegant solution.'

'Elegant! I'm not a fool, Max. We both know perfectly well there will be no marriage. I have no intention of marrying anyone. Ever. The only people at fault here in this whole damned fiasco are myself, for succumbing to homesickness, and your fat-headed uncle, for thinking the world is an opera and he the conductor. So the only person who should in all conscience be making me an offer is that histrionic nincompoop. And if he *did* make me an offer I would take great pleasure in making him eat each and every one of his execrable vests. Inch by grotesquely embroidered inch.'

Max rubbed his cheek to quell the smile that threatened. It was insane that with his orderly life crumbling around him she could make him want to laugh.

'I would pay to see that, Minnie. Though I doubt he'd learn his lesson.'

She threw up her hands and set to pacing up and down the conservatory.

'I can't talk sense into any of you! Can't you see this is a disaster?'

'I don't think *disaster* is the right word. A challenge.'

'Don't play word games with me, Maxie! Trust me, your aunt will be using much stronger words than *disaster. Calamity… Catastrophe…*' She paused her pacing, fists clenched, visibly struggling for words.

'*Cataclysm*?' he offered.

'That, too. And worse.'

'What is worse than a cataclysm?'

'A Cavendish trapped into an engagement with a disgraced bastard.'

'You didn't trap me. I knew what I was doing.'

'To save Peter.'

He ought to tell her the truth—that he hadn't been thinking of Peter. At least not in terms of saving him.

He drew a deep breath and pushed away from the door.

'Would it be so terrible, Minnie? At least you know what you are getting.'

She finally stopped pacing, the anger receding and revealing confusion, pain and that fatalism that life had imprinted on her. That hurt him far more than her anger and dismissal.

He took her hands and every cell in his body contracted with this damnable yearning. For a moment he could think of nothing to say. Nothing that wouldn't send her running for the first ship to New York.

'We were friends once,' he managed. 'And what happened at the theatre proves there is an attraction between us…' He brushed his thumb over the back of her hand, a gentle caress that was anything but innocent.

She stared down at their hands, her lashes veiling her gaze, but a flush arced over her cheekbones. The heat he was trying so desperately to leash was beating inside him, making it hard to breathe.

'Is that what your Cavendish conscience is battling with?' Her voice was as rough as her words, but there was a tremor in her hands. 'But you forget—I'm no debutante. Someone with my scandalous past is mistress material, not marriage material. So if that is what you're after, you can have it without the grand gestures... I'm certain you've had your share of discreet arrangements.'

There was no reason for her mocking words to strike deep, but they did. Lust and anger were tangling dangerously and he tried to draw them both back.

'There is no such thing as a discreet arrangement. Eventually people find out. Do you honestly think I would subject you to what would follow?'

Her flush deepened. 'I suppose that *would* look bad—you bedding your cousin's once fiancée. Almeria would throw a fit.'

'Devil take Almeria. This is about us!'

She turned away. 'There is no us. In a few days I'll be on a ship to New York and this...this farce will be over.'

'I think you've proven that it will never be over if you keep running from it. The worst thing to do at this point is turn tail.'

'This isn't a business venture you can engineer, Maxie. There are no rules to follow here.'

'There are always rules. And ways to fight back.'

'Not always. Sometimes it is best to accept defeat and move on. What on earth are you trying to prove?'

'I'm not trying to prove anything. I'm trying to right a wrong.'

'So that is it. You feel guilty about what happened to me and you've decided to set everything right, *à la* Maxie,' she taunted. 'You just hate feeling you aren't in control, don't you?'

Alarm flickered behind her bravado as he moved towards her, but she held her ground. He stopped a step away, watching the flush spread over her too-pale cheeks, her eyes darken as the silvery grey was pushed back by widening pupils. The mechanics of attraction. He had that in his corner. She might want to strike him over the head with one of the potted plants, but she couldn't control the heat that sizzled between them any more than he could.

'That isn't quite true, Minnie,' he murmured. 'Sometimes I very much enjoy not being in control.'

'That's not what I meant.' Her voice was hoarse and even in the gloom he saw her swallow. Good, he wanted her as unsettled as he was.

'At the theatre, for example. If I *had* been in control, I would have chosen a less public venue. Someplace private. Perhaps with a nice, comfortable chaise-longue. Like that one.'

Her gaze flickered from his to the indicated piece of furniture by the wall, and her tongue touched her upper lip.

'And if I was in control,' he continued. 'I wouldn't be trying to seduce you in my cousin's conservatory with half the *ton* under his roof. But, I'm not, you see.'

'Not?' She cleared her throat. 'Not trying to seduce me?'

'No, not in control. I am *definitely* trying to seduce you. The question is, how best to go about it?'

'You're *asking* me?'

'Who better to ask? Who knows better what makes your heart beat faster...' He took her hand, his fingers finding the swift pumping of her pulse. 'What makes your skin...tingle.' He brushed his palm lightly along her bare arm. She shivered and her teeth pressed into the plump rise of her lower lip; his own lips felt singed with heat and he wanted her to sink her teeth into him, into any part of him. The need to make her lips part, open for him, was a compulsion. He needed to be closer, he needed to feel her pliant, lithe body under him, over him. He needed her scent, her heat... He needed to be inside her more than he needed to breathe.

He was still sane enough to know he had somehow fallen off a cliff, but there was nothing to grasp to slow him down. He wanted her to be his already. Beyond doubt. He wanted to push her back onto the chaise, bare her. He wanted everything. *Now.* He wanted her to cry out with need for him…

He moved closer, still holding her wrist where her pulse, rapid and sharp, beat against his fingertips, feeding his own rising fire.

'Who knows better what sets all that heat at your core blazing, Minnie? What makes you cry out with need…'

'Max. *Stop.*' She panted, planting her free hand on his chest. 'Is this some kind of game with you? Are you going to…to bring me to the brink of something and then waltz off like you did at the theatre? Like you did on the ship?' Her fingers curled into the fabric of his shirt as they had on the *Aquitania* and she gave a faint, helpless moan. 'You keep doing this to me…'

'I keep doing this to *you*? If anyone is pushing anyone over the brink it's you. This is no damned game…'

He drew her hard against him, his hand sliding under her bottom and raising her against him, his arousal pulsing hard and hot against her core. The fusing of their bodies was a striking of flints—hot, immediate, explosive.

He knew it was madness. Kissing her in the theatre had been reckless enough, but this was beyond foolish. It was also beyond him to stop.

He splayed his fingers deep into her hair, coaxed her lips apart with his, drawing them between his, dampening them with his tongue, tasting and suckling them. Her lips opened, her tongue darting to meet his, the moment of contact sending a shudder through her, or through them both. With a faint, desperate mewl of surrender she wrapped her arms around him, pulling herself even closer.

'It feels so good...' Her words were just a whisper of warmth against his mouth, but they felt like a blow from a piston.

He pressed her back until the chaise-longue impeded their progress. She drew back a little, her hands on his chest, the languor in her stormy eyes dissipating for a moment. Only for a moment. Then her fingers dug into his shirt, fisting, drawing him with her as she sank down, her skirts bunching as his leg slid between hers.

His hands shook with the need to crush her to him. To make her his. To make this final, irreversible.

'God, Minnie...'

'Don't tell me it's madness again,' she panted, misunderstanding his momentary resistance. 'I don't care.'

Neither did he, certainly not enough to stop his hand from sliding up her thigh, his fingers tracing featherlight caresses on the exposed flesh as he brought his mouth down to hers once more. Each shiver that shook through her drove echoing shocks to his erection. God, he was hungry for her, ravenous.

It was all happening too fast, and he wanted to feel every second of this, imprint it on both of their minds. Make it irrevocable.

He inched the skirts higher, his thumb just brushing the juncture of her thighs. Her nails bit into his shoulders as a shudder rode through her. Knives of pleasure were slicing through him at her excitement, anticipating her precious, joyous release.

'That's right, Mina. Take what you want.'

She didn't answer, but it set her hands free. They moved over him, feverishly, mapping him, struggling to press under his shirt.

'Take your shirt off.'

He laughed at her command, but obeyed. Her hands slid up his chest, her eyelids fluttering closed, her lips parted. He held himself immobile, absorbing the feathering of her palms against his skin, the shifting expressions of wonder and pleasure on her face. Her lips moved faintly as she explored his chest, dipping to encompass his waist and move up his back, her tongue touching her lower lip before she drew it between her lips. A vicious bolt of need ripped through him, as sharp and uncompromising as an iron stake.

He groaned as if she'd sunk her teeth into his own lips and bent to taste that sign of her pleasure.

'Your turn.'

'My what?' she whispered, her breath shallow.

'Take your dress off.'

Her hands fumbled at the catches and he gave a grunt of frustration and took over. The ice-blue silk finally slithered onto the ground, and her corset followed with a sullen thunk.

'Stupid things,' he muttered, and she gave a faint laugh.

'I hate them. I would burn them all if I could.'

'Excellent idea. I don't want anything between us, not even this lovely creation.' He traced the delicate frilled line of her chemise, drawing it slowly downwards. The thin straps gave way, sliding down her arms. Another shudder ran through her, sending the rest of the thin fabric slipping about her waist. Her eyes were shut tight, as if afraid to see him now that she herself was bared. He held himself still, taking in the raw beauty of her curves, her hair a tawny tangle on the cushion, her skin creamy in the half dark, the vulnerable yet defiant curve of her mouth.

For a moment he just stood looking down at his fantasy come real.

Mine.

He had to grit his teeth against the need to say it.

He rested one knee on the chaise and traced a slow line from her collarbone down to her navel, dragging the bunched fabric of the chemise ever lower, stopping just short of the darker curls that hid her sex. He didn't say the word, just shaped it with his lips as he bent to follow that line with his mouth.

Mine.

She breathed in deeply as he moved, her body arching into his touch, her hands moving over his shoulders, threading through his hair.

'I like it when you touch me…' she murmured. 'It feels like…there's quicksilver under my skin…setting me on fire…'

Her voice was setting him on fire. The taste of her. The feel of her skin. It made no sense, but her skin felt utterly different against his, a completely new texture.

A decent man would stop, not take advantage either of that vulnerability or that defiance.

Apparently he wasn't very decent.

He sank down on the chaise, gathering her to him. The fusing of bodies was a striking of flints—hot, immediate, explosive. Max groaned, his leg parting hers, pressing against her heat, his hands taut against her behind, his arousal pulsing hard and hot against her. She arched, bringing herself closer, and her eyes opened, more black than grey in the shadows.

He wanted her so much it hurt. At this rate, he was going to die before either of them climaxed.

'I like this.' Her words were rushed and hushed, as if her own needs frightened her.

'Like? Is that all? Obviously I'm not doing a very good job of coaxing you.' He ran his hand over her behind and the soft skin of her thigh and fitted himself more firmly against her heat. A shiver coursed through her, her eyelids flickering. Her voice was hoarse when she answered.

'More than like, then. And I don't think I need much coaxing.'

He laughed.

'Too bad. I like coaxing you. I want you on the edge of a cliff before we both fall off it. I want you hanging there, desperate, completely untethered, while I coax…'

He grazed the plump curve of her breast with his teeth and she rewarded him with a moan that clenched about his erection like a fist. He licked a circle around the rosy aureole and blew on her dampened skin, watching her nipple gather and pucker. His fingers parted the soft curls, grazing the slick heat of her sex, caressed her core with his fingers. His body bucked as his fingers slid down the moist fire of her loins and he almost exploded there, like a schoolboy, just from touching her.

Her body shuddered at his touch, but the shudder turned into an almost animal cry as his thumb brushed that small, essential inch of skin.

Her eyes opened briefly, gleaming like translucent shadows as he ran his thumb across the sensitised nub again and again in a circular, drawing motion. He bent to brush his lips across one hardened nipple, pulling it into the moist heat of his mouth, coaxing it as he coaxed her with his fingers, his senses filling with her, he could even feel the animal whimpers against his lips. He drew back slightly and saw disbelief, wonder, and an incredible need in her unveiled eyes.

He was shaking now as she rocked against his fingers. He had never seen anything even close to that look on her face and he wanted it. God, he needed it. Her eyes closed again as he increased the pressure and speed of his fingers then relieved it to brush her just lightly. Her nails dug into his back as she tried to pull him to her, but he kept the few inches between them, the effort bringing a pale sweat to his back.

'Look at me,' he commanded. He wanted her looking at him as she climaxed, he wanted to see the need, the pleasure in her incredible eyes. He wanted his face burned in her mind when she came.

Mina obeyed, locking her gaze with the dark storm visible in his eyes. Full exposure was a small price to pay for such…such…

Her body leapt as his thumb brushed the centre of her agony. She felt herself stretch, fill, she wanted more… She squirmed against his hand, trying to increase the pressure. His rhythm controlled her breathing now and she just followed, shaking and panting with each touch, her eyes drowning in his midnight gaze. Where their bodies were fused she felt a deep groan shake him and he bent to take her mouth again, his teeth closing briefly on her lower lip, then his tongue entering her mouth even as his fingers controlled her.

'Max,' she moaned when his mouth released her again. 'Do something. Stop this…'

'Patience, sweetheart,' he whispered against her skin. 'I'm not done coaxing. Not by a long shot.'

Patience.

She groaned.

He must be mad. How could she be patient when he

was demolishing her? When his touch and kisses—light as feathers, then hard and demanding—were driving the ache at her core into a storm of need she hadn't known was possible.

It was terrifying to be so stripped of her defences, but she wanted to let him coax her to wherever this was heading. Off the edge of the cliff he'd threatened her with.

Coaxing was clearly alchemical magic. It was an amalgam of quicksilver and hot flowing lava and bursts of lightning and joy. She tried to stifle her moans, still aware enough of her surroundings to worry they might be heard. But even that control was being stripped from her and she gave in and let the sounds, the sensations, the sheer utter joy of it take her over.

She heard someone crying out his name again and again and suddenly she burst, her hands closing convulsively on his arms, her eyes squeezed shut and that voice was sobbing his name now with each beautiful wave that crashed over her, tossing her like an angry, delicious surf, carrying her higher on each wave until everything fell away and she fell until she settled at that point between sea and sand where tiny, pulsing waves rocked her with decelerating speed. She floated down, warm and pulsing and beautiful.

Max didn't move.

Braced on one elbow, one hand still cupped over her loins, torturing himself with the last quivers of her hot, wet skin. His eyes still on her face as she turned her head slowly to one side, as if falling asleep, her features relaxing from their intensity. At that last moment before she had closed her eyes, he had seen the wonder, the sudden, incredible joy. She had almost laughed. And he had cursed himself for wanting to see that.

But he had marked her. He had seen her as no one had ever seen her. And in his present state he thought he might kill before he let anyone see her like that. The primitive possessiveness of this thought shocked him back into some sanity and for the first time he felt how cold the night had become against his damp flesh.

He looked down at her relaxed body, her leg still tangled in his. Blood was pounding in his groin and temples. He couldn't remember the last time he had felt such burning need. Desire he knew well, but need was different.

'You said we would fall off together,' she murmured.

'I lied,' he managed. 'I wanted to see you.'

'Unfair. I want to see you fall, too.'

Her hand brushed down his back, his hip, her fingers grazing his sensitised skin.

He ought to stop her before he did something even more foolish than make love to his cousin's ex-fiancée in his other cousin's conservatory while half the *ton* was gossiping about them just a dozen yards away.

Whatever sensible thoughts were trying to form were burnt into cinders when her palm brushed against his heated erection. He groaned, pushing her hand away.

'I didn't stop you. You don't stop me,' she whispered, closing her hand on the hot, pulsing evidence of his desire. She caressed the velvety skin over the hard flesh beneath. 'It's soft as velvet and hard as steel. I can feel it harden when I do this...' she murmured, clearly revelling in the surge of heat that hardened him further in her hand.

He held himself as long as he could until her exploration became unbearable. Then he closed his hand around hers, leading her until he shot right off that cliff and into blissful oblivion.

Nothing in his life had ever been so utterly, wonderfully beautiful in itself. There was no world outside this moment, no threats of scandal or heartbreak waiting to strike. Just two people who had coaxed each other off a cliff and into heaven.

Chapter Twenty-Four

Who was the idiot who said mornings brought good counsel?

Mina paused three paces short of the breakfast room door. The cowardly part of her had contemplated stealing out of the house at dawn with her meagre belongings. Perhaps leaving a few messages behind. A warm and encouraging one for Eliza and Mrs Oakes. A well-wishing one for Peter. An excoriating one for Septimus.

And for Max… She could think of nothing at all. That much was beyond her.

After she'd returned to her room last night and surfaced fully from her lustful stupor, reality had returned with a vengeance. She had no idea what she'd expected after their lovemaking… She let out a long breath and corrected herself. *Lustmaking* was a more appropriate term.

Max had been gentle as he helped her dress in the silence of the darkened conservatory, but he'd also returned to being his usual inscrutable self, though underneath she'd felt an element of... What? Satisfaction? As if he'd won. Well, he probably believed he'd removed her imagined threat to Peter's well-being. She wasn't even angry at him for that any longer. She knew how fiercely protective he was of his adoptive family. And she had certainly been more than willing... Just as she would be more than willing if he decided to accept her offer of an affair.

It would end in heartbreak, she knew that, but at least she would have memories to take with her to balance out the pain.

What if he didn't want an affair? What if last night's encounter was victory enough for him... If she was sensible she wouldn't wait to be hurt more than she was already. She could take her meagre belongings and walk out right now...

She sighed in exasperation. She was too old for such dramatic gestures. She would indeed leave Cavendish House and probably return to New York, but at the very least she was owed wages and she fully intended for Septimus to purchase her return ticket. And not in steerage. He owed her that much.

She finally drummed up the courage to enter the breakfast room. Septimus was the only one at the table and her mangled heart proved to her once again why she was an utter fool.

The real reason she had stayed was for Max.

Septimus waved her inside, brandishing the newspaper he had been reading.

'A triumph! A veritable triumph! Listen to this review by that little weasel Burgess. *"Never has a mezzo-soprano upon Her Majesty's stage sung with such abandon and pathos. She has the impulsive gaiety of a Madame Vestris, but the vocal depth of a Miss Graddon. This author has seen Carmen interpreted two years since in Brussels by the wondrous Minnie Hauk..."* That's the other Minnie, Minnie, and to be fair she is wondrous, one must give credit where credit is due. I was at that performance as well and that is what gave me the—'

'Yes, you told me already, Septimus,' she interrupted, unsure whether she ought to be relieved or offended that he was making no reference to last night's multiple disasters. She poured herself some tea, wondering if perhaps Lady Murchison had for once in her life managed to keep her word and her silence. Perhaps it would all just...melt away? She tried to smile. 'Do go on, Septimus, what else does this Burgess fellow say about Eliza?'

'Ah. Yes. Here we are. This is the good part: *"But when Don Jose plunged his dagger into Carmen's chest in a fit of towering jealousy, this reader felt the strike in his own quivering organ. Rest assured, dear readers, that your humble servant will attend again tonight to assure himself this newest treasure is yet alive and singing like the angel she must surely be.*" Well? What do you make of that?'

'That he should not leave his job as critic to become an author. That is rather florid.'

'Nitpicker. He adores her. And this is the man who said Signora Valenti howled like a dog with a cat strapped to its back.'

'Oh, that's awful!'

'Well, to be fair, so was she,' Max said as he entered the breakfast room. Septimus frowned at him.

'You think most opera singers howl like dogs.'

'That's because they so often do.' He sat down and glanced at Mina as he poured coffee into his cup. 'Good morning, Mina. You look tired.'

'How sweet of you to point that out,' she replied tartly, much more flustered than she would like. She'd been dreading this moment, but there was safety in conducting their first meeting after last night's combustive encounter in public. Damn him for looking so calm. Well, so could she. 'You, in contrast, look annoyingly well-rested, Mr Cavendish.'

'That's his natural look in the morning,' Septimus said cheerfully. 'Looks the same after a hard night on the town. Very aggravating.'

'He is,' Mina grumbled and turned back to Septimus. 'Is that it? In the newspapers?'

Septimus lowered the edge of the newspaper, his eyes flickering to Max and back to her. 'You sound almost disappointed.'

'I'm not, but... Why isn't there more scandal?'

'Why should there be?' Septimus objected.

'Because Lady Cartwright snubbed me in the most public manner possible. Because...' She was incapable of mentioning the scene in the garden, so she changed track. 'Because ten years ago I jilted Peter and disappeared and now I am back and staying at Cavendish House and none of you are throwing rotten cabbages at me, which was what they must naturally have expected.'

'I hesitate to prick your vanity, my dear, but setting aside your rude prude of a half-sister, I'm afraid you credit yourself with far too much notoriety. I agree you caused some fluttering of the gossip wings ten years ago, but in the end, what was there to wonder at? After all, you were not yet of age and so your father was fully within his rights to dismiss your engagement to Peter. And as for your so-called disappearance, Lord Bascombe must naturally have wished to keep the destination of your exile quiet so as to prevent poor, heartbroken Peter from pursuing you. It was naturally understood that once your respective ardours cooled, you would be allowed to return to England and marry a man of Bascombe's choosing. Unfortunately, Bascombe's failing health prevented his plans from coming to fruition, and you remained with your mother in a perfectly respectable venue. So respectable, in fact, that, once widowed, your mother eventually married into the highest levels of the court of Mexico. Have I covered all eventualities?'

Mina's jaw had been dropping with each fabrication.

'Septimus Cavendish! Do you mean to tell me you have been spreading this...this manure about town?'

Septimus looked aggrieved, but Max burst into laughter.

'Was that what you and that prime gossip Lady Dunforth were whispering about in the corner, Sep? I commend you.'

'And so you should, Max, my boy. I was worried it was a little tame for Society's taste, but like good quality manure, it stuck.'

'Not with Lady Cartwright.'

Septimus waved a dismissive hand. 'No one cares for the Cartwrights. They're no fun at all. No, the real problem that faces us is that now everyone is awaiting the sequel.'

'There is a *sequel*?' Mina demanded.

'Of course. The star-crossed lovers in these tales are always given a second chance. I've heard quite a few people say they were struck by how well you and Peter look together—quite as if you had never been apart.' He sighed loudly. 'It is quite the fairy tale.'

'Careful, Septimus.' Max's voice lost its warmth as he caught and held his uncle's gaze. 'Don't overplay your hand.'

'Don't play it at all,' Mina interrupted. 'If you *dare* give any credence to that piece of prime bull, Septimus, I shall... I shall tell Eliza she would do far better with James Mapleton.'

'You wouldn't! "*Ah, you serpent, whom I have in my kindly bosom warmed, till I am stung to death.*"'

Mina wrinkled her nose. 'If anyone is a serpent here, it is you, Septimus Cavendish. You know full well there is nothing between Peter and me.'

'Now, now, there's no harm in letting Society spin its wheels. The more wheels the better in fact. Like all spoilt beings, it is less dangerous when its attention is occupied on various fronts.'

Mina didn't answer. Under the table her leg began twitching. She should be pleased, and grateful. But all she felt was as tense as a sail in a storm and a little queasy. She cast a quick glance at Max. Was he feeling relieved that nothing had come of that horrid scene? That he ought no longer feel obliged to follow through on his offer? He met her gaze with the blank one that gave her no purchase whatsoever.

'You look almost disappointed,' he drawled. 'Were you expecting something else?'

'You know damned well what I was expecting.'

Septimus clucked his tongue at her language, but Max merely tapped the teapot.

'Have some more tea. Or should I send for chocolates? They seem to improve your mood.'

'Now, now,' Septimus chided, ruffling his newspaper. 'You are not wed yet. There will be plenty of time for marital tiffs once the knot is tied.'

Mina dropped her teacup. It bounced off her hardening toast, rolled off the table, and landed in her lap.

'Good thing you didn't have any more tea yet,' Septimus said consolingly.

'You told him what happened?' she demanded of Max, her voice shaking.

'Lady Murchison told him,' Max replied in the same even, infuriating voice. 'Did you expect her to keep silent?'

She'd hoped... Or had she? She set her cup back on the table and shut her eyes.

'Oh, did I forget to mention that little titbit has made its way into the newspapers as well?' Septimus chirped as he pulled another newspaper towards him. 'Nothing definite, just something coy about hopefully soon hearing the sound of wedding bells. Most picturesque. Where was it... Ah, here: *"The return of the late Lord Bascombe's youngest daughter from the Americas was reflected in her choice of the finest in fashion to be offered by that great sister city across the seas, New York. Her gown with its hint of a Grecian line, and of the finest silk reflecting the celestial blue of her eyes..."* Celestial blue indeed! Whoever wrote this needs glasses. But I digress... *"and her charming countenance proves that the Bascombe beauties may be deserving of that title even in their summer years..."* Summer years, I ask you! Why, you are a spring chicken yet, my dear. Still, I daresay that is better than saying autumn years. Where was I? Ah, yes.

"*It is hardly surprising that her reappearance is said to be accompanied by the hint of forthcoming wedding bells.*" There, you see? Quite charming.'

Charming. Her heart was thumping so hard she could hear it.

Max couldn't seriously contemplate such a ruinous move. It had been a ploy, a necessary act on his part to prevent Peter from taking an even more ruinous step.

'But what of Lord and Lady Cartwright?' she asked, her voice a little too high.

'I doubt the gossip rags like them enough to trumpet their attempt to snub you. Too puritanical by half.'

She shook her head again. 'It won't go away. Things like this don't. And we aren't getting married,' she added, a little late, but with emphasis.

Max refilled her rescued teacup.

'I'm certain there will be a great deal of gossip. Ignore it.'

'Oh, is *that* how it is done?' she asked brightly, eyes wide. Max finally looked directly at her and smiled. It made it all worse. She bunched her fists and stared down at her tea.

'The most important thing,' said Septimus, 'is to meet it head on. Cut straight through the waves, so to speak. This afternoon Eliza is invited to sing for the Duke of Albermarle. A small setting, no more than fifty people. An excellent opportunity not merely to gauge the waters, but shape them.'

'Water doesn't take well to humans believing they can shape it,' she snapped.

'Actually we shape it all the time,' Max replied. 'Canals, dykes, sea walls, ice cubes, cups... Speaking of which, careful you don't break your much maligned teacup gripping it like that, Minnie.'

Septimus sniggered and reached for another newspaper. Mina rounded on him.

'Speaking of not breaking things, you gave me your word you would pay me my wages and arrange for my passage back to New York, Septimus.'

'And so I shall, and so I shall. I shall send word to my banker and you shall have your wages tomorrow.'

'And arrange passage.'

'Naturally.'

He seemed affronted at her suspicion, which only made her want to do precisely what Max had warned her not to and toss her poor teacup at one of these complacent, infuriating men. She rose.

'I think I prefer to have breakfast in my room. It is safer for everyone, including the crockery and certain people's hard heads.'

She strode out, cursing them all, but mostly herself.

Chapter Twenty-Five

Max set down his knife as the door closed behind Mina with a decided snap.

'Phew!' Septimus exclaimed cheerily. 'At least you know what you're in for, lad.'

'She won't marry me,' Max replied far more calmly than he felt. He'd goaded her knowingly. She was better angry at him than defeated by her own thoughts and fears. He ought to have known... He *had* known that their incendiary encounter in the conservatory wouldn't magically convince her she had to marry him. If anything she seemed even more determined to leave.

'Maybe, maybe not,' Septimus conceded. 'But she's here, isn't she? Didn't pull a runner yet.'

'She can't until you pay her. Why did you say you would pay her tomorrow?'

'I lied. It will take at least another week. Stringing her on.'

Max relaxed a little and smiled. 'She'll be furious. Rightly so.'

'Excellent. She's magnificent when she's fired up. If between us we keep her angry she might yet pull through this briar bush with most of her reputation intact. We need Almeria.'

Max straightened in alarm. 'Good God, Sep. Don't involve Almeria. She'll knock the last nail into the coffin without a backwards glance.'

'Humph,' said Septimus and retreated behind his newspaper.

Max glared at his uncle. He didn't trust him an inch. 'Septimus. Promise me you won't…'

'Ah, Lucas!' Septimus interrupted, beaming over the rim of the paper. 'Excellent morning, yes?'

'I'm in no mood for your games, uncle,' Lucas snarled and turned to Max. 'I left you and Peter alone with her for five minutes! Five minutes! How could you manage such a royal cock-up in five minutes? I know you want to protect Peter, but… I'm damned if I understand you, Max. Couldn't you have sent those two gossips packing without throwing yourself onto a flaming pyre?'

'Oh, you needn't worry,' Septimus chimed in. 'She has no intention of marrying Max. She plans to return to New York.'

Lucas snorted. 'You actually believe she'll turn her back on a fortune and the Cavendish name for a governess's life and salary? This isn't a blasted play. You might have skulked off to your rooms, Max, but the rest of us heard the gossip loud and clear after we returned to the ballroom last night. They only stopped short of accusing her of witchcraft!'

'Sit down, Lucas.'

Lucas blinked at Max's tone. Surprisingly, he sat.

'What the devil is going on, Max?'

'What is going on is that it is also our fault that she is in trouble, so I will need your help fixing this.'

'How is it our fault?' Lucas demanded. 'Maybe we *should* accuse that hellion of witchcraft. First Septimus and now you.'

'Me?' Septimus paused in the act of pouring Lucas some coffee.

'Yes, you. You always had odd notions about her. Ten years ago you told me this mad notion Max fancied her and now you pluck her off the streets of New York and waltz her and her scandals back into our family.'

Shock coursed through Max, and a strange sensation of being stripped. He turned to his uncle. Septimus was busy fiddling with the top of the coffee pot, his mobile mouth pursed into a tight knot.

'Septimus.'

His uncle's shoulders hunched a little, his focus on the coffee pot redoubling.

'I know—it's ridiculous,' Lucas scoffed. 'I told him he must be either mad or drunk.'

'What precisely did he tell you, Lucas?'

Lucas frowned. 'What does it matter?'

'Tell me.'

'I say, Max...' Septimus tried, but fell silent when Max raised his hand.

Lucas shrugged, clearly uncomfortable now. 'Some nonsense about keeping an eye on you. I'd just returned from Paris, straight into the middle of the chaos that followed her running away, remember? He said you'd taken the whole thing very hard.' He turned his gaze to Septimus and some of the fire returned. 'It's a damned good thing you're the third son, Sept. If you'd been head of the family, we all would have gone up in flames long ago.'

'That's unkind, my dear boy. Well, if we've done raking up the coals, I'll be toddling off...'

'Sit *down*, Septimus,' Max snapped.

'But, Max...' Septimus gave a petulant shove to the coffee pot and sank back into his chair. 'Oh, very well. No point in beating about the bush. You certainly took your sweet time catching on. I would have thought you'd be grateful.'

'Grateful! You think I should be grateful for you playing ducks and drakes with Mina's and Peter's lives. And with mine.'

'Well someone had to. You couldn't expect me to just walk away and leave her there in the museum tea shop. One doesn't thumb one's nose at fate.'

'Just at one's relations apparently.'

'I see. So if I could go back and do it differently you would have me walk away? Say nothing and do nothing? Even knowing she'd broken your heart ten years ago.'

'*Peter's* heart.'

'No, my dear boy. Don't forget I spent a fair amount of time at Fairweather that summer. I may have many flaws, but give me credit for being a fair judge of hearts. She dented Peter's heart but it was soon mended. She crushed yours. So tell me—should I have left her there? You might never have met her again. Ever.'

Max wanted to do some crushing right now.

'Damn me,' Lucas muttered. 'I hate it when you're right, Sep.'

Septimus revived enough to beam at his other nephew. 'You really should come to the opera more often, my boy. You might learn something useful. Might help you stop a war one day.'

Max didn't react to this absurdity. His blood was still thrumming with shock. And there was nothing he could say. Because Septimus was right. Whatever happened he didn't...*couldn't* regret Mina had entered his life again.

Even if he had to pay for it for the rest of his life.

'Just...don't interfere again.'

Septimus smiled brightly, back in character.

'You see me in the guise of Voltaire's watchmaker deity—I merely set matters in motion once and let the mechanism do the rest. I am the very personification of non-interference.'

Max left the breakfast room.

Chapter Twenty-Six

The Duke of Albermarle's music room could easily have been mistaken for a greenhouse. Potted palms lined the walls, interspersed with moss green sofas plump with pink cushions. The wallpaper was an exquisite hand-painted green silk covered in a wide variety of orchids, which Septimus assured Max were as true to life as a botanical bible. Even the scent was an overpowering mixture of roses, perfumes and earth.

Eliza was swiftly appropriated by their host as he led her to the dais that had been erected at the end of the large room in her honour.

'Don't tell Eliza,' Septimus whispered to Max as they followed, 'but Haydn himself conducted an orchestra here. And Chopin played on that very pianoforte.'

'I've no intention of telling Eliza anything at all. Where the devil has Mina gone?'

They paused beside a clump of potted palms, scanning the thickening crowd, Septimus swivelling his head like a curious owl. The green fronds masked their view of a group of women seated on a cluster of sofas, but did nothing to mute their conversation.

'She *assured* me it was Max Cavendish who was engaged to Lady Wilhelmina,' whispered one Society matron.

'No, no, she must have meant Peter Cavendish, my dear. It stands to reason,' whispered another in response.

'Well, she was most insistent, but perhaps…'

'And did you hear Lady Cartwright gave her the cold shoulder? She is quite, quite disgraced. Like mother, like daughter, they say. I remember when she made her debut ten years ago. She always was a flighty hoyden.'

'That is quite true. Hopping from one fiancé to the other as if they were flowers. I ask you! And now Lady Bascombe is living with some Chinese fellow!'

'Mexican, my dear Mrs Ponsonby. A nobleman. And she did marry him once poor Lord Bascombe passed away.'

Max resisted the urge to snort at that one. *Poor* Lord Bascombe indeed.

'Well, a Mexican nobleman isn't quite the same as a real nobleman, is it?' insisted Mrs Ponsonby. 'It makes one wonder what Lady Wilhelmina has been up to all these years. No doubt she heard about poor dear

Emily Cavendish and decided to try her luck luring Peter Cavendish back...'

Septimus tugged at Max's sleeve and they moved away.

'Usual nonsense,' he said, and cleared his throat. 'It'll blow over soon enough.' He tucked his thumbs into the pink and green rose garden vest he'd chosen for the occasion, but his tone carried less assurance than usual. Even he must realise the ship was taking on water and sinking fast. At this rate there would be no third act on Society's boards for Lady Mina Davenport.

Max just wanted the evening over with so they could take Mina away from the bubbling vitriol. Preferably back to the conservatory. Where the devil was she?

Septimus cleared his throat once again. 'I think I have left Eliza long enough... Or should I stay and help you find Mina?'

Max shot him a mocking look.

'Are you finally regretting hiring her? Maybe next time you'll be less cavalier with other people's fates. Go play with your latest toy, Sep. I have more important matters to deal with.'

Septimus ignored him. 'Never mind all that, there she is, by that alcove. You see? You worry too much, my boy. All is well.'

Max barely resisted the temptation to reply to that outrageous platitude. Mina was indeed standing in the shade of the alcove leading to the supper room, far from the bustle that was gathering around Eliza near the dais where the orchestra was arranging itself. She watched as he approached, but there was nothing on her face to betray her feelings. Neither a glimmer of awareness of the threat she was facing nor of the passion they'd shared the previous night. It was almost as if she wasn't present.

'Why aren't you with Eliza?' he asked, resisting the urge to take her hands. To take her away from this sucking swamp.

'She doesn't need me. It was foolish to come tonight.'

'What is foolish is playing a wilting wallflower in an alcove.'

'Oh, am I embarrassing the almighty Cavendishes?'

'The almighty Cavendishes are impervious to embarrassment.'

'That's right, you can get away with anything. Even an illicit tryst in your cousin's conservatory must be quite commonplace for you.'

He reached out, but stopped himself in time. *He* might be impervious to embarrassment, but he had no intention of adding any more fuel to the fire the *ton* was lighting under Mina's feet.

'I don't think this is the best place for that discussion...' He broke off as a footman emerged from a door hidden behind the alcove and barely avoided upending a tray crowded with audibly fizzing champagne flutes. Max drew Mina away from the harried servant, but she swiftly detached her arm from his hold.

'That was close. Perhaps the universe is trying to tell you something,' Mina said as she brushed her hand over her glove as if to sweep away any sign of contact with him.

'You're enough of a challenge without bringing the universe into it, Minnie. Now, we are returning to the fray and you are going to show these idiots how little you think of them.'

'I don't take well to directions, Maxie,' she snapped, but she strode through the crowd to position herself beside Eliza with her chin at an angle that Septimus would have applauded.

Septimus himself sidled over to Max in a manner he must have learned from one of his productions.

'Talked some sense into her, did you? Good show, good show, eh?'

Max glanced at his uncle and realised he was playing his role as caricature with less attention than usual, his gaze flickering around the room.

'Anyone else missing, Uncle?' Max inquired drily.

'Missing? Not quite… Ah!'

He broke off as the tone of the crowd shifted, paused and then returned with increased enthusiasm. Max turned warily. In the doorway, talking with the Dowager Duchess of Harwood, was Peter. And Almeria. Peter spied them and smiled, detaching himself from his mother and heading in their direction. Lady Ashworth followed more leisurely, greeting friends as she went. Max moved forward, intercepting her halfway across the room.

Her smile was tight as she looked up at him.

'Good evening, Max. Do come introduce me to my dear brother-in-law's newest protégée. I wish to congratulate her on her success tonight. I hear she sings like a chorus of angels.'

'Why are you here, Aunt?'

'That isn't very polite, Max, dear. You should be grateful I am by the sound of the scandal bubbling and brewing about our ears.'

'Aunt, whatever you are planning, don't do it.'

'Do what? Come. You shall give me your arm.'

He did as he was told, but he looked past her towards Mina. She'd already seen Lady Ashworth. She stood like a prisoner in the dock, her pallor even more marked next to Eliza's emerald gown.

Lady Ashworth's hand tightened on Max's arm for a moment as Peter stopped before Mina. The buzz in the room fell, and for a second the silence revealed the soft sound of the violins that had begun to play on the dais—sweet and cheerful and wholly inappropriate. Peter bent over Mina's hand and smiled as if there was no hailstorm about to burst above their heads. Then Mina's face softened and she smiled as well, the colour returning to her cheeks as she drew Eliza into the conversation.

Max slowed his pace, his heart a fist of pain. She'd shared passion with him last night, but that look—

affectionate, inviting... The same tenderness he'd witnessed when he'd come upon them in the drawing room.

It burned into him like acid. He wanted to march over and pull Mina away. He didn't want Peter touching her. He didn't want him anywhere near her.

He almost pulled away from his aunt's arm, but her grip tightened, recalling him to the other danger. All Almeria had to do was replay Lady Cartwright's drama by addressing Eliza and ignoring Mina, and that would be that as far as Society was concerned.

'Aunt...'

'You worry too much, my dear. Come.'

Mina's smile evaporated as they neared, her chin rising. Not defiance, but acceptance. Max hoped his aunt saw that, for once. But Almeria merely continued her leisurely way through the crowd, nodding and exchanging greetings with people as they went. Finally, they reached their objective and Almeria smiled at Peter and at Septimus who had bravely come to stand beside Mina. Lucas had also joined the tableau, standing a little to the side, watching his mother with a curious look. Lady Ashworth ignored them all and turned to address Eliza.

'I have not been in London ten minutes and already I have heard Carmen is a success *fou*, Miss Serena. I congratulate you. And you too, Septimus.'

'Thank you my dear, but the praise must all go to

La Serena. Eliza, allow me to introduce my sister-in-law, Lady Ashworth.'

'And you remember Lady Wilhelmina Davenport, Aunt,' Max added, his hand tight on her elbow.

She cast him a slight, mocking smile, but turned to Mina, pitching her voice just a shade higher, her cool patrician tones carrying nicely above the buzzing conjecture.

'Of course, Max. Our Dear Mina requires no introduction.'

She held out her hand and Mina, looking paler than ever, extended her own hand like an automaton. His aunt took it in hers and then shocked Max by leaning forward to brush a light kiss to Mina's cheek. 'You have been away far too long, Mina. It is good to have you back amongst us, my dear.'

She stood back, but Mina was completely stripped of her poise and just stared at her, as if afraid to move with the sword still hovering.

'Tomorrow we shall both have tea at Cavendish House and you shall tell me all about your travels, yes?'

Mina blinked, waking from her stupor. 'Of course. I shall be happy... I... Thank you, Lady Ashworth.'

Peter and Septimus beamed at Lady Ashworth and Lucas shot Max a quizzical look, half amused, half amazed.

'Now, which of you boys shall fetch us a glass of champagne?' Lady Ashworth continued blithely. 'It was a long ride from Fairweather today and trains are so very rough. Oh, how lovely. The music is beginning. Is that your doing, Septimus? Your timing, as always, is impeccable. Peter, why don't you and Mina secure us the choicest seats. I am so looking forward to hearing dear Miss Serena sing.'

Peter held out his arm to Mina without hesitation, and again, like an automaton, she placed her hand in his. As they melted through the crowd Lucas gave a low whistle under his breath and turned to Eliza.

'Sep, you go fetch the champagne. I shall claim my right as head of the family and lead *La Serena* to the dais. No, Septimus, she's had enough of your company. Let another fellow bask in her glory.'

Eliza flushed and laughed and the two made their way towards the dais. Sep opened his mouth, but after a glance at his sister-in-law he wisely mumbled something about champagne and hurried off.

'Thank you, Aunt,' Max murmured as they made their way to their seats.

'Whatever for? You did not think I was so petty as to punish Mina for her foolishness ten years ago? Nineteen seems even younger now than it did then. And it was all for the best. I would have perhaps preferred a rather less dramatic exit from our stage, but in the end it achieved what I wanted all along. Peter returned to Emily far readier to fall in love with her than he had been before Mina broke his heart, and I now have George and Amy. I can afford to be generous.'

'Sometimes you amaze even me with your Machiavellianism.'

'Us Bellinghams are just as adept at strategy as any Cavendish.'

An alarm went off in his head and he turned to her.

'You came here, to London, today, for this...'

'Of course. I knew it had to be done the moment you told me she was back.'

'And Peter?'

'You needn't worry about Peter. He is my concern. Look how well they seem together.'

He had been looking, a stone the size of a cannonball pressing against his lungs.

'They might look well together, but she is engaged to me.'

'Ah, yes, Peter explained what happened. You needn't worry about a thing.'

'I'm not worried,' he lied. 'But she most definitely is not about to marry Peter.'

She ignored him. 'I came across Lady Murchison.'

'Came across. By chance, I suppose.'

She patted his arm. 'Naturally not. Septimus provided a rather more coherent version of events than Peter, so I decided to pay Agatha Murchison a quick visit to thank her for being so considerate on my behalf. Agatha and I understand each other.'

'What the devil does that mean? What are you doing, Aunt?'

She smiled and patted his arm once more.

'Righting old wrongs, Max. Now do come along or we shall miss Septimus's songbird.'

Chapter Twenty-Seven

'Good morning, Mina.'

For the second morning in a row the person Mina least wanted to see was the only inhabitant of the Cavendish breakfast room. This morning she would actually have preferred Septimus.

'Good morning, Lady Ashworth.'

'Do sit down, child. I have been looking forward to having a word with you. In private.'

Mina forced a smile and chose a chair opposite and a little to the right of her hostess. She had waited until she knew Septimus had taken Eliza to the theatre for a new costume fitting and Peter had gone with Max into the City on business. She hadn't reckoned Lady Ashworth would ambush her, but she ought to have known the reckoning was bound to come. Best get it over with sooner rather than later. She owed Lady Ashworth her pound of flesh.

'The breakfast room isn't precisely private.'

'It shall do for now. You've changed, Mina.'

'I was thinking the same of you, Lady Ashworth. Or perhaps it is merely that I am no longer engaged to Peter.'

'Of course. I can afford to be magnanimous now I have two lovely grandchildren.'

'Of the correct variety.'

Lady Ashworth sighed. 'You haven't changed that much, Mina. You always say the most outrageous things.'

'I wouldn't necessarily call the truth outrageous. Unpleasant, rather.'

'I disagree. I happen to think you and Peter would have had rather wonderful children. I was far more concerned that your unhappiness in the union would make Peter unhappy.'

Mina wanted to protest that Lady Ashworth had no right to decide whether she would be happy or unhappy, but she knew the woman was right. Even without Max upending her world, in time she would probably have become frustrated and unhappy with Peter.

'Is that what this is about? Having me admit you were right?'

'I don't need validation from you, Mina. When you are a mother, you will understand that a parent doesn't need to balance and tally those books with anyone but themselves.'

That hurt far more than Mina would have imagined possible. She pressed her hand to her sternum, her heart whipping itself against her palm. It was hard to breathe.

'I won't be a mother, so that point is moot,' she mumbled and hurried to ask the one question that had been on her mind since yesterday: 'Why didn't you snub me last night? You could have been rid of me once and for all. Everyone expected it.'

'I answer only to my conscience, Mina. You are not your parents, nor should you be tarred with their brush.'

Tears reared their annoying head again. 'I don't even know who my father is. Peter told you, didn't he?'

'He did. So did Septimus. Really, my brother-in-law is quite a romantic behind all his bluster.'

Mina gave a faint laugh. 'Yes. He thinks my life story very operatic.'

'Well, it certainly has been dramatic. The question is, what next?'

'That is my concern.'

'I disagree. Septimus tells me you are pressing him to provide your wages so you can return to New York. Is that correct?'

Mina pushed away the pain and nodded.

'Yes.'

Lady Ashworth nodded and set a blue silk purse on the table between them with a thunk and clink of metal.

'Your wages in full and enough to purchase comfortable passage to New York. I have also arranged for a carriage to be outside in half an hour. It will take you to the train to Southampton where a ship, the *Gallia*, will be departing for New York tomorrow. My footman will accompany you to help you with your luggage and the arrangements.'

The silk purse glistened in the morning sun, looking as smug and heavy with gold as the woman in front of her. Mina reached out and touched the soft fabric. It was warm.

This was what she had wanted, wasn't it? Or rather, this was what she ought to want. She had no future here. She could stay for a while as Max's mistress, until... Until he tired of her, or decided it was time he married and produced a host of privileged little engineers, or found another mistress with more experience and less uncomfortable baggage. One of those scenarios would eventually, inevitably trot onto life's stage.

You could always play on his guilt and marry him. He would, you know. That stupid conscience of his runs deep. Just like Peter's. He would marry you because it is the right thing to do.

She looked down at her lap, fighting the burn of tears. The moment was less dramatic than that rotten, awful day ten years ago. But just as painful. More so. She'd not known then she would love Max for so long and so pointlessly.

Half an hour.

'I should say goodbye...'

Lady Ashworth leaned forward. 'My dear child, you

know as well as I that some things are best done… cleanly. It is not by chance that you and I are the only ones at home at the moment. Peter went with Max to his office in town and Septimus and Eliza are at the theatre. It was thought best I should be the one to say farewell on behalf of the Cavendishes. You can of course choose to make things…difficult. But I know you, child. You don't wish to hurt anyone, do you?'

It was thought best…

So they had all sat down and discussed her. Mina knew how attached Max was to his aunt. She would have played on that. Convinced him to set aside his foolish conscience and this inconvenient lust and do the right thing. And she would have done it with that horrid gentleness. Mina knew it was sincere. There was kindness and even affection in the woman's eyes and it burned Mina from the inside. If only her own mother had looked at her that way. Had fought for her the way Lady Ashworth was fighting for the boys she loved. If only…

She shook her head. There was no point to that. And the woman was right about her.

She'd caused enough damage. Twice now. It was time to pay the price.

She reached across for the purse. It was surprisingly heavy. Enough gold to support her for a while. At least Lady Ashworth played fair.

She rose.

'I'm sorry… For everything.'

'Don't be sorry, Mina. Be everything you are. I wish you all the happiness the world can provide you.'

Mina shook her head again and left the room.

Upstairs a maid was already packing her belongings and her travelling dress and coat were laid out on the bed.

Lady Ashworth might not be a blood relation of Septimus, but she was just as cunning.

Chapter Twenty-Eight

Ten years ago Mina had stood on a darkening quay in Liverpool, staring at the rust-caked SS *Speedwell*, her mother weeping by her side. Her body had been numb, but her mind had buzzed with fear and resentment and anger.

Today she was numb again, but the sun sparkled merrily on the water and the SS *Gallia* had the gleam of a ship eager to embark on an adventure.

It only made everything worse.

If only she could go back in time and refuse Septimus's offer... No. That would mean she wouldn't have met Max again. That thought was even more agonizing than the thought of leaving. She could not imagine erasing these past weeks, no matter how painful.

'Miss?'

She turned to the steward and reflexively extended her boarding ticket. The steward took her meagre luggage and led her up the gangway. Her windowless berth was a far cry from the one she'd had in Eliza's suite, but it was all she'd allowed herself. Her wages would have to last her a long while once she reached New York.

She sat on the edge of the narrow bed. Her bag slumped against a plain wooden chair and a curtain hung across one end of the room in lieu of a dressing room beneath which a puddle of greenish water swayed gently. She closed her eyes and took herself back to a veranda overlooking the sea, the stars drawing a sliver line on Max's profile, the sharp line of his cheekbone.

She ought to have stayed, at least long enough to seduce him into having an affair with her before she returned to New York. That way she would have more memories of the pleasure he had given her to keep her warm during the freezing New York winters.

She closed her eyes more tightly as a tangle of agony and need tore through her.

She still could do it...

There was a clanging as some object was dragged along the corridor outside, followed by boisterous male voices. Either stewards or fellow passengers. They would not be leaving until the evening tide. There was still time...

She shoved to her feet. There was a small silver-pocked mirror on the door and a woman stared back at her from an unremarkable face, her grey eyes dark and empty. An unremarkable, illegitimate woman nearing thirty years of age.

More clanging and rumbling beyond the door marked the arrival of more passengers. She wished they were already on their way so the temptation would be removed.

She locked her door, let down her hair and lay down. Perhaps she could sleep her way to New York.

She didn't sleep, not at first. The silence of her tomb-like berth only made room for the grief she'd been holding back, expanding into every part of her until it was hard to breathe.

I can't do this.

There is only so much I can bear and this is beyond me.

I can't lose Max. Not again. Not again.

In the end she must have fallen asleep because the knocking inserted itself into her dream. Monstrous granite-hued whales were pummelling the ship, pounding it into a pulp. She woke with a gasp as the hull crumpled and a great wave rose above them, curling over, closing in... Knocking...

'Open the door!'

She surged awake and stumbled towards the door. Perhaps the ship *was* sinking. The knocking resumed, more forcefully, and she unlocked and tugged it open, falling back as a tall figure filled the frame.

'Why the devil didn't you open the door? I thought... We thought something happened to you!'

Mina blinked up at Max. He looked pale and quite, quite furious.

'We?' she asked dumbly.

'The steward. He went to fetch the master key.'

'Oh. Why?'

'Because you wouldn't answer, damn it.'

Her stupor finally began to recede.

'Stop yelling at me. I was dreaming. I thought you were a whale.'

'A whale.' He drew a deep breath and pushed past her into the berth and promptly stopped. 'Bloody hell. This is smaller than a closet.'

'Thank you for stating the obvious.' She pressed back against the wall, her body thrumming far more intensely than any ship engine. She was so absurdly happy to see him she could cry.

'What are you doing here?' A horrid thought occurred to her. 'Has something happened? Is it Eliza?'

He waved a dismissive hand before shoving his hands into his pockets.

'Eliza is fine and probably making Septimus proud in Haymarket Theatre right now.'

'Oh. Good.' It shouldn't have hurt that Eliza and Septimus could so easily continue with their lives without even caring she was gone, but it did.

'So why are you here? To make sure I am safely on my way? Was Almeria worried I might decide to take the gold and stay after all? I *was* rather surprised she trusted me to keep my word.'

He canted his head a little to the side, his face back to that inscrutability that always left her exposed.

'You gave her your word?'

'Well, not exactly. She assumed, correctly, that I would agree to your arrangement. You may report back to her that I am safely on the *Gallia*, waiting to be transported away from her precious family.'

He glanced around. 'She booked *this* cabin?'

'No. Your aunt was very generous. So you can put that silly conscience of yours to rest, Maxie.'

'My conscience.'

There was an ominous weight to those two words, but Mina ignored this sign of her nemesis's pride.

'I can't imagine it was easy to let Almeria do your dirty work. But I don't hold it against you. She did it very...elegantly.'

'You think I had Almeria...' He drew a deep breath but didn't move away from the cabin door. 'Pay you off.'

'Naturally she did not put it so crudely. Almeria is nothing if not smooth.'

'Yes. She is that.'

Mina shrugged. 'She cares for all of you. You're lucky.'

He gave a short laugh. 'I'll tell her you said so. And a few other things.'

Something in his tone pulled her out of her little knot of pain.

'I don't understand... Why *are* you here, Max?'

'Why didn't you at least tell us... Tell Peter you are leaving?'

'Oh, for heaven's sake! Not Peter again!'

'Yes Peter again. Everyone saw how comfortable the two of you were at Albermarle's yesterday. Don't tell me you don't...don't feel any affection for him.'

'Why should I? Of course I feel affection for him. My judgement might be off, but it is not completely faulty. I feel comfortable with him because despite being such a good man he doesn't judge people like me who aren't as good as he. But that doesn't mean I have an evil plan to enslave your innocent cousin. I thought I'd made that clear.'

'You made your intentions clear. Your emotions are another thing entirely.'

She scrunched her eyes closed against the need to pummel something. To yell to the skies.

'How many times must I say it? I don't love your pretty little cousin. I don't love him now and I didn't love him back then. Not in any way that mattered. I was nineteen, for heaven's sake! Does anyone really know their own heart at nineteen?'

She broke off at the absurd tragedy of those words. She *had* known her own heart. It was still the same heart. The same folly.

The same man.

She plopped down on the side of the bed, rubbing her numb cheeks.

'I don't understand why you came, Max, but they'll

be weighing anchor soon so you'd best leave before it's too late.'

She heard his indrawn breath above the rising rumble of the engines. He let it out on a halting laugh.

'It's already too late.'

The knocking on the door took them both by surprise.

'Miss? I have a key. May I…'

Max opened the door, shielding her from the steward's view.

'Thank you, Perkins. Miss Davenport will be disembarking with me, so please have her belongings sent to the Pelican Inn…'

'I am *not* disembarking.' Mina bounced to her feet, but Max had already locked the door and turned back to her with a fierceness he usually kept well hidden.

'Yes, you are. It's either that or I'll have to make the journey to New York as well. Choose. Either back to London or put up with me on board for the next two weeks. You thought I was a nuisance on the *Aquitania*? I can be a damn sight more annoying, believe me.'

'Why are you doing this, Max? Is this some last-moment spurt of conscience or chivalry? You must know I won't hold you to that silly engagement. It's over and done with.'

'No, it bloody well isn't.' He dragged his hands through his hair and began pacing up and down the very narrow confines of her room. With a twist to her already mangled heart she realised he was looking distinctly, and uncharacteristically disheveled. 'I'll never forgive her for this!'

'Forgive who?' she asked, thoroughly confused.

'Almeria! Do you honestly believe that even if I wanted you gone I would have been so cowardly as to allow her do my *dirty work* as you called it? At least now I know how little you think of me.'

'Oh. So you didn't know.'

'No, I bloody well didn't. You should have known that.'

Mina sat on the edge of her uncomfortable bed. Said so baldly, she realised it was true. If she had been thinking clearly at all, she would have known Max would never leave such a task for his aunt. Not that it made any difference. The result was the same.

'It hardly matters. I always meant to leave once I was paid. I'm only sorry I didn't say goodbye to Eliza...' She broke off as the lie stung. That regret was miniscule compared to her regrets regarding the angry man glaring down at her.

The thrumming of the engines increased. Max raised his chin, listening. He threatened to remain on board, but she didn't really believe he would do that.

'Aren't you worried you'll be stranded here?'

A smile twisted his mouth.

'There's no hurry. The *Gallia* won't be leaving tonight.'

'It won't?'

'No. Once I made certain you were on board I paid

a visit to the engine room. The engineers are going to have a long night figuring out why the piston and the propeller are communicating as poorly as you and I seem to be. Knowing you, I wanted to be certain I had enough time to counter whatever outlandish argument you came up with.'

'You…you disabled the ship?'

'You don't have to sound as if I've sunk the thing. It is perfectly safe. It will merely cause a little delay until the next tide.'

She stared at him in awe.

'You disabled a transatlantic ocean liner carrying several hundreds of passengers just so we could argue.'

'Probably closer to twelve hundred passengers and probably a hundred or so more in crew.'

'You're mad.'

He laughed and extracted a metallic ring from his pocket and tossed it onto her lap. 'That is one way of putting it. Here. Hold on to this. You'll need it if I lose this argument.'

'There is nothing to lose because I shan't be arguing with you. What I shall be doing is delivering this to the first steward I can find.' She rose, clutching the little nut. It was surprisingly warm, its sharp edges pressing into her damp palm. 'Back to your hobby of blocking doorways again, Maxie? Kindly step aside.'

He crossed his arms. 'Imperious as always. Ask me nicely and I might consider it. Or you could try pushing me aside again. It seems to be a hobby of yours, too.' The engines changed timbre, the growl lowering into a sullen rumble. 'Ah, good. They're realizing something is amiss. There's your chance to save the day.'

She was tempted. She could picture it—striding in to the engine room, nut upheld like a heraldic talisman, denouncing Max's perfidy...

'If I were ten years younger that dramatic entrance might have appealed to me,' she grumbled. His mouth softened at the edges. Not quite a smile.

'I think you still have it in you, Minnie. I won't stop you.'

'And you'd leave the ship?'

The smile faded, his eyes narrowed and for a moment he merely stood there. Then he shook his head.

'Not a chance. You can't win all the battles, sweetheart. If you hand that over, I stay. And since I haven't had time to book a cabin, we'll have to share.'

It wasn't the threat that made her cheeks flare. He'd called her sweetheart that night in the conservatory, but this was different. It sounded so...tender. As if he truly meant it. As if beyond the undeniable tug of lust he felt for her, the affection that had sprung between them all those years ago was still there, reaching out to her.

She sank back down on the berth, clutching the nut.

Hope was a foreign sensation for her. Far more unsettling and frightening than danger. She knew what to do when she was threatened. She had no notion what to do with this uncomfortable pressure growing somewhere between her stomach and her lungs.

She spoke very carefully.

'If I agree to stay. For a while. So we can...can have an affair... Could we do it without your aunt and everyone knowing?'

His hands fisted in his pockets.

'I can't do that, Minnie.'

'Why not? It is the most sensible choice. That way you needn't feel guilty.'

'Guilty? I don't feel any guilt. Ten years ago, yes. Not anymore.'

'Ten years ago? Why on earth? You weren't responsible for what happened.'

'I was responsible for falling in love with my cousin's fiancée. I was responsible for what I felt that day you jilted him in the village... You thought I was angry with you, but I was far more furious at myself for being so bloody relieved you wouldn't marry Peter. I should never have come to Bascombe that day, but I had to see you. See if perhaps I was why you'd... It was as stupid as stupid can be, but I couldn't believe you jilted Peter because you really intended to marry some wealthy old man. I'd actually hoped... It's no excuse for my behaviour, I know. But I felt like the worst of traitors, being happy at Peter's pain. I didn't trust myself, or you. So when you put on that act it was easier to believe you were every selfish thing you claimed to be.'

He gave a single, harsh laugh. 'You put on one hell of a show. Septimus would have hired you on the spot.'

Mina clung to the edge of the uncomfortable bed, trying to contain the foreign sensations inside her that grew and grew.

'I did what I had to.'

He smiled, but there was sadness there that pinched at her.

'Yes. That could well be your motto, Minnie.' He went down on his haunches before her and took her frozen hands. 'I'm not losing you again, Mina. I've held everything together all my life since that damned accident. I've shaped the world to meet my needs and I've calculated every move I made in life. There's only been one thing that's been completely outside my control, that I absolutely knew was right for me even if I fought to deny it. It's always been you, Minnie. Probably from that cursed day you bullied me into eating that ridiculous cinnamon cake and dictating my letters. If I'd know that day was the first step on the worst and best experience of my life I might have had the sense to run for the hills. But I'm glad I didn't. Because whatever happens from this point on, I don't regret falling in love with you. It was the smartest thing I've ever done, even if I was a complete idiot about it. I only wish I had been a better friend to you. I failed you when you needed me.'

She shook her head, her innards a roiling mush of hope and pain.

'You were an excellent friend. It's ludicrous to blame yourself for my own stupidity.'

'It's ludicrous to call yourself stupid. Unless you're fishing for compliments?'

She gave a snort of disdain. 'If I was, I wouldn't start with you.'

'I'm not a bad hand with compliments. When they're merited.'

'You're awful. You never once complimented me on my secretarial skills. And I was an excellent secretary.'

'The best. It wasn't just my heart that suffered when you left. Please come with me, Minnie. Give me a chance. Give us a chance.'

He shifted to sit beside her on the bed and held out his hand.

She wanted so badly… *So* badly to reach out… She covered her eyes. Even if she dared believe him, that he cared… It didn't really change anything. She was still Mina not-Davenport. Scandal-ridden. Almost thirty.

If she cared—and, heaven help her, she cared so much it crushed her just to think of taking his hand—if she cared, she should do the right thing. Just as she had done ten years ago, but for all the right reasons now. Because she loved this man.

'Max, you must know it is impossible—'

'Oh, no you don't. Not again.' His abrupt interruption cut her short. 'I'm not engaging in another village square scene with you playing the noble sacrifice and me the weeping willow being kicked to the side of the road. This time you stay and face the music, Minnie. I don't give a damn who your father is. Not one bloody damn. I know who you are—you're a damned thorn in my side and I want *you*. You're the only woman I wake up wanting and go to sleep wanting...'

'Max...' It was more of a wail this time. She searched for some way to take what she wanted and not harm him. 'Can't you see that the most sensible thing to do is to have an affair? That way we could do something about this...this attraction without hurting anyone. Including yourself. I can't bear hurting people I—I care about. I can't.'

'Well, you'll just have to risk it because attraction is just the tip of the iceberg when it comes to you. You manage to drag every emotion I never thought I had to the surface, good and bad. I knew you had that capacity ten years ago, but I didn't realise how precious that is. Accepting that I'd never fallen out of love with you has been a tough pill to swallow, but it's nothing compared to the thought of losing you again. I won't survive that blow, sweetheart. I'm no longer young enough or arrogant enough to fool myself into thinking I don't need you in my life, Minnie.

She could feel his heart thudding against her palms and hear the bruised, yearning need in his voice, calling for her to reach out to him just as he was reaching out to her. He could have let her go, given them both time to consider all the implications. But he had chased after her... Disabled a monster of a ship for her...

For them.

Her own heart was pounding so hard it was painful. She wanted so much to give in. Believe everything he said, forget her birth, Society... Forget the damage that might follow and fall into this beautiful dream just like she'd fallen into endless, fruitless daydreams.

She wanted so badly to stay. To tell him the truth.

I love you, Max. I can't bear leaving. It was unbearable before, but now...

Max felt her hands tighten on his and, for the first time, sensed a swing of the scales in his favour. It was like trying to coax a wild animal out of the cage they'd spent their whole life in.

He stroked his thumb gently over her knuckles.

'If you leave, where else will I find a woman who could infuriate me and make me smile at the same time?'

A smile finally touched her lips and he had to resist the urge to lean in to that simple sign that he had the power to bring her some happiness.

'That's quite a tribute. Getting a smile out of you was always harder work than infuriating you, Max. That was easy.'

He smiled, too. Damn, he loved that she gave far better than she got.

'Strange. I remember smiling quite a bit after you invaded my study. Though mostly on the inside at first. I must have been afraid.'

'Of what?' Her eyes softened again, worried, hopeful. Another excellent sign. He gathered her hands a little closer.

'Of admitting how much I enjoyed letting you win me over. Of how much I wanted to win you over... I loved your smile, Minnie. Mischief and warmth and... quiet. Something in you quieted when you were happy.'

Her smile wavered and fled. 'You have to stop *doing* that.'

'What have I done now?'

'You keep breaking my heart again and again. Snapping off the brittle pieces and warming them and sticking them back on and it *hurts*.'

He gave in to temptation and pulled her into his arms, breathing in her scent. It always had the power to make his insides melt and turn everything else hard.

'Now you know how I feel, love.'

She shook her head against him, but he merely pulled her closer, nuzzling the sweetness of her neck, gathering her scent, letting his body absorb everything. No fear, no guilt, just his Mina. His love.

'I know you love me, sweetheart,' he murmured. Again, she shook her head, but her arms held tight. He brushed his hands down her back, over the beautiful bottom he hoped would very soon be lying bare with the rest of her—body and soul.

'I know you want me to love you,' he whispered, brushing the curve of her ear with his mouth. She shivered and mumbled something inaudible, but he felt the truth. 'I know you want to believe every word I say. I know you want to trust me and let go…'

Her hands fisted on his shirt, her body stiff. He kissed her neck, her cheek, and, very softly, her lips.

'Part of you believes me when I say I love you. Someday soon the rest of you will, too. I'll do everything I can to earn that trust, love.'

'I do trust you, Max,' she whispered. 'It's only… I'm terrified.'

'I know about being terrified. It's a state best shared with someone who loves you.'

He waited, holding her. He could feel her struggle, so silent and so powerful. Then the shaky breath as she let go of another knot in the rope.

'I could only ever share it with you, Max. I knew that before I even realised I was in love with you.'

'Minnie.' He barely managed to speak her name, his arms tightening around her, beyond his control. He'd waited, wanted, so long…

'I knew that day in the graveyard, Max. That it was already done and there was nothing I could do to turn back. I was afraid I must be just like my mother and I would fall in and out of love with dozens of men. Except the truth was even more terrifying.'

'What truth, love?'

'Seeing you on the *Aquitania* and realizing it had never gone away. That I was still in love with you. It was awful.'

'I don't think that's awful at all.'

'Well, you ought to because it would have been far better for you if I had fallen in love with someone else far away and married them and let you get on with your very comfortable life and find some perfectly lovely and fashionable woman to marry. And don't tell me you didn't fall in and out of love with dozens of women in the interim…'

'Not in love, sweetheart. I'm afraid I must be as tediously constant as you because nothing I've felt towards anyone has come close. I've never been as much myself with any woman as I am with you. I don't just love you, I trust you.'

Her shoulders hunched in his embrace, but her hand tightened on his.

'You didn't trust me ten years ago. Nor should you have.'

'Actually, I should have. But that was my mistake. If I hadn't been in love with you and wracked with guilt over it, I might have had enough sense to realise something was terribly wrong. But I was and I didn't. I can't change the past, love.'

'I'm not blaming you.'

'I know. Just trying to warn me off. It won't work. You are well and truly stuck with me. Now, I have no objection to spending the next week in this cramped cell with you, but I would rather respect all the hard work Almeria put into pushing us together…'

'What on earth are you talking about? She did everything she could to be rid of me.'

'Including informing me that you were on your way to Southampton and that if I was indeed serious about you I should hotfoot it down here?'

'She...she did? But then why send me here at all?'

'I rather think both my aunt and Septimus are secret romantics and this was a test of sorts. For both of us. She told me that ten years ago she'd hoped I would soon forget about you, but after ten years of observing my resistance to caring for anyone else and then my response to your return, she realised she'd been wrong. She sent you away because she believed that any decision you made should be a real choice on neutral ground, not boxed in on Cavendish territory and without a penny to your name. If you have any doubts, she also said we should act sensibly for once and have a very boring wedding ceremony at the Fairweather chapel.'

She brushed her fingers over her damp lashes. 'Boring would be nice. But Max...' She grasped his hands, her fingers pressing into his palms. 'Are you truly certain? It is one thing to make that decision for yourself, but you haven't considered. What...what if there are children... My birth...'

He raised her hands, resting them against his heart.

'Minnie, if we do ever have children, they will be lucky to have you as their mother and I hope they will be the kind of people who care as little as I do about something as ridiculous as your paternity.'

'But Max…'

'Damn it, do you want to marry me or not?' The words burst out of him and the unnatural stiffness melted out of her.

'More than anything, damn *you*, Maxie.'

'Bloody hell, that's better. There's nothing I love more than being damned by you, sweetheart. No, that's not quite true, there are a few other things…'

Mina's laughter faded the moment his mouth touched hers. The impact was immediate—her body contracted as if she had touched an electric wire, then heat rushed through her, burning and biting. He seemed to share her shock, drawing back, all laughter gone.

'No more coaxing. You're mine.'

She nodded. There was no point in denying what was so blatantly true.

'Good. And I'm very glad you're wearing one of your old dresses—they are so much easier to remove. That's better. Now your chemise.' With a few deft moves the chemise joined the dress on the ground. She was about to protest to this cavalier treatment of her clothes when his mouth captured hers again.

She forgot about her crumpled clothes, about the fact that he was still fully clothed. And when his mouth finally released hers she tried to bring it back with a whimper that became a gasp as it descended to her throat, teasing and licking the sensitive skin. The sensations were so intense that she didn't know what to do and merely closed her eyes, biting on her throbbing lips. All her senses followed the descent of his mouth as he pressed her back onto the bed.

'I think this sad little bed is even narrower than the chaise-longue, sweetheart,' he murmured as he brushed his lips gently along the swell of one breast, then the other, and she could feel her nipples harden as his warm breath just grazed them. Then he took one into his mouth, caressing it with his tongue and her whole body contracted under the thrill it sent through her. Even the cool air on her damp flesh as he raised his head was sweet agony.

'Next time, my bed,' he said roughly. 'Our bed.'

She couldn't answer, was afraid to. So she merely shoved his coat from his shoulders and tugged his shirt up and off so she could feel him.

'I want you, Max. I have for so long.'

She felt him shake as he returned his mouth to hers, kissing her more and more deeply, with desperation even, she felt, as if he was expecting to be pulled away at any moment.

She felt the same fear that the threat might become reality, pressed her hips against his, hooking her legs about his waist, pressing her tortured heat against his hardened loins.

'Take them off. Your trousers. I want to feel you.'

'Oh God, Mina…' he gasped.

'Now!'

He laughed and twisted off her to obey, kicking them off onto the floor as well. He moved back towards her but she held up her hand.

'Wait... I want to see you.'

He stood still, his eyes raking over her body, as she did the same to him. The heavy pulsing in her limbs was becoming a throbbing ache. She wanted to feel him again, she wanted his heat inside her.

'You're so beautiful,' she whispered, in awe.

Max's body flared as if he were a lucifer match dragged across a slab of granite. He wanted more than he could ever achieve. He wanted to taste every inch of her, torture her as much as he had been tortured since he had laid eyes on her. He wanted to sit back and just look at her.

But he knew none of these wishes would survive this mad heat in him. More than anything at that moment he wanted to feel her heat around him. To become part of her and make her part of him.

He shook his head slightly and stretched himself beside the woman he loved. He ran his fingers lightly along the curve of her hip, down to the soft warmth of her thighs. Her breath came out in a little moan and she shifted towards him, her legs pressing against his. He slid his knee between them, rubbing softly between her thighs, his fingers teasing their way upwards as he bent to brush light kisses to her breasts. She breathed his name, her body leaping beneath as he found each sensitive spot. He groaned at her hot response, at the undeniable dampness of her loins…

'Wait, wait,' she gasped. 'I'm not going over first, this time. Together.'

He held himself still as she caressed him with her palm, the back of her hand, just brushing up and down as he had touched her, slipping her hand to his thighs, watching the tension on his face, the fire stoking higher and higher in her eyes. He could feel the sweet agony echoing between them, heightening the yearning, the heat, the need…

Some distant corner of his mind gathered every sensation—the rawness of her breathing, the vibrations of their bodies, the slick heat of his skin against hers as she opened to receive him.

'Together,' he repeated, but he needn't have worried. She was with him. He watched the pleasure build in her eyes, her cries slipping her control, her body twisting and rocking into the pleasure of his fingers even as he drove into the tight heat of her sheath.

'Max,' she cried out as she shuddered her release, her legs wrapping themselves around his waist, her heels digging into his buttocks, drawing him deep into the rippling convulsions that tore through him, scattering him, unravelling him into intense waves of pleasure, and then into nothing at all.

* * *

It was the distinct sound of the ship's engine rumbling into life again that recalled Mina to their surroundings.

'Max?'

He groaned hoarsely, pulling her closer.

'Hell, the ship's engineers are better than I thought.'

'Will they make the tide?'

'I don't know. I'd rather not wait and find out.' He reached over the side of the bed and retrieved her dress. 'Let's make a run for it before we have to swim back.'

They were halfway down the gangway when one of Max's comments finally registered and she paused on the bottom step.

'Why did you say Almeria *and* Septimus are romantics?'

He smiled at the suspicion in her voice.

'Apparently Almeria wasn't the only one who realised I was in love with you back then.'

'But… You can't mean that…that Septimus hired me because…'

'Yes to whatever you are thinking.'

'Max! He's… He's…'

'I know. There are no words. In fact, now I think of it, I realise there is one very serious drawback to marrying you. He will be insufferably smug about the whole thing.'

'Oh no, you're right! From now until eternity he'll

be spouting on about his third act philosophy of life and we shan't be able to say anything at all!'

Max drew her into his arms and lowered her onto the quay.

'Having from now until eternity with you will just about make that bearable, my brilliant, beautiful nemesis.'

Epilogue

'A little more. Yes. No, deeper. Deeper!'

Max grunted and pushed it deeper.

'It is in?'

Mina gave a sigh of satisfaction. 'Yes. It was just stuck before.'

'Good. Let's try again.'

She leaned across and pressed the button. The engine purred.

'Oh, Max, you're a genius. No, I'm a genius for marrying a man with such talented hands.'

Max extracted himself from the hatchway above the yacht's engine and grinned up at his wife.

'I told you it would be worth it one day.'

'Well, it took long enough. Five whole years.'

'Five whole years, two children, and far too many opening nights at the opera. And you put up with it all so bravely, my long-suffering Minnie.'

'I'm practically a saint. Why did you remind me of the children? Now I'll feel guilty again about leaving

Lily and Tom at Fairweather while we are sailing the seas in your new yacht.'

'*Your* new yacht. I built it for you, love. And I refuse to feel guilty about having you to myself for a few weeks. We both deserve this.'

He pulled his discarded shirt towards him, tucking it under his head like a pillow as he stretched out on the deck. The Mediterranean breeze molded Mina's white dress against her curves and tangled her loose hair about her shoulders. The sun had warmed her skin and happiness had softened her eyes and mouth.

She looked beautiful, happy, comfortable. His.

She smiled back. 'You're just going to stay there lying on the deck?'

'It was hard work. Besides, I like the view from here.'

She laughed, clasping her skirt and drawing it up a little. He could almost feel the shiver of the fabric on her skin and the heat of the sun migrated into a different kind of heat.

'Keep going.'

She glanced around them. The small bay was encompassed by low sandstone cliffs and shaded by cypress trees. 'Are you certain no one can reach this bay from the island?'

'Not unless they sprout wings, sweetheart. Come here.'

'Not yet. I'm enjoying the view, too. I like you spread out at my feet, shirtless.' Her gaze moved over him, her lashes lowering. Even after all their years together those grey eyes could wreak havoc on his body. Her gaze lingered on the undeniable proof of her power over him.

'You seem to like it too, Max Cavendish.'

She moved forward, brushing the inside of his calf with her bare foot.

'There's grease on your trousers. Here. And here. And up here...'

He drew in a sharp breath. 'That's not all there's going to be on them if you keep doing that.'

'Well, take them off, then.'

'You first.'

Her eyes widened at the challenge, but with another quick glance behind her and then out at the empty expanse of the aquamarine sea, she tugged the dress over her head and tossed it at him. His heart lurched and stumbled ahead, and his erection strained against the soon-to-be-removed trousers.

'This is embarrassing,' she laughed, her hair tangling over her beautiful breasts.

He shook his head. 'You're magnificent. A Greek goddess rising from the sea.'

'Here to punish a handsome mortal for daring to invade her secret bay... Goodness, that sounded suggestive. You were planning to invade my secret bay, weren't you?'

'Often. And with vigor.'

She rested her foot against his erection, kneading it gently. He groaned, shifting against the pressure.

'Very firm vigor, I see.'

His free hand closed on her other foot, sliding up the sun-warmed skin. Her tongue touched her upper lip as he found the sensitive point behind her knee.

'I didn't give you leave to touch me, mortal.'

'Us mortals are weak. We can't help…ourselves. Especially not when you do that…' He broke off with a groan. 'Enough. Come here before I expire.'

'I shall indeed come here, mortal. Often. And with vigor.'

His laugh was cut short as she sank to her knees, unfastened his trousers and straddled him.

For a moment she remained unmoving, heat against heat. Only her hair danced and played, catching the sun as the afternoon wind gently rocked the boat.

'I love seeing you happy, Max. Watching you here on the yacht.… Reading a book with Tom and Lily… It fills my heart. I don't need anything else in the world.'

He rested his hand on her cheek. He couldn't speak. Love did this to him sometimes. It bordered on fear that all this might never have been. That he might have lived his life, half empty, without even knowing his full capacity for feeling, for caring, for love.

She nuzzled his hand. 'I love that I can still leave you speechless sometimes.'

'So long as you don't leave me,' he mumbled and she shook her head.

'No woman with an ounce of sense would leave the man who stopped an ocean liner for her.' Her eyes glistened with sudden tears and her voice turned hoarse. 'Sometimes it frightens me how close I came to making the greatest mistake of my life, Max. If you hadn't fought for me and forced me to realise I deserved to be selfish...'

'Not selfish...'

'Yes, selfish. We both took a risk, Max. I'm so happy you helped me be brave enough to take it. Even if Lily and Tom might suffer for it one day, I know they will work their way through it because they have your strength.'

'And your stubbornness.'

'Goddesses aren't stubborn. They're resolute.'

'That's better. Now stop squeezing my heart into useless putty and go back to squeezing something else.'

'Goodness, this mortal is very demanding.'

'Not demanding. He just knows what he wants.'

'And what is that?'

'I want you to be happy.'

'Oh, damn you, Max. I hate it when you make me cry. Now take off those trousers. This goddess is about to coax you into heaven.'

* * * * *

*If you enjoyed this story, be sure to read
Lara Temple's The Return of the Rogues miniseries*

The Return of the Disappearing Duke
A Match for the Rebellious Earl

And why not check out her other great books

The Duke's Unexpected Bride
The Earl She Should Never Desire
The Wrong Way to Catch a Rake

MILLS & BOON®

Coming next month

ACCIDENTALLY WED TO THE PRINCE
Lucy Morris

What should I say? Magnus had made his decision in the library earlier, but now he was at a loss for words. The next sentence would seal his fate and that of his beloved Thrudheim forever.

He supposed he should just get it over with. 'Miss Mortimer, in light of our recent...accident. I think it only best that I ask for your hand in marriage.'

'What?' Miss Mortimer screamed the word so loudly that his ears rang and he winced.

She glanced up at the stagecoach, and he noticed that several people had gathered at the windows and doorway. Staring down at them expectantly like a nest of hungry chicks. Miss Mortimer scowled back at them and they hurried back into the shadows.

'Have you lost your wits?' She hissed, and then added, 'Your Serene Highness.' Belatedly and with a perplexed expression, as if she wasn't sure how she could remain polite and question his sanity at the same time.

'As we are going to be married, you may call me by my Christian name, Magnus, at least in informal settings such as this.'

She blinked with a slack expression as if she couldn't quite comprehend his words. After a moment of blankness, a strange iron-will seemed to take over her. She raised her chin and her spine stiffened, that odd conviction hardening within her eyes like granite. It was spectacular to watch, a goddess emerging from a fiery pit. 'I did not agree to your proposal!'

Continue reading

ACCIDENTALLY WED TO THE PRINCE
Lucy Morris

Available next month
millsandboon.co.uk

Copyright © 2026 Lucy Morris

COMING SOON!

We really hope you enjoyed reading this book. If you're looking for more romance be sure to head to the shops when new books are available on

Thursday 21st May

To see which titles are coming soon, please visit
millsandboon.co.uk/nextmonth

MILLS & BOON

FOUR BRAND NEW BOOKS FROM
MILLS & BOON MODERN

Indulge in desire, drama, and breathtaking romance – where passion knows no bounds!

OUT NOW

Eight Modern stories published every month, find them all at:

millsandboon.co.uk

LET'S TALK
Romance

For exclusive extracts, competitions and special offers, find us online:

- MillsandBoon
- @MillsandBoon
- @MillsandBoonUK
- @MillsandBoonUK

Get in touch on 01413 063 232

For all the latest titles coming soon, visit
millsandboon.co.uk/nextmonth